SWIPE RIGHT FOR MURDER

SWIPE RIGHT FOR MURDER

DEREK MILMAN

FOREWORD BY JAMES PATTERSON

JIMMY Patterson Books
Little, Brown and Company
New York Boston London

The characters and events in this book are fictitious. Any similarity to real persons, living or dead, is coincidental and not intended by the author.

JIMMY Patterson Books / Little, Brown and Company
Hachette Book Group
1290 Avenue of the Americas, New York, NY 10104
JimmyPatterson.org

First Paperback Edition: May 2021
First Edition: August 2019

JIMMY Patterson Books is an imprint of Little, Brown and Company, a division of Hachette Book Group, Inc. The Little, Brown name and logo are trademarks of Hachette Book Group, Inc. The JIMMY Patterson Books® name and logo are trademarks of JBP Business, LLC.

Cataloging-in-publication data is available at the Library of Congress.

ISBN 978-0-316-45106-2 (hc) / 978-0-316-45102-4 (pb)

Printing 1, 2021

LSC-C

Printed in the United States of America

For my family, as always: Mom, Dad, Jordan, Lorin, Isla, Henry, my shining light Brian Murray Williams, and the great Victoria Marini, who inspired and encouraged me to write this book and never let me quit.

FOREWORD

The stories that I look for all have one important thing in common—true, heartfelt emotion. Whether you're cheering on a girl with wings who's saving her loved ones from destruction or gasping in fear for a boy with a troubled past running for — and *from*—his life, as in *Swipe Right for Murder,* I want all the books I publish to make you feel things. Intensely.

Make no mistake, *Swipe Right for Murder* is absolutely the high-octane thriller that the title promises. But during the course of the chase, we follow Aidan's race through emotional highs and lows as well. Joy, heartache, loneliness, infatuation, grief—his character comes to life on the page in a way that has you thinking he's a real kid, maybe a lot like someone you know. Or maybe a lot like you.

I hope you'll be as entertained and moved by Derek's deeply nuanced story as I was, because *feeling* things is never overrated.

—James Patterson

SWIPE RIGHT FOR MURDER

CHAPTER 1

Death Rays

It's late afternoon at the Mandarin Oriental Hotel, and we're splurging on ridiculously overpriced tea and discussing sudden death.

Unfortunately, the topic is all too relevant at the moment.

Spring break during my final year at Witloff Academy took something of a turn when two things happened.

The first thing was that my Aunt Meredith, who I barely know, was injured by a Vegas Hotel Death Ray.

So what happened is, they built this new hotel in Vegas. But the Swiss "starchitect" who designed the thing was apparently more concerned with his ego than the desert sun's relationship to the concave shape of the building and how it might reflect off the glass front. They're technically calling it a "solar convergence," but let's be honest: *death ray* sounds way cooler.

Everyone who was on the pool deck at noon caught on fire like caterpillars trapped under a magnifying glass. Okay, maybe not literal flames, but my aunt is hospitalized in Nevada with second-degree burns, and now we have to go visit her.

"It was hot enough to melt *plastic cups,* Aidan," my mom told me on the phone, muffling a histrionic cry over a sister who she talks to once every seven years. Before I had a chance to consider how depressing it was that people were drinking out of plastic cups at a high-priced resort in Vegas, she added (as if she realized she hadn't been judgmental enough yet): "I wish she would make better choices. And stop all that gambling. *Vegas? Alone?* She does these travel tours with endless casino stops. She just can't stop moving."

The second thing that happened involves my heart.

I've been having these stomach issues. I have a lot of stress at school and the nurse thought I might have an ulcer. So I saw a doctor in town who prescribed antacids and for the hell of it gave me an EKG, which yielded an "abnormal result," meaning they thought my heart might be enlarged or something.

Of course my mom freaked out, because that's what she does. She's always been something of a high-functioning hysteric, but her freaking definitely got more severe after I hit seventh grade; it's been on a downward spiral ever since. Immediately, specialists were called, tests arranged, appointments scheduled. I can't count all the e-mails over this.

"Aw, your heart's too big for this world!" my best friend Jackson told me, laughing.

Right off the train this morning, I cabbed it to a hospital on the Upper East Side for my echocardiogram. This involved a very nice lady pressing a transducer into my chest for half an hour.

I could hear my heart beating on the monitors—not the dull thud you're used to. It had a liquid whipping sound, like a stingray moving through the sea. When the test was over, they gave me a towel to wipe away the cold gel smeared all over my chest (which reminded me of a rushed sexual encounter) and showed me my heart on the monitors, pointing out all four chambers.

"Oh, look at that," I said, seeing this muscle that's been keeping me alive for seventeen-and-a-half years. And I wondered, then and there, if I would ever see it again. Hopefully not, I guess. So I spent a second or two watching it do its thing and feeling grateful for all its work on my behalf.

I won't know if there's a real problem with my heart for another week, when I see our family cardiologist and he interprets the echo results. But that's cool because now the world has this romantic gloss to it. I mean I might die young.

I might die young. My heart, you see.

I've been practicing that line in my head.

We were supposed to go to a fancy-schmancy resort in Maui but now we're not because of my burned-up aunt. And that's okay. I mean about Maui, not my aunt. Although I swim, I'm not as athletic as the rest of my family. Sometimes that can get pretty annoying on family vacations what with the surfing and the tennis and the hiking and shit.

In Cabo last year, we went horseback riding along a beach.

The rest of my family galloped off like they were in *Red Dead Redemption,* but my horse just lumbered along, sticking to the edges, eating every weed in sight. I finally gave him a sharp little kick and was like, *C'mon, buddy, let's move!* The horse stopped munching and slowly turned his head to look back at me with this expression like: *Bitch, please.*

I wound up stumbling back to the hotel hours later, covered with dust and grit, to find the rest of my family glistening and supine, tanning by the pool, lazily swirling straws through bright-yellow drinks with little pink umbrellas. "Oh, Aidan, honey, did we lose you?" said my mom, sitting up a tad and only slightly lowering her sunglasses from her novel—the second *Fifty Shades of Grey* book.

The bronze-skinned pool boy gave me a sympathetic smile. I found him later stacking chairs, and felt vindicated when we hooked up in a blue-and-white-striped changing cabana while my family ate shrimp tacos without me (I was still pissed) at the only passable restaurant at the resort—Pasión Del Amanecer.

The pool boy's name was Santiago. I remember that while he kissed me, I gazed through the cabana flap into the dark pool. The water reflected squiggles of light from all the hotel windows above. Between kisses, I mouthed his name because I liked it.

Jackson taps my knee, exposing that impressive bicep of his. The jagged edge of his red lightning-bolt tattoo peeks out from under his cobalt-blue, short-sleeved button-down.

"Should we get more hot water?" he's asking me, gesturing

at one of the waiters framed by the tall windows. The view is amazing: Central Park splitting the beige glittering buildings of New York City like a vegetal invasion climbing out of the planet's core. Tatiana, Jackson's girlfriend, is nodding, texting, reaching for a mini pastry on a tier of plates. The sandwiches are gone already. "Yes, please," she says.

Jackson and Tatiana are the perfect couple: both of them black, gorgeous, super-smart, athletic, total Renaissance types. Jackson got into MIT, where he will probably stay for a year and create the next Facebook. Tatiana is already at Harvard. Pre-law. They met on a secret Tinder-like app that only accepts people who are a certain level of attractiveness and intelligence. I'm not kidding. Digital eugenics. It's happening.

I look practically homely next to them. At least three people (that I know of) already walked up to Jackson today, revealed themselves as modeling scouts, and dropped business cards in his lap. I get why. Jackson is tall, toned, has an amazing smile and perfect bone structure. I call him "Rational Erik Killmonger." He calls me "the flaxen-haired ghost of a J.Crew heir who died choking on an almond croissant."

He has no interest in modeling. But he smiles at anyone who asks.

Sometimes I think my feelings for Jackson might go deeper, but I don't want to complicate our friendship, so I never let my mind fully go there.

I gaze down at the cars racing around Columbus Circle. Being so high up makes the world seem quiet. I snap a few photos. I use Instagram, but not as much as everyone else does. I prefer to upload photos to my Tumblr. It makes me feel like a serious photographer. I number and title every photo.

I look at Jackson. "Is Leo coming?"

"Leo is flaking," says Jackson. "Surprise, surprise."

Leo is our other friend. Half Asian. Hipster. Coder. Puppyish. Flakes a lot. Goes to Comic-Con. Total stud anyway. Loves *Minecraft, Fortnite,* and Tarantino (but nothing after *Inglourious Basterds*). Heading to Brown next year. Full scholarship. Will probably create the next Snapchat or go into finance.

Yes, all my friends are intelligent and attractive. It's just nice in a world of dust, blood, and fire to always have something lovely to look at. And I like being intellectually challenged.

In the fall I'll be attending a small liberal arts college in New England. I don't like telling people which one because then I get put in a box and people think they know me. Not that it matters. I'm sure everyone there will be named Aidan, too. Liam or Aidan. A sea of Liams and Aidans wearing Sperry Top-Siders and cardigans with catalogue colors like "heather" or "toast."

That's my big fear, I guess—that I'm a clone; that I'll never be different; that my whole future is just mapped out for me and I essentially have no free will at all.

I grew up in a Rhode Island suburb where church bells chime at the top of the hour and everyone drives a Volvo SUV. People become lawyers and doctors like it's written out in their DNA. My dad is a pediatrician on his way to retirement and my mom is a periodontist. So freakin' normcore, I know.

I guess that's why, when I finally left my hometown, I made

sure I was not going to be friends with other boring, belching white dudes who watch ESPN obsessively and think the Chainsmokers are a really deep band. I pretty much hated my (highly rated) public school. There were definitely specific factors behind my wanting to get the hell out of there. I mentioned my unhappiness at school—painting it more as a general malaise—only once to my parents, in passing, while we were in a department store. I mused out loud about maybe going away to a boarding school. And then *boom,* off I went—shipped to Witloff at sixteen. TO BECOME A MAN.

"So this dude Drew," Jackson is telling me.

I run my fingertip around the rim of the teacup. "Drew."

Right: our sudden-death conversation. Jackson is telling this story because of my heart and my aunt. In the theme of: bad random shit can just happen.

"My cousin Alex goes to Amherst with this dude named Drew," he says. "And Drew took a semester abroad. And he was skiing in the Swiss Alps during winter break last year. And he died. In an *avalanche.*"

"That's terrible," says Tatiana, clapping a hand to her throat.

"Amherst dude named Drew died in an avalanche while skiing in the Swiss Alps during break?" I say, leaning forward.

"Yep," says Jackson.

"So basically he died *the preppiest death of all time.*"

"Basically." Jackson covers his mouth with his hand.

"Don't laugh at that." Tatiana waves her finger at me, mock-scolding.

"Yeah, don't," says Jackson. "Could be you."

Tatiana gives him a look. "Don't tell him that."

"What? His heart could explode!"

"I could go at any minute," I say, flopping back, making the sound of a flatline.

Jackson laughs.

"I wonder what started the avalanche," I say. "Do you think Drew stopped skiing to make a really loud phone order to Lacoste or something?"

"His questions about Slim Fit versus Regular echoed too loud and then *whoosh,*" says Jackson.

"This is not funny!" Tatiana protests.

Jackson calls her Tats. And I call him Jacks. And she's right. Sometimes we can be assholes.

"His family," she says, looking stricken. "Can you imagine?" She looks around, trying to get the waiter's attention. "The service here could be a lot better."

"Yes," says Jacks, rolling his eyes, "we know. Tea service is better in Singapore."

Tatiana gives me a look, like *Can you believe this is who I'm dating?* I take her hand in mine to commiserate. I like Tats. She grew up in Singapore. Something with her dad's corporate job, I don't know. But she loved it there. Misses it. Says it was beautiful and perfect. Everything always sucks because we're not in Singapore.

She does go on about that a lot.

I never mention the fact that you could go to prison for being gay there.

I surreptitiously check my phone, but there are no new calls or texts. I *even more surreptitiously* check a certain hookup app under the table and find out pretty quickly this hotel is Cruise Central. I look around but see no immediate possibilities. There's some sort of bridal shower happening in one corner of the lounge. A gaggle of tourists with shopping bags from the Time Warner Center hold court at the low Chinese table in the center of the room. An elegantly dressed older lady wearing an eye patch walks by clutching an orange Hermès bag. I snap her photo. I always snap a burst, so I can meticulously choose the best shots later. "Lady with Hermès" is the working title of that one.

They finally refill our hot water and do it with a smile. Personally, I think the service is fine. They're just busy. The entire lounge stops and stares as Jackson gets up to stretch. Literally, there's a hush. His arms go over his head in one smooth motion like a dancer, and he turns left then right, his shirt lifting just a bit so you can see the thin band of white underwear poking out from his skinny jeans.

Tatiana seems oblivious to this little display. But I know Jackson. This is the kind of shit peacocks do. He likes to be noticed. He knows the power of everything about him that works. And perfect as the two of them may be, or close to it anyway, I know for a fact that Jackson has a wandering eye.

Jackson lives in northern New Jersey. Like mine, his family isn't super rich or anything. But he's staying the night with Tats (whose family *is,* and has an apartment in TriBeCa) because he has a ton of interviews for high-octane summer internships—*Vogue, The New Yorker, Vice,* various tech start-ups and consulting firms, the freakin' UN.

I'm telling you, man, you get singed if you stand too close to his flames.

My parents put me up for the night at the Mandarin because it's popular with a lot of kids from Witloff stopping through New York. The echo test is done now, so I have most of tomorrow to kill ("go to the Neue Galerie, honey, see the Klimts") before we all have dinner somewhere downtown at five p.m. sharp, like the rock stars we are.

"What are your plans?" Tats is asking me.

"My plans?"

"Don't look so scared," she says. "Not your life. Just for the rest of the day."

"Yeah. We have to bounce," says Jackson as he pats down his jeans, which is what he always does before he bounces. It happens very suddenly. You think you're hanging out, you think it will last somewhat longer, but then there's the jean pat-down, and he's gone—off to the next great adventure.

"We're having an early dinner with my parents," says Tats. "And tomorrow morning he's interviewing with Deutsche Bank."

"Nice," I say, staring into my lap. I haven't been on top of this whole summer-internship thing as much as everyone else has, apparently. Personally, I think they're bullshit. But maybe they aren't. One of my uncles is a survivalist hunter-type who lives in Maine. But my other uncle is a Hollywood script doctor, and there were some vague plans for me to go out to LA for a few weeks, be a pseudo research assistant for him, and "meet people." The movie business sort of interests me (although so does a lot of stuff), my uncle is gay, too, and for five seconds I thought maybe I could be the next Dustin Lance Black. That's as far as I got with my summer. Now I wonder if that's lame. "I'll probably just take a nap," I say, softly.

"We were up pretty late," says Jackson.

"He made me watch a movie," I tell Tats. "Forced it on me, really."

Maybe I'm the only one in the world who finds Netflix stressful. Granted, I find fairly mundane things to be stressful, but how is it fun to spend hours cycling and arguing through their limited selection of mostly second-tier Elijah Wood projects and then be unable to pick something decent? The good stuff you've already seen. So what happens is—I mean *what happened last night* is—you just give up in the end and wind up streaming a Dutch lesbian movie called *Loving Klara*. And then it's ninety-four minutes of two Dutch ladies with strange haircuts running down a rocky beach while one of them keeps shouting: "Klara! Wait! No! Klara!"

That was the whole goddamn movie.

"We were up past three," says Jackson. He explains the plot to Tats. "It kind of sucked. And it was very foreign. But I wanted to see what happened in the end."

"And what happened?" she asks.

"Klara jumps off a cliff," I say.

"Why?" Tatiana's hands hover over her cheeks; she looks so stricken.

"Because she's Klara. And that's what Dutch lesbians named Klara do, I guess," I say.

Jackson signals for the check.

"Poor Klara," says Tatiana, shaking her head, looking even more stricken. She's good at looking stricken.

We pay the ginormous bill. Or Tats does, anyway, saying the tea is on her. Jackson gives me a bro hug—slingshot into the body, sharp slap on the shoulder, and then a quick pivot off. Tats gives me a hug and air kisses me on both cheeks because she's way cool and *that's what they do in Singapore*.

"I'm so glad we got to see you," says Tats.

"Yeah, well, thanks for coming all the way up here," I say, trying to quell an unexpected surge of anxiety that I'm about to be alone in a hotel in New York City.

Jackson whispers in my ear. "I might go out later. Friend of my cousin is hosting a warehouse party. Bushwick. Want to come with?"

"Wait. What about Tats?"

"What about her? She falls asleep early."

"Okay. Maybe?"

"Don't be worried about that test. I'm sure your heart is fine."

"I'm not that worried."

"If I don't see you, have fun with your folks tomorrow."

"I'll try."

"And sorry about your aunt."

"She'll be okay."

"I hope my story didn't freak you out."

"What story?"

"Drew. The avalanche."

"I don't really like skiing, so..."

"Shit does happen." He squeezes my shoulder. "But not to you."

I smile. "Be good."

"No. *You be good.*" He sticks a gold toothpick in his mouth. Only he could pull that shit off. He points at me. "And you know what I mean."

I do know what he means. But I probably won't behave.

"Later, gator," says Jacks.

Then they bounce. Like beach balls.

I take the elevator to my room, where I still haven't unpacked. I throw myself on the bed, wanting to do something productive. So I read a little of this book I like called *The Age of Wonder.* It's about all these cool scientific discoveries made in the late eighteenth century leading into the Romantic period.

I think history is pretty cool. All those different time periods, each characterized by a different tone, different values, and different ways of thinking. Maybe the Romantic period could get exhausting with everyone swooning and being emotional, but I bet the Renaissance was a pretty badass time to be on this planet—maybe a little cliquey, though, if you weren't sculpting enough.

Now, the Age of Enlightenment I'm not sure about. You couldn't complain at all. People would be like: Wait, you didn't love the second season of *Westworld*? It's amazing! And you'd be like, eh, too many minor characters, and everyone would go on about you needing to be more enlightened about the character arcs in *Westworld*. You'd probably have to pretend you thought the Chainsmokers were prophets or something.

But the freakin' Dark Ages? People gave zero fucks. And it

lasted forever! The Roman Empire was in ruins; you could die in the Crusades, catch the Black Death, get burned alive if you pissed off the wrong guy. And all those medieval torture devices? Holy shit. You probably had no idea if you would survive any given week. And people would be like: *What?* Your dad is giving you shit about using the car? This is the *Dark Ages,* dude. I just beheaded my whole family with an ax because *I felt like it.*

You could get away with anything.

CHAPTER 2

War in Heaven

I fall asleep, but only for a minute or so. I turn on the TV and take in some of their "digital content on demand." I love how hotels think phones don't exist. Sure, Mandarin Oriental, I'll pay thirty bucks to watch the latest Jason Statham movie.

I've always thought hotels are romantic and disorienting, but vacations in general are weird. Being lost in time as the days tick off in a mad rush to return you home. The weeklong sunburns. Those eerie, empty hours before dinner. The soapy-sweet smell of hotel rooms. The muted sound of television voices through the walls. People whispering as they sift down the carpeted halls. Deep, strange dreaming in stiff alien bedding. And those heavy curtains you're reluctant to close.

I take out my phone and open DirtyPaws, the gay hookup

app I was checking earlier under our table during tea. But I had a blank profile because I had just re-downloaded it on the train in. Nothing good can come from this, but I cobble together a profile ("on break" says my headline), forgo a screen name, throw a few photos on, and get seven hits right away.

Two messages from faceless profiles: "Cute," they both say. I delete these.

One headless torso (screen name: TDawgPA) on PrEP just gives me a room number. Delete.

One dude in his late twenties (screen name: YoungLawyer) has a great smile, but he's into unprotected sex ("bb only"), offers a negative HIV result from over a year ago ("phew!"), and just gives me a Thumbs Up emoticon. This shithead gets blocked.

One European-looking gentleman (screen name: JetLag) who could be a Bond villain, and whose profile photo is of him in a white tux raising a glass of champagne (celebrating his latest kill?), offers me the honor of performing oral sex on him.

They keep coming: little buzzing vibrations on my phone from the lonely, horny denizens of Columbus Circle. I scan through my options. Everyone is approximately 205 feet away. So many dudes doing that thing where they hold the phone slightly below the jaw in a full-length mirror, looking aloof, wearing only briefs.

Whoa, *wait*. . . .

My thumb freezes on a face I recognize, and I actually gasp a little.

Darren Cohen.

Well, well, well. Darren freakin' Cohen: Witloff track star.

Blond, blue-eyed all-American Hollister-type headed to Dartmouth next year. Dating Ashley Henderson, a cheerleader on her way to Wesleyan, who looks like Alicia Vikander. The app says he's 56 feet away. I imagine him lying in bed right over my room, concurrently checking out my profile with a nervously excited expression on his face.

His screen name is JockNxtDoor. I crack up at that. He doesn't say much on his profile; just lists his height and weight, which seems accurate. I lay the phone face down on my chest and consider this.

Now I regret putting my face on my profile. I should have just put a photo of my chest like everyone else. I'm not sure what to do now. Darren is a total rock star at school. We haven't crossed paths much. He's someone I *might have had a crush on,* but he never seemed accessible enough. And I assumed he was straight. But, *oh snap,* I guess Ashley Henderson did, too. I pick up my phone and just stare at his face. The app says he's still online. I purse my lips.

Bond Villain is now offering me money. BLOCK.

Then Darren freakin' Cohen freakin' messages me!

Okay, Jamison, we've both seen each other.

ME (playing it all cool): **What do you want to do, man?**

DARREN: **What is there to do, Jamison. Let's hang.**

ME: **You're not really my type.**

Why did I just say that? I dance my fingertips nervously across my forehead.

Darren just responds with his room number, as if he knows he's everyone's type and STFU. This simultaneously annoys me and really turns me on. Then Darren sends me more pics. My eyes go wide. Track does amazing things for your arms, abs, and legs, apparently. He's genetically just a winner in all other categories.

It takes me a moment to realize what these secondary pictures mean.

He's saying: *we're on.*

I swim, I remind myself. I'm not *not* in his league.

I hop off the bed. I flick the lights on in the bathroom and stare at myself in the mirror. I look dazed. I squirt out some hair gel and swipe it through my hair, but that just makes everything worse. Boy-band spiky. Ugh. I wash my face, wondering about the world of Witloff, the shells we all hide in, and how once we exit those gates, where we all have these set roles, we emerge as different people. Am I nothing more than a horned-up skeeze who cruises hook-up apps?

Then I glance at Darren's abs again.

Who. The. Fuck. Cares.

I rummage through my luggage. I try on three different T-shirts and two different pairs of jeans before I decide to go more casual and put on some khaki shorts and a chambray shirt with the sleeves rolled up.

It's the longest elevator ride of my life and it's only ten floors up. I nearly strangle this lady who takes forever with her nine suitcases. Is she staying here for a year?

Darren has left his door unlocked. "Just come in," he calls.

I walk inside. He's on a higher floor, so his view is impressive, way better than mine. He's sitting on the edge of his bed, facing away from me, as if almost shy, framed by the lush park below. The sun is just beginning to set, rays of crimson and gold streaking through the mass of trees.

Death rays.

Now I feel like a total dork for worrying about what to wear. He's wearing only one of those fluffy white robes they leave in the bathroom. I raise an eyebrow, but he's used to parading around locker rooms.

So am I, I have to remind myself. Although I don't *parade*. It's more like a rushed hustle.

A breeze kicks up outside, and in the distance, over the tree tops, a funnel of white blossoms spirals around in a fury.

Darren follows my gaze out the window. "That keeps happening. I keep thinking they're feathers. That it's a war in heaven. And all the angels are fighting."

There are several things I might have expected from Darren as a conversation starter. This was not one of them.

"Milton," he says. "*Paradise Lost.* Have you read it?"

"Uh, no, have you?"

"No. But I want to. I hear good things." He turns to me. "Come in. Close the door."

Right. I walk inside. His TV is on mute. Bloomberg News. He stands up. He's holding a glass. Ice clinks. "Want a drink?"

"I'm good," I say.

"I don't want to drink alone, man."

"Um. I'll have what you're having, then."

He goes to the desk. He's unpacked his luggage. Flaps of expensive suitcases lie open like some sort of surgery that got interrupted. He has ice filled to the brim in a bucket. Playa. It was going to be me or somebody else.

Better the devil you know, I think.

He grabs a glass, a mini bottle of Absolut from the minibar, scoops ice, and pours me a drink. As he hands it to me, I hear the cubes crack. He clinks my glass with his—a bit too hard, so I sway back a little on my feet. "Cheers," he says.

"Yeah, cheers."

I take a sip. I don't really drink. The sheer chemical burn of the Absolut makes me wince, and I'm sure it's abundantly clear now to Darren that I don't drink...or go to those parties where people do. For a second we just stand there, really awkwardly, holding our glasses like we're at some corporate mixer or something, staring at each other. Then Darren turns, and confidently lies down on the king-size bed, patting the space next to him.

I bite my lip.

What do I do with my drink? Darren has placed his glass on his stomach, so I lie down next to him and do the same. This is even more awkward. We're just lying next to each other now, pretending to be engrossed by the soaring price of strawberries on Bloomberg News. Then Darren brushes his bare leg against mine.

"Take off your shoes at least," he says.

Yes. That was rude of me. "Sorry," I say, sitting up, kicking off my red Vans.

"No worries." Darren sips his drink.

I suddenly feel like we're going to make this spectacular connection and we'll be friends forever and I'll always remember this moment we had together, this first time, with the blossoms falling outside. But then Darren puts down his drink, presses the side of his hand sharply into my chest so I immediately think of the EKG test and the transducer because I'm kind of sore right there. My drink tumbles onto the carpet.

And then Darren just leans over me and kisses me....

It's almost as if I hear an authoritative British voice narrating a nature documentary: *Do you know what an anglerfish is?*

Holy shit, okay.

It's a fish with a huge mouth and tons of needle-like teeth sticking out. They have that lure thing dangling over their heads like a fishing rod that attracts prey. They're hideous. But Darren is so damn pretty it takes me a full minute to rationalize the soul-crushing fact that kissing him is what kissing an anglerfish might be like—all teeth, no tenderness, total aggression.

I can't even begin to understand how someone could kiss so badly. It's *kissing.* It's *innate.* I reposition myself a little so his mouth will come at me from a slightly different angle, but that just makes it worse. I feel like I'm being... *chewed.*

I begin to realize, slowly, sadly, that his mouth can never go near any other part of my body. I push him off. "Sorry," I say. And I mean that in so many ways.

He lies back, makes this *ahhhh* noise like that was the most satisfying moment of his life. We don't say anything for a little while. I can't unwiden my eyes. His robe has partially peeled away from his chest and I can't help staring at his rigidly defined pecs. He's way more ripped than me. I'm really just a skinny kid with some definition. My body hasn't yet decided how hunky I can actually become. Darren must work out regularly, or have a trainer. I don't have that. I don't do that.

"I always thought you were kind of cute," he says, staring at the ceiling.

I pull at a thread on my shirt. "Really?"

"I mean since I saw your photo on DirtyPaws."

"That was ten minutes ago."

"Well, before, too. I realized it for sure when I saw your photo, though."

What?

"I'm not really sure about anything," he says.

This sudden nonsensical vulnerability makes me like him a little more—but only a *little,* and not enough to kiss him again. My stomach feels sour.

I tend to physicalize sadness, I think.

"I just never thought about you much," he says. I can sense him trying to articulate more, but his voice has become distant. "I mean I'd see you around. But. You know...I guess that's what I'm saying?"

"What's your deal?" I ask him, a little more sharply than I intended. I don't really want this to end, oddly enough. I want to rewind five minutes before the terrible kissing and start over and have it be something else, something so much better than what it is.

"What do you mean?"

"Do you like dudes?"

"Well, yeah," he says, like it was so obvious all this time. "But not, like, at school. I can't there. I have...you know. Because. No offense. I..."

"Yeah. I get it. You're someone else at school?" He's in the closet. I'm trying so hard. I'm piloting a wounded plane into the sea.

"I think I'm bi," he offers, with a firm nod. "And this is all NSA, by the way."

I blink exactly three times. "National Security Agency?"

Darren laughs, but it's forced, polite laughter.

There's a button undone on my shirt. I button it back up.

"Can I, like..." He's reaching for me now, all wiggling fingers like he wants to tickle me. I recoil a little bit. I think of a crawfish or a lobster.

I have no idea why all this ocean life keeps popping into my head right now.

"What."

"I don't know," he says, still reaching. "I gotta get to bed early. Interview in the morning."

He's saying one thing, but his body is doing the opposite. I start to get a tension headache in my neck.

"I'm meeting with Condé Nast," he adds.

I roll my eyes. *Jesus.*

Darren curls up and holds on to me—more like *grips me,* like I'm dangling off a cliff. I feel the hard muscles of his body pressed up against me, which is really the only pleasure I get out of this whole thing, to be honest, and it isn't much, and it's all sort of vague. He starts patting my arm. He says something, but it's muffled into my shoulder.

I actually *feel* his loneliness and confusion coming off him in waves, like it's something physical, but there's nothing I can offer him; there's no way in for me here. I stare out the window, and I do think of angels killing each other now.

Darren says something.

"What?"

"I think I want you to go," he mumbles, still holding on to me.

Yep. I'm already disentangling myself, sliding off the bed.

"Thank you," says Darren. And then, as he falls asleep, he just keeps repeating that over and over again: *thank you, thank you, thank you,* as if he's willing me away as quickly as he can.

Crouched on the floor, I slip on my sneaks so fast I burn a patch of skin on my right index finger. I turn to look at him. He's sleeping: his mouth open a little, his arm still placed where I was, outstretched next to him.

He is beautiful—and it hurts to think that even, because I don't know what to do about it. I can't have him. And I have to stop myself from storing this image of him for later; mental thumbnails for when the juices start flowing, because it'll come with a heaping of sadness and frustration and I don't want that other stuff.

I remember Santiago and the way his hand gripped my upper thigh, a little possessively, while he was kissing me. That one chunk of memory has come in useful at times. I don't want any chunks of this.

I practically tumble out of his room with my eyes closed so I don't see any more of Pretty Sleeping Darren.

I hit the elevator button sixty times. I lean against the wall across from the elevator bank, looking down at the carpet. I don't get in with the family of four. As I get in the next car, I let myself laugh as I straighten my shirt collar. At least that's over. And I guess it could have been worse. But when I get back to my room, I'm in a different frame of mind already, and the absolute wrong combination of shit happens.

CHAPTER 3

Before the Devil Knows You're Dead

They turned down my bed. There's a piece of chocolate on my pillow. I tear off the wrapper and stuff the whole thing in my mouth. I flip on the TV, lie on the bed, and mindlessly watch an episode of *Bob's Burgers* I've already seen.

I want to make a point here: I would not have gotten back on DirtyPaws except for the fact that I had just had the most frustrating, unfulfilling experience of my entire life and desperately wanted to wash the taste of that out with something else.

I try everything. I half watch that Jason Statham movie. I down a mini bottle of Southern Comfort (awful!) and order room service. I try to go to bed early. Fail. I read some more. I spend a few minutes uploading all the recent photos I took—including the ones I snapped today—to my Tumblr.

But I'm horny and restless. So I open the DirtyPaws app again, and when I see the perfectly polite greeting ("Hello there, young man") from the Silver-Foxy-Anderson-Coopery-Roger-Sterlingy dude who is 49 feet away, it trips all my wires.

I send a smiley face back.

His name is Benoît.

"Pronounce it *ben-WAH,*" he says, with a wide grin. Nice, straight, white teeth.

"You're French?"

He gives me a quick, sharp, curious look. "French Canadian. But I live in the States."

"Cool."

I'm standing in his room—second room I've visited tonight, and don't think I'm not overly aware of that fact. Hotel rooms seem to manipulate human behavior into certain patterns. Darren and Benoît have pretty much nothing in common. But they've both put their luggage in the same corner, on luggage racks. The ice bucket is in the same place, too. Both their phones are charging in the same location, on the mantel below the TV, and their toiletries are laid out in the same spot beside the sink in the bathroom.

I guess we're all creatures of habit. Or maybe secretly we look for guideposts, so when we're away from home we don't feel like we're flailing. We never want to flail.

"You brought it with you," says Benoît, mouth open, expectantly, and not really asking a question.

For a second, I don't know how to respond. Is this some sort of line older men use? Is he referring to my...*skills* or something? My prowess? I laugh a little bit and sit on the edge of his bed, hands clasped between my legs. When he sees me do this he seems amused, like he was expecting something else, but just got a bonus. I'm aware of the alcohol in my system. My head is not clear. But, given what we're about to do, I'm okay with being a little removed.

He sits beside me. He smells expensive, like a guy who regularly takes luxe vacations and stays in nice hotels: wafts of cedarwood and coconut. When he puts his arm around my shoulder, I allow it. He rubs my back, lightly. We sit there like that for a moment and I notice his TV is off—one notable difference from Darren: Benoît isn't distracted in any way.

"We'll do it after, then?" he asks, his mouth curling up at one side.

My head shudders, subtly, once, from side to side. *We'll do what after what?*

Is this how French Canadians talk? He's French Canadian. That's what he said, right?

I nod, not really knowing what he means, and not really caring because that's become the theme of tonight. I lie back and close my eyes.

Immediately Benoît takes that as his cue, and moves into action as I exhale.

He undresses me. Then I tell him what to do, in a whispered

torrent of optimistic stage directions. He does it, but he puts his own twist on things to let me know I'm not necessarily the one in charge here. And also, I think, to make things less regimented. He has firm hands and he's in good shape for his age.

Even as I reciprocate, I have yet to open my eyes. Which has nothing to do with him. He's a good-looking guy, with a sexy accent. But right after we bring things to a satisfying denouement, Benoît sits up and cups my chin, making me look right at him. This unexpected moment of tenderness startles me, so I just wind up apologizing because I've been shutting him out the whole time.

"*Très adorable,*" he says.

"Yes. I mean... thank you. *Merci.*"

"We should eat... maybe sleep a little? And then you can give it to me?"

I smile and go "Mm-hmm," assuming he's talking about more sex, which impresses me because we did not exactly hold back just now. He has a lot of energy, and he doesn't seem to want to kick me out. And I don't want to make a break for it like I usually do. I kind of like him.

Benoît orders room service and we eat cheeseburgers in bed and watch some travel show on the Food Network. We don't say anything for a while, even as my eyes find his gold wedding band on the bedside table beside a black-and-gold Bulgari watch and a pile of loose change. I look at him. His eyes are the color of icebergs when icebergs look blue. I rest my head in the crook of his arm while a lot of stuff swills around inside me.

I haven't been 100 percent honest about everything.

My public school back in Rhode Island was fine, perfectly fine. In fact, I even had a few friends I really liked. It wasn't the school's fault that I was unhappy. The main issue was...I made a pretty big mistake.

I had a good friend there named Shane. And I was sleeping with his dad.

I know. It was wrong, very wrong, and I'm a terrible, awful person. The worst part about it was that I started to...*feel things* for Shane's dad. And when that happened he knew it was time to cut me loose. He felt I was becoming attached, which I was. He broke things off, and it pummeled my heart into a million pieces, even though I knew it would have to happen eventually.

No one ever knew. No one ever found out. Not even Shane.

Jackson and Leo are the only two people I ever told.

Shane is disabled and his mom was sort of the breadwinner of the family; she traveled a lot, because she was the chief legal officer of some Fortune 500 company. They lived down the street. And one day his dad, Mr. Reid...I mean, Tom...his name was *Tom*...asked me if I could help mow his lawn and I agreed because he would pay me well. Shane was out of the house a lot of the time doing physical therapy. And one thing led to another. I know. It's like the plot of bad gay porn. But that's what happened.

After we ended things, I just couldn't deal with seeing him every day outside my window: mowing his own lawn, pulling out of his driveway, taking in the morning paper, or whatever. And with that pain came other stuff. Regret. Anger. Guilt. I felt like I had betrayed Shane. And his mom—who I never really knew, but she seemed perfectly nice, just super busy. I felt dirty, like a scheming teenage homewrecker. I didn't like who I was anymore.

So that's why I brought up the whole *going-away-to-boarding-school* thing with my parents. They quickly agreed, probably because I had pretty much stopped eating or sleeping at that point, and they must've figured new surroundings would do me good, that leaving home would be a healthy change of pace. I can't really give them credit for having figured out what was going on. And even if they did, I doubt they'd care. My family is pretty much like what Jackson guessed about us: Waspy-repressed. Staring down silently at our breakfast, silverware clinking, in a kitchen full of windows with everything buried under sweaters.

He was joking, but he was kind of spot-on. When things weren't worried-hysterical with my family, they would settle into the silent-funereal. After a while, I couldn't figure out which was worse.

I just needed to leave.

When I wake up from a restless doze, Benoît is asleep, curled away from me, and I feel like not much time has passed. There's an odd, focused draft in the room. It's dark, but my eyes are drawn across the room because there's a nimbus of cold light emanating from the dresser. I realize it's my phone and some-one is texting or calling. I hop out of bed, run over and grab the phone, unplugging the charger. There's a text from an unfamiliar number.

The message says:

May you be in heaven a full half hour before the devil knows you're dead.

I stare at the message for a second, and when I slide into the home screen I realize my phone isn't locked. No password. And then I realize someone has erased the contents of my phone. Then I realize this isn't my phone—it's Benoît's. I left mine on the nightstand. Then I realize I'm stark freakin' naked. Shit.

I grope around and turn on the nearest lamp, bathing the room in a golden hue. Benoît doesn't stir, so I commence the search and rescue to locate my underwear, which I find wadded up under the front of the bed, where it usually is. I gather the rest of my clothes and quickly get dressed. I pocket my own phone (no calls or texts, and it's twenty to midnight). Then I look through Benoît's phone, which is kind of a naughty thing to do, but whatever.

Here's the weird thing.

His iPhone is blank, like it did get erased. Or maybe it's brand new, although the scuffing on the back and a small scratch on the screen the size and shape of a fingernail clipping would say otherwise. There's no e-mail account set up. There are no apps. Even DirtyPaws seems to be deleted. There are no contacts or phone calls made or received. No voice mails, no other text messages. I open up his Photos, and that's when my throat gets tight and sweat beads up on my brow.

There are photos only of me.

They start from me asleep, in his bed. That's creepy enough:

that he took photos of me while I was asleep. Except, as I keep scrolling down, the photos of me go back in time.

He was taking photos of me in the lobby having tea with Jackson and Tatiana.

There are photos of me *at school.*

My hands are shaking as I stare at photos of me going to and from class, talking to friends, walking down the steps of my dorm. But they look like paparazzi shots—something taken with a telephoto lens from far away. These photos were *sent* to him, I think, rather than taken with the camera phone itself—although I don't know for sure.

I lower the phone and stare at his unmoving form, fast asleep under the covers.

Then there's a knock on the door.

When I look through the peephole, I see a bellhop standing outside.

"Room service," he says, two or three octaves away from being jovial.

I look toward the bed. "Hey," I say to Benoît in a tense whisper. I clear my throat. "Hey," I say again, louder, but he doesn't move.

We already ordered room service. Did he order something else?

I open the door.

The bellhop is a sharp-jawed blond guy who looks like he stepped out of a daytime soap—a different bellhop from before, but wearing the same hotel uniform.

"Room 4509," he says, pushing the cart inside with a silver tray on it as I stand aside. I look toward the bed, but the bellhop, trained in the art of walking into hotel rooms and encountering a wide array of messy situations, politely doesn't follow my gaze. Nor does he wait for a tip, or lift the lid off the silver tray.

"Have a good night, sir," he says, closing the door behind him.

When I lift the lid off the tray there is nothing under it. The tray is empty.

I walk over to Benoît, ready to wake him up, and that's when I see the blood.

And his eyes...

Glassy. Wide open. He's lying on his side, head resting on his arm. It's as if someone scooped out a dime-size hole in his temple with a cherry pitter; blood is trickling out of this hole, over his arm, down the side of the bed—a little crimson waterfall pooling in a puddle on the carpet. And it actually makes a sound: a little *drippity-drip-drip* as more blood soaks the carpet, further darkening the Rorschach stain.

I jump back, looking around wildly. Directly across from Benoît's head there is a similar-size hole in the window, a sprinkling of broken glass on the carpet below.

I realize, almost immediately, that I should get the hell away from the window.

And then I see a green laser beam slowly crossing the room.

I drop to my stomach, hyperventilating, trying to steer clear of the blood.

I am giving DirtyPaws a one-star rating in the app store. *This is bullshit.*

I slither across the floor, trying to move toward the door as fast as I can.

And I think about Tinkerbell. That's right, the stupid fairy.

As a kid, I saw a local performance of *Peter Pan*. Tinkerbell was just this squiggly green laser flitting across the stage. I'm reminded of that now, watching this horrible laser sight seeking me out.

I wasn't exactly enchanted by the show. I think I was just pissed those kids got to fly, and I wanted to fly. I wanted to be Peter and Wendy and whatever the hell those other kids are named. I was jealous because I felt ordinary and landlocked. So when it came to *clap if you believe in fairies* I didn't clap. I didn't really care if Tinkerbell died. My mom was clapping hard, and she looked over at me, somewhat concerned, and said, "Don't you want to clap and save Tinkerbell?"

But I just shook my head.

As I wriggle across the carpet on my belly, chafing my elbows, trying to get to the door, I can't help thinking this is Tinkerbell's revenge. Evil Tinkerbell has come to kill me because I didn't clap. I'm a bad person and I deserve to die.

Evil Tinkerbell arcs across the ceiling and down the walls as I continue my impression of a panicked mollusk, getting closer and closer to the door, praying that laser sight doesn't nail me when I reach up to turn the handle.

There's a buzzing in my hand. Someone is calling my phone.

No, my phone is in my pocket.

This is Benoît's phone. I'm still gripping it hard in my hand. The number calling his phone is the same number that left that weird text message. I recognize the area code. So I turn over onto my back, lie flat, and answer it.

CHAPTER 4

On the Lam

"Hello?"

A pause. "And who am I speaking with?" The voice is steely, smiling.

My lips are tingling. I don't know what to say. Should I give my real name? A fake name? I don't know why I just answered a dead man's phone. Was I hoping for a magical resolution to whatever I just got myself into here? Some quick and easy answers that would make the laser sight—or *this whole situation*—go away?

The voice seems to register my petrified indecision with a slightly impatient *hmpf*. "Considering he didn't answer his phone with our code word, signifying the exchange was made, I have to ask: what has happened to our dear friend?"

Code word?

"Who? Benoît? He's dead."

There's a disappointed but knowing sigh on the other end. "And here I am thinking we already had a deal in place. But apparently you had other plans."

"What... are you talking about?"

"We have a confirmed visual of you," he says.

My mind races. "The bellhop with the empty tray?"

"We know what you look like. What you're wearing. And, obviously, what room you're currently in. Do not hang up."

The adrenaline pumping through my system is clearing my mind. I wasn't really listening to what Benoît was saying when I first walked into his room—"You brought it with you... we'll do it after... and then you can give it to me." None of that made sense. He obviously thought I was someone else. And now so does this guy on the phone.

"What do you want?"

"What we discussed," he replies. "The item in question."

Briefly, absurdly, I feel a surge of hope. This misunderstanding can be cleared up lickety-split, no problemo. I keep my voice level. "I think you have me confused with someone else. I don't think I was supposed to be here."

He laughs at that. "How exactly did you plan on getting away? I'm... curious."

It's kind of crazy, but I just start laughing back at him: involuntary and unhinged. I can't believe all this is really happening. It feels like a prank.

The kind of prank where there's a dead guy in a hotel room, blood pouring from a bullet hole in the side of his head.

Weirdly, my reaction changes the tone of the conversation—the timbre of the man's voice lightens a bit. "Of course," he purrs. "You're wounded. I'd forgotten."

Despite the creepiness, I bristle at that. How would he know what I am?

"You light fires and watch them burn," he says, knowingly.

"Uh, no..."

"Do you have dreams of running?"

What. The. Fuck.

I take a deep breath, deciding to play along, because maybe that's my best option here. "Sometimes I have dreams about tornadoes," I say, scanning the room, trying to spot the laser sight. I don't see it anymore.

There's a silence that goes on too long. I press the phone into my ear so hard it hurts. "Hello?"

"Tornadoes are very destructive, Mr. Preston."

"That's not my name." They definitely think I'm someone else. Shit. What if they don't believe me?

"Would you disagree?" he asks.

"About my name or about tornadoes?"

"Tornadoes."

I clear my throat. "They are. Yeah. Running through a field to escape the funnel. The sky all black and green, upturning like that, sucking everything inside itself."

"You can't even trust the sky. Especially when it's the color of a bruise. Right?"

I reach for the door handle. "Right."

"Don't leave the room."

My hand freezes on the handle. "Can you see me?"

Silence.

I sink to the floor, lying flat on my back again. I still don't see the laser. "Do you have sights on me or something?"

"What are those tornado dreams *really* about, do you think?"

These random questions are hitting me like stray shrapnel. "Are you, like, a psychologist? I just want to go, man."

"Answer the question."

I lick my lips, desperate for this to end. Will they kill me if I try and leave? Will they kill me if I stay? "Losing my family. Seeing everything blown to smithereens as I run." I wipe away tears. I didn't even realize I was crying.

I shift my focus out the window in case the laser returns.

"You wouldn't talk about what happened...not to me, anyway...that would cheapen everything, right? Your memories of him are all that's left."

What is this?

His probing questions are so excruciating, my hands start shaking. "Please stop."

"Why would you want there to be more loss?" he asks.

"I don't!"

"You care deeply about your family. That's touching."

That's a threat.

"I'm trying to tell you I'm not who you think I am!"

"Did you take the money?"

"What money?"

"Is that why you killed him, Mr. Preston?"

"*Who is Mr. Preston?*" I spit into the phone. "I'm the only one here."

There's another silence. The room is so eerily quiet. Jesus. They think I killed Benoît. That's what this is all about. But why would they think I killed him, if they're the ones who shot him through the window?

Unless they weren't the ones who shot him through the window…

Then who did?

I keep thinking honesty will somehow get me through all this. "I didn't kill anyone," I say in a slow, steady voice. "I don't know anything about money. Or an item. I'm the wrong guy."

"We will fetch you very soon. And this time you will have what we need."

He's not hearing me. He doesn't believe me.

"If I'm not him, how could I have what—"

"You will have what we need," he repeats. "No more playing around, hun."

"But listen, please—"

"Promise? Otherwise you will have had your last tornado dream."

They know about my family.

"Okay." I know I'm making impossible promises. This is dangerous. And stupid.

"I'm willing to give you another chance," he says. "Because I know your pain."

How the hell would he know anything about me?

"Who are you, please?" My voice sounds like a teakettle that's been whistling too long.

"You forget so easily." He laughs. "*We*...Mr. Preston...We are the Swans."

I squeeze my eyes shut. "The...*Swans*? I don't know what that is."

"It all begins with a number."

"A number?"

"That night. When it all began."

WHAT.

"We don't get played, Mr. Preston."

"Please—"

"Apologies, but I have to smoke you out. I wouldn't hang around the Mandarin Oriental for too long, hun. A 911 call has already been placed. Looks like somebody just reported a dead body in room 4509."

"Shit, listen—"

"If you get detained by the police, I won't get what I need." He laughs a little, amused by his own game. "So do what you do best in all those dreams—"

"Wait—"

"Run like there's a tornado cutting through the sky."

"Please—"

There's a click.

"Wait, GODDAMMIT!" I scream into the phone.

Shit.

Shit, shit, shit.

I stand in the middle of the room, frozen like a mischievous elf just cast a spell on me in a Nick Jr. movie. I hear my heart drumming in my ears. I'm functioning on pure survival instinct now, every move I make either the right one or a deadly one.

If this fool really called the cops on me, I probably have only two minutes *max* left in this room. If the police find me here they'll definitely detain me. I MEAN THERE'S A DEAD BODY IN THE BED. And if I'm detained, will these Swans actually hurt my family because I couldn't deliver this item to them? Would they do that?

Dumbass, I think, *you have no time to debate this. GET. OUT.*

I reach for the door, but then I stop.

One thing I know for sure right now is that I am in some serious trouble. And it might be smart to find out everything I can before it's too late.

So I quickly search the room.

One of the two open suitcases holds just expensive-looking clothes. If I was going to take *anything* in this room, it might be one of Benoît's James Perse linen shirts.

In the other suitcase there's an accordion folder sticking out. It's full of cash: thick stacks of bills bound by currency straps—labeled $10,000 each.

Well, there's the money.

I estimate there's about a hundred grand in the folder. Some major deal was obviously about to go down here. I consider pocketing the cash, or *some* of it, but that's playing right into the hands of whoever the Swans obviously *think* I am: a con man who was supposed to make a deal but instead just killed the middleman and took the dough.

Plus, I can't carry this much cash around. Plus, if I leave the money I feel like that's a measure of good faith—they'll know I didn't kill Benoît because I would have taken the money.

Do I need to worry about being *implicated in a murder*?

No, no, no. Any kind of ballistics team will realize in five seconds the bullet was clearly shot *through the window from outside,* not fired from inside the room.

But just in case, I grab a towel from the bathroom and do a sweep of the room. I wipe my fingerprints off everything I remember touching, thinking this is probably the most useless action in the world, knowing I'm mucking up a crime scene here. That's probably bad.

Well, I mean it definitely is, that's a crime.

I should probably just wait here for the cops. Or call them myself and explain what happened. But these goddamn Swans know what room I'm in. What if they just want me dead?

I decide to pocket one of the stacks—ten grand—because they already think I killed Benoît and I may not be able to use a credit card or get to an ATM if I'm on the run. And fuck, is that what's about to happen? *Am I on the lam here?*

I gulp air raggedly, filling my lungs. *THINK.*

The basic facts as I know them: some really scary guys think I have some kind of item and threatened me and my family unless I give it to them. The real Mr. Preston was supposed to exchange the item with Benoît for the money. Benoît thought I was Preston last night, but got shot before he figured out I wasn't. The real Preston never showed up. Benoît is dead, so obviously something went very wrong here. Maybe he tried to keep the money? I don't know.

I need to find out who this Benoît guy really is.

I rip the covers off him, wincing at the squish of a used condom as it flies away. Benoît's skin is waxy, turning a freaky gray color, and his body is already stiffening. I get a sudden punch of nausea but I manage to allay the gagging by bending over, grabbing my knees, and breathing in and out through my nose. Then I straighten up and continue. Benoît has a tattoo I didn't notice on his upper arm. I lean in: it's the outline of a swan, with the numbers 6 28 69 curving around the inside of the swan's throat. *A swan.*

It all begins with a number.

I take my phone out of my pocket and snap a photo, accidentally dropping Benoît's phone as I do. My hands are sweaty, fumbling. There's a laptop on the desk. I hurriedly tap a bunch of keys, waking it up—there's nothing on the screen. No folders, no documents—a blank just like Benoît's phone. However, there is a flash drive in the USB port. I pocket it.

I notice the camera on the laptop isn't taped over. Maybe that's how they were watching me? The camera indicator light isn't on, but I'm not sure it has to be. I quickly take a pic of Benoît's body and the bullet hole in the window. I search everywhere for his wallet, or any form of ID. I open every drawer using the towel wrapped around my hand—but there's no wallet, no passport, no credit cards, nothing of any kind. Fuck. All that stuff has gotta be here *somewhere*, but I don't have any more time to search.

I don't feel safe here. I have to get out NOW.

I slip out. As the door closes, clicking behind me and locking, I realize I have everything of mine on me. But I forgot Benoît's phone. It's still lying on the carpet, and that's one thing I didn't wipe my fingerprints off of.

I also left the condom.

I almost laugh out loud. I'm really shitty at this.

I inch along the hallway, flattening myself against the wall, but there's no one here. The floor is empty and hushed, like the hotel was evacuated and no one told me. For one brief, wild second I think of messaging Darren that I need help, or even knocking on his door, but I don't think that will get me anywhere; plus he's probably asleep. So I text Jackson a quick SOS, even though he's not exactly known for being prompt about answering texts. I wish I could just call the police.

Is it safe to go back to my room?

I can't process the concept quickly enough—where I would be safest right now (what if the sniper who killed Benoît is waiting for me outside the hotel?)—so I decide to go back to my room to recoup: my hands are still shaking badly, and my stomach hurts. I hit the button on the elevator, looking over each shoulder a million times, but when the elevator takes forever I run down the stairs, two at a time, until I get to my floor.

When I open the staircase door and step out onto my floor, I see only one person, and he's coming toward me. It's Blond Bellhop, who delivered the empty silver tray. He stops about midway down the hallway and gives me this lascivious grin, which is *so inappropriate* for a uniformed hotel bellhop. He has a white cloth napkin draped over his hand, and there's something bulging underneath. I don't like that. I back away. He comes toward me at a quickened pace.

I guess they're going to try and just kill me.

I open the door to the staircase and run down the stairs so fast I trip, nearly spraining my ankle, careening down, hearing my footsteps clatter beneath me, the sound of rubber streaking, echoing. When I get to a lower floor, I take an elevator the rest of the way to the lobby, freaking out the whole way down.

The lobby lounge is actually on the second floor. This hotel is so Fancy Weird. But there are people here, milling about, suitcases stacked next to them—late arrivals checking in, on their phones, gazing longingly at the last gasps of the emptying cocktail lounge. I feel a little safer here, with people around me.

I look around but don't spot any obvious threat. Maneuvering around the trippy glass sculpture of a plant or something, I walk up to the check-in desk and calmly wait my turn, keeping my eyes peeled for anything bad.

"Hi," says the woman behind the desk.

"Hi," I say, and my mind goes blank for a second. Then: "I'm staying here...."

She waits for more but then becomes confused when that's all I can get out. She just starts nodding, her mouth open a little, waiting to pick a rote response from a memorized roster of Hotel Speak for whatever I'm about to throw at her at this late hour. I want to find out if the dead man in room 4509 is actually named Benoît, and if so what his full name is (or *was*). Any info gleaned about him might be useful, but my mouth isn't forming words.

The desk woman, sensing something is off, throws a blank,

all-purpose smile my way. "And what can we do for you, Mr. Preston?"

I have to steady myself by laying my palm flat on the desk.

"Why...why do you think my name is Mr. Preston?" I stammer.

Her mouth goes a little crooked. "Well, isn't it, sir? Room 4509, right?"

Am I in the fucking Twilight Zone here?

"We know all our guests." She flashes a proud smile. "This is the Mandarin Oriental," she states, like I may have forgotten. "Now, what can we do for you?"

I'm starting to really lose it. "I'm not Mr. Preston. My name is Aidan Jamison...and I'm in room 3715." I take out my wallet (thank God I still have it) and slide my driver's license, as well as my school ID and my room keycard, over to her. "I think...I'm in some sort of trouble. I don't know...."

What are you doing, dumbass, what are you doing....

I'm so freaked out I'm not thinking clearly, yet I'm also cruelly aware of that fact. "I think...maybe you need to call the police actually."

"Is everything all right, sir?" She looks concerned.

"There's been a mix-up. I'm getting...uh...harassing calls... and knocks on my door...from people who *think* I'm Mr. Preston. How, uh, was this mistake made?"

I have no idea what I'm even saying. They are random words just pouring out of my mouth.

She frowns at the ID cards in her hands and checks her computer, tapping the keys. There's a pause, then a deeper frown. "One moment, please," she says, not making eye contact, leaving her place behind the desk and disappearing inside an interior office.

Now I'm just standing at the check-in desk waiting for her to come back. The longer I stand here, the more panicky I'm getting. Something is seriously wrong. I want to get out of here now, *like right now,* but the lady took both my ID cards.

I look behind me. Oh, shit...

Blond Bellhop is standing at the bottom of a staircase, with that napkin still wrapped around his hand. He licks his lips. He looks positively murderous. But his expression changes when the elevator doors open, on the other side of me, and my eyes follow his. About twenty police officers pour out of the elevators.

Oh, God, that guy on the phone was not kidding around.

Blond Bellhop slowly shakes his head at me, a finger pressed to his lips. And then he runs off.

The Swans may be trying to kill me, but if the police get me first, the Swans won't get what they think I owe them.

And then they could go after my family.

They have all those photos of me; they seem to know a lot of personal shit about my life.

There's a cacophony of voices in my head right now, arguing with one another about what the hell I should do, like my consciousness was contained within a fragile vase all this time, and it just got atomized by a mortar shell.

Is this what pure panic sounds like? The voices rise and blend into a humming chant. But then one voice carries over the rest and it's telling me, in no uncertain terms, to get as far away from the Mandarin Oriental as fast as I can.

So, shit, yeah.

I take a step away from the desk just as the police crowd it, muscling me aside. Everyone in the lobby turns to watch them. Their radios crackle.

I make a break for it—sprinting, hurtling myself inside one of the still-open elevators. The last thing I see before the doors close is the check-in clerk pointing at me, and twenty police officers turning their heads in unison just in time to watch me disappear.

I fly out into the night, potentially a fugitive now. I'm hit with the whole city at once: the humidity, car horns, sirens, slick streets, blinking traffic lights reflecting off the windshields of idling Ubers, and the sweet rot of European perfume mixed with curbside garbage.

I run toward Central Park, past the Maine Monument—Columbia and her seahorses bronze and unfazed, rising gloriously from their pylon. I'm thinking: *trees, darkness*. I just want cover. I look behind me. I'm not being chased (yet) and I see only one thing that's curious, because it's the only thing besides Columbia that isn't active in some way.

It's a guy on a vintage Yamaha café racer motorcycle—shiny gold front forks and a leather seat the color of a baseball glove; hard to miss. He's dressed all in black leather, right in front of the Time Warner Center next to the hotel. He's wearing a black helmet with a mirrored visor that mimics the iridescence of a green bottle fly.

His head seems to be tracking my movements—very, very slowly—and I have a sick feeling that he's one of them.

As I hit the edge of the park and begin running as far and as fast into it as I can, I hear the motorcycle starting up behind me. But I just keep running. My pocket vibrates.

Someone's calling me.

"Hello," I gasp into the phone.

"Whassssup!" says Jackson, and I know immediately he didn't see my text. It's so annoying when he does this. But hell, I don't know what it's like to be him and receive four thousand text messages and nine hundred e-mails an hour—his phone is just a mess of red notification bubbles with numbers so high it gives me anxiety every time I happen to see his screen.

"Jackson!" I scream.

"Yo, where are you?"

"In the park."

"Central? Kinda late, isn't it? Alone?"

"Jacks!" I scream again. I look around. I've penetrated the southwestern corner of the park, which is about to officially close for the night, so cops might spot me. I'm running down a pretty well-lit path. I veer off it, onto a lawn, staying clear of lights until I'm next to a pond, still and becalming. For some insane reason I think of that hotel pool in Cabo and Santiago's hand gripping my thigh, and I feel myself blush everywhere. What the hell is wrong with me? Even now? *Seriously?*

"Are you okay?" says Jackson.

It's hard to catch my breath. "Some shit went down, man."

"What happened?"

I glance at my phone. The battery indicator is red. I have 15 percent power left. *And I don't have my charger with me.* "My phone... almost dead."

I find a bench and sit down hard, panting, heart pounding. I'm in partial darkness, away from the dusky streetlights, but the sky is overcast; the skyline reflects off it like the clouds are engorged with LEDs—a black-and-white movie flickering in the sky.

"Dude," says Jackson. "I forgot to text you. But I didn't really know if I was going to go and then I did."

"Where are you?"

"I'm here!" I hear heavy background noise now: thumping music, laughter, shouting. "I don't know exactly," he says. "This place is awesome! There are two DJs. I think they're both younger than us. EDM with this, like, influx of Northern Soul. You gotta check this shit out. There are these brainy tech babes here, man. They're like—"

"*Where are you?*"

"Dude, I don't even know."

"Then how can I meet you? Where is Tats?"

"She's asleep at home. She didn't want to come out. She's being annoying."

I scowl. "So you're out... flirting with other girls while she's home sleeping?"

"Word, I'm like... *not ready to settle down.*"

I understand I'm being chased by murderers and cops, but... I really like Jacks and Tats as a couple; they are great together, they are something stable, and the fact that this stable unit, which indirectly stabilizes me, is endangered makes me immediately unhappy.

"I thought you guys were all about each other?"

"Shit got weird with her parents—yeeeeaaah *YA ARE*—" he shouts out to someone, with a forward gallop of a laugh, his voice sliding away from my ear, into the wash of noise, and then right back to me. "I don't know where we're going."

I don't know if he means his relationship, or literally, like he's heading elsewhere. I keep my voice steady. "Jackson. Listen to me...are you...drunk?"

"A little."

"Juuling?"

"Vaping with Garrison. I'm good. Been dancing. I met this girl."

"Who the fuck is Garrison?"

"Guy I met here."

There's a shadow moving through the trees. Someone's coming toward me; maybe it's someone walking a dog, maybe something else. I get back on the path and start walking rapidly. The luminous funnel of the black-and-white sky follows me like a powdery spotlight. I think of the Bat Signal. Gotham City. Pulpy comic-book adventures. My brain desperately trying to suppress the string of horrors I just witnessed and can't quite reconcile yet. Evil Tinkerbell. My family being threatened by a stranger on someone else's phone. And Benoît, a man I barely knew, who was cute, and was kind to me, and knew what to do with his hands, before someone blew his brains out.

I see flashlight beams, then *groups* of flashlight beams in the near distance, coming through the park. I lower my voice. "Look. I'm in trouble and I need you to pay very close attention to what I'm saying."

"I'm here," says Jackson. "It's okay."

"My phone is almost dead. And I need to get to you."

"Get on the L train. Head east. Jefferson-Wyckoff."

"I'm in Central Park. That's not helpful!"

"Dude, Uber it."

"I don't have an Uber account! I don't have the battery power to download the app. And I don't know where you are, asshole!"

"Oh, shit, just use mine, just use my Uber. Where are you?"

Okay, good question. *Where am I?*

I glance at my phone. As if knowing my distress level and wanting to ensure my weakened heart gets a nice hard pummeling of pure seismic fear, my battery has precipitously dropped to 9 percent. Shit. If this phone dies, I might die. This is real.

"Stay on the phone with me," I tell Jackson, thinking it'll use more battery power to hang up and call him back. I don't know if that's even true. I know nothing.

"Yeah, yeah," he says. "No worries. It's fine."

I work my way through the foggy, moonlit park, a dark jumble of low hills, stone arches, and winding paths, until about ten minutes later I see lights and hear traffic and emerge on Central Park West and 89th Street. How the hell did I get this far up from 59th? I have 4 percent battery power left. I tell Jackson where I am. I see clumps of police vehicles at various intersections, flashing lights—nervous-disco reds and blues. I can't possibly think they have anything to do with me.

"Look for an Acura MDX. Your driver's name is Nazrul," says Jackson. "Three minutes."

I hide behind a tree until I see a car slow down. "Nazrul," I repeat. "Okay."

I open the door and slide inside. Nazrul barely acknowledges me as we drive off. He's involved in an intense phone conversation with his brother, who apparently may or may not be getting out of prison tonight. I hang up, relaying the Uber drama to Jackson via text.

They're always on the phone with their brother, Jackson texts back. IDK why.

Then my phone dies.

CHAPTER 5

Bushwick

It was a warm Saturday morning, on the cusp of noon, when Tom first asked me if I wanted to go for a swim, playfully throwing me one of Shane's old bathing suits. I had just finished mowing. I was all sweaty; I smelled like soil and freshly mowed grass, and my knees had patches of dirt on them, *so sure why not*. I changed in their downstairs bathroom while I heard Tom, outside, dive into the pool, getting a head start. I peeked out at him through the blinds, my curiosity piqued in a very specific way.

They had a nice round pool in the middle of their backyard, very out in the open, so when you were swimming you were aware of the vastness of the sky. The wooden fence around their property was really low. Neighbors could easily peer over it if they wanted to; an infusion of innocent suburbia—every shout and splash heard three houses down.

I thought of Archie Comics and that sunlit town of Riverdale, lost in time. I had just started reading them, with a keen interest in the Kevin Keller stuff, obviously, but had back-ordered older issues because I was interested to see what Riverdale looked like through the ages, and I was happy to discover it hadn't changed all that much. I find weird things comforting like that.

I never had much interest in *Riverdale,* the TV show. That was something else. Although the guys in it are super cute.

Tom and I swam laps together. He had been a swimmer in college, so he gently adjusted my form. Then, still shirtless, towels wrapped around our shoulders, we escaped into his kitchen, where he microwaved us a plate of pizza rolls and poured lemonade over ice. I could see that he was uncomfortable in his kitchen, and was making food only for me, was doing all this just for me. We ate from the same yellow plate, sitting on barstools facing each other across the kitchen island, keeping our feet off the cold tiled floor, and didn't say much at all.

I had ideas from Insta and Snap who gay boys my age crushed on, or were supposed to be crushing on—Troye Sivan, Roy Harper on *Arrow,* the dudes from *Supernatural*—but I was interested in the way Tom's muscles moved when he reached for the glasses in a cupboard over their stainless-steel fridge. I liked the shape of his back, how tall he was, and the way his mouth crinkled on the sides when he smiled. And I did wonder if that made me different from the ways I was already different—a double whammy of not fitting in.

Leave it to me: simultaneously worried about not fitting in, yet terrified I was a boring suburban clone with my whole life laid out before me.

We went swimming a bunch of times after that, any kind of physical contact filed under the casual guise of a late-morning impromptu swimming lesson. But gradually the lessons didn't seem quite so impromptu anymore, and the distance between us closed.

I think I was attracted to something I sensed in him that I didn't completely understand yet, but identified with anyway: a quiet desolation. As our activities evolved, I realized he was home alone a lot of the time. I began to see more of Tom than I did Shane, which felt weird at first, but then not weird at all.

We started watching TV together—post-swim, post–pizza rolls—and each time, we slid closer to each other on that beachy white sofa. If you fast-forwarded all those moments together you would definitely see the perceptible shift, like one of those nature documentaries that show a flower growing out of the ground in sped-up time.

I can't remember what we were arguing about. I think we were watching a silly TV show, some buzzy Hulu drama, and he predicted where things were going to go. I disagreed in a really sassy way and kicked at him, nudging my bare foot into the side of his leg. And he just went for me.

We pseudo-wrestled on the carpet. When I was clearly winning (or he was letting me win), pinning him down, I said something like: *I guess swimming really WAS your thing in college cause it sure as fuck wasn't wrestling.*

He scooped me up and slung me over his shoulder. He spun me once around the room, which was enough to make me dizzy. He was stronger than I thought. Then he just stood there, with me still dangling over his shoulder, his arms wrapped tightly around my legs, holding me in place. I was conscious of his breathing, of his body working. It was clear he didn't know what to do next, and it was clear he didn't want to put me down. So I rested my hand against his lower back and said:

Take me upstairs, you stupid dumbass.

I can't believe I said that.

But I did, and he did.

When he first put his hands on me after that moment—the very first touch after the game between us changed, and our playfulness became something way more serious—I was like: *oh, shit.*

I remember touches, where people first put their hands, and he put his palm right below my throat, on my upper chest. I instantly felt a charge run through my body, something clicking into place. It was the first time I ever felt that I mattered to someone, felt accepted, or cared for in that way. I didn't want to let that go. Something scary emerged in me then: I realized I would fight to keep this. This was a part of me I didn't know I had. And I didn't know where it would lead, because the rational side of my brain was screaming that this could never be, that this was very wrong.

And I wondered if I was willing to see people get hurt to keep this, to keep him.

Over time the risk became part of the thrill, I think, each of us doing something wrong for different reasons. I became a little obsessed with Tom and with what was going on between us. That was probably my biggest mistake.

The night flies by the car windows in hurried wisps of light and muddled sound. After about twenty minutes, we go over a bridge. The view of the city stretches out; it feels momentous, the skyline almost toylike as we skitter along its top edges, as if it's trapped and glittering in a jar. I think I hear the sound of motorcycles twice, but each time I look out the rear window I don't see anyone following us.

Eventually, once we're over the bridge, the Uber slows to a stop on a quiet corner outside a liquor store. I don't see much of anything around us. Nazrul insists that we've arrived at the correct address, so I get out of the car. As soon as I close my door, he skids away, still on the phone.

At first I think I've been left in an abandoned industrial wasteland, but then I see pockets of life: bars in sneaky corners, spills of light, tight clusters of people smoking, laughing—the neighborhood slowly revealing itself, undoing its creases and folds. I don't know which direction to walk. Jackson never gave me the address, he just plugged it into the Uber app and now the fucking Uber is gone.

Goddammit.

I walk across the street, trying to get my bearings. I'm facing a large warehouse. The windows are lit up gold, shapes and words painted on them from the inside; some of the windows are colored with hanging sheer cloth. But the place seems deserted to me. I walk farther along the street, looking around, hitting a string of cafés, some of them still open even at this crazy hour, the loud festive voices and the clank of silverware from inside momentarily soothing. The traffic lights change, a few cars zoom by, then a bus, and suddenly the neighborhood doesn't seem as sleepy and dead to me.

Then I see the motorcycles.

They round a corner, facing me, facing the wrong side of the street. My heart starts to play a Led Zeppelin song inside my chest. It's the same motorcycle I saw outside the Time Warner Center, and now there are two of them—two dudes on vintage bikes with iridescent green visors. They followed me all the way to Brooklyn.

So I run.

I turn a corner. I'm on a side street now, where it's super dark and quiet. There's an empty parking lot behind a fence, a few dilapidated apartment buildings with cracked windows, an elementary school set back from the street, partly hidden by clusters of trees. Sneakers hang from power lines.

I keep running, past another fence with rusty automobile skeletons and piles of mangled metal junk behind it. I hear the distant roar of the motorcycles, growing closer. I round another corner. I'm just getting myself more lost, tunneling into the bowels of a neighborhood I'm not familiar with in any way.

Intense psychedelic art, painted on low brick walls, pops out: Q*bert wearing Beats headphones and devouring a purple octopus; a flying saucer shooting red rectangular laser beams; Pac-Man eating a laptop while being chased by government-agent ghosts: vintage video game imagery updated with millennial hacktivist angst.

I hear music. I feel a beat. I just can't tell where it's coming from.

I turn another corner, trying to run toward the music, but the sound of a rumbling train, somewhere overhead, drowns it out. I hear the motorcycles again, closer now, and then a hand reaches out and grabs my shoulder and I scream and jump five feet in the air.

"Dude!" It's Jackson. His phone is halfway to his ear, casting a little pool of light against the side of his face. He has a slightly dumbstruck expression. A throng of girls in groovy-patterned tops, his latest admirers, all move aside like a wind. They pretend to check their phones, swaying, keeping one eye on me, curious.

"Oh, my God," I say, and hug him hard. I have never, in my whole life, been more relieved to see someone.

"I was looking all over for you," he says. "Where the hell did you—"

"We need to *go*," I tell him. "*Where is this thing?*"

The twin motorcycles appear at the other end of the street. They gun their engines. The two bikers, shielded mirrored faces growing more chilling each time I see them, turn their heads in unison to stare me down. I point at them.

Jackson looks at the bikes, then back at me. "Seriously?"

"YES! Let's go!"

"It's right here," he says.

Jackson grabs my hand and we hop around a corner, partway down an adjacent block, past a gate. Then an unmarked door, scribbled with pink graffiti, is thrust open, and we're inside.

Everything is doused in acid-green light. Cloud rap is echoing through the cavernous, multi-tiered space. Everything is cloudy in general—blurry, off-kilter. Shadowy bodies, silhouetted against the light, bounce up and down to the music. Lines of people wearing Day-Glo bracelets and necklaces that change color in tandem snake around makeshift bars, the bottles illuminated from behind with an underwater glow. Sequined acrobatic dancers with greased-up hair hang from poles, gyrating. I see a lot of unusual tattoos, choppy asymmetrical haircuts, girls in black miniskirts, dudes in muscle tees bearing mysterious insignias.

Projected on one wall is the original *Space Invaders* arcade game. But it's tricked out with molten colors and twitchy-looking aliens. On the opposite wall, the bright-blue sky and puffy clouds from *Super Mario Bros.* serenely scroll by.

"It's a fashion-and-tech theme!" Jackson shouts, pointing out a group of revelers in one corner wearing Adidas jackets and Oculus Rift headsets. "This whole party is virtual reality–ready," he says, but it's really hard to hear him over the music.

"What does that even mean?" I shout, as he leads me across the dance floor.

"I think you can put on a headset and parts of this place become a 3D wonderland or some shit. This whole thing was organized by a group of post-conceptual artists who work across different mediums. Like Cory Arcangel." He points at the *Super Mario* clouds. "Got famous for hacking Nintendo NES cartridges."

A girl in a slinky blue dress—older, with severe eye makeup and an Amy Winehouse-y beehive—hands Jackson a drink that glows blue from ultraviolet light. "You want anything?" says Jackson, pointing at me.

"No, no."

Jackson is totally wasted, clearly has been for some time, and I have to figure out how to bring him back down to earth, because I need him to focus and help me right now.

"This is Charlotta," says Jacks, pointing at the Amy Winehouse girl. She smiles, faintly. "She does PR for—"

"I'm a digital marketing strategist for Xavier Lightbeam," she corrects him.

I nod. She might as well be speaking Portuguese.

"It's a Brooklyn-based tech start-up," she explains, looking around, bored.

"Charlotta is from Sweden," says Jackson, winking at me. He's got on his turquoise muscle shirt, which is what he wears when he's actively on the prowl. Another girl in a black dress wraps her arms around his neck, like she's known him forever, whispering into his ear. Jackson nods, and looks at me, bringing two fingers to his lips. "Do you want to . . . ?"

"*Smoke?* Not now, man!"

I turn around. The two bikers, still wearing their helmets, are inside now, moving toward us through the crowd. The lights reflect off their visors, making them gleam in a really off-putting way. They look like hostile aliens in black leather biker gear.

"Jackson!" I scream, pointing at them.

"My friend thinks he's being chased by Daft Punk," says Jackson, pretty cavalier about it all, and everyone laughs, sips their drinks. "He thinks they're trying to kill him."

"What's your name, sweetie?" says a girl with kinky red hair, who appeared out of nowhere and is rocking this white-and-blue zipped-up jumpsuit thing with a matching purse. She gently cups Jackson's elbow.

"Aidan," I tell her.

"I'm Corinna," she says. "I'm in from San Fran. I work at Clarium Capital."

I nod, distantly.

"For Peter Thiel?" she explains.

"He's gay," says Jackson, indicating me, sipping his drink.

All the girls nod as one, and take an almost imperceptible step back, because I'm suddenly off the market, *something they can't have.* Corinna smiles warmly at me, though, stirring her drink once with her little finger. "I have a friend here I'd love you to meet . . . if I can find him. He works in Chelsea. The David Dorbean gallery?"

I shake my head. She looks over my shoulder and giggles, hand to her mouth. "Are you really trying to kill our friend?" she says.

I turn around, slowly, and see she is addressing the two bikers, who are now standing right behind me like grim reapers.

I freeze. Sweat beads on my brow. They could kill me at any second, and there is too much going on in this space for anyone to notice or care. If I try to run, they could just grab me, break my neck, stab me, inject me with something . . . This whole place—where they're ironically now playing trap music—*is* a fucking trap.

The biker dudes don't move or react. They both wear black gripping gloves—probably deerskin leather. Good for strangling.

Jackson downs his drink, throws down his cup. "Yo, what is *up*?" he asks them. "Do you have a problem with my friend?" He moves in. *"Do we have a problem here?"*

But I'm with Jackson, I remind myself, my superhero best friend.

The biker dudes don't move. Their silent stoicism is deeply unnerving.

"What do you want?" Charlotta asks them. "When is your next album dropping?" But Jackson's already made that joke and it isn't as funny the second time, especially in an unsure, drunken Swedish accent.

After a moment, the biker dudes turn in unison and walk away.

"Yeah! Go on!" says Jackson. He gives me a look like: *See?*

"This isn't over," I shout in his ear. "They'll probably be waiting for me outside, where I'll be more isolated."

Jackson frowns at me. "Who did you piss off? How real did shit get?"

"Pretty real," I tell him.

"Okay. Let's go out the back way. C'mon," he says, leading me through the crowd, breaking away from the throng of fancy ladies who have no idea we're underage. Jackson probably told them he was the world's youngest venture capitalist. He does shit like that.

Every room we pass by in this insanely huge warehouse—Jackson tells me it's called the Rocket Factory; they once manufactured rockets here, or whatever—is playing different music, different DJs, catering to an entirely different subset of reveler.

I almost want to linger in the room decorated with glow-in-the-dark sculpture-monsters made out of orange yarn, where the DJ is playing a deeper cut from the Clash's *Sandinista!* album, but I follow Jackson out to a wide courtyard, where people are gathered in tight groups vaping and chugging PBRs.

"I need a minute," says Jackson.

"Jacks, we really need to get out of here."

"I need to clear my head."

He leads me over to a bunch of hammocks strung between trees, and soft round chairs hanging from chains. We nab a swinging chair after two girls with pink hair depart, blowing us a kiss as they melt into the party. Jackson sucks on his vaping pen, the light on the end glowing like a comet, then hands it to me. I take a long drag because at this point, why the hell not.

"You know I love you," says Jackson, exhaling, staring up at the sky.

"I love you, too, man," I say. But my words sound strained. Jackson is more in touch with his emotions regarding other dudes than I am. But he has less of a past in that regard, too. He doesn't bear the same handprints.

Dirty paws.

Jackson wanted to be friends with me precisely for the same reason I wanted to be friends with him—we remind each other of nothing we're familiar with from back home. We're in the same residence hall—Welton. He was the first person at Witloff who I came out to because we just started talking one day after our American Lit class. Know what he did? He put his hands on my shoulders, gave me a big kiss on the mouth and said: "Well,

I guess we know for sure I'm straight now *'cause ya sure are pretty.*"

"I need your phone," I say.

He hands it over. I remember the numbers tattooed on Benoît's arm: 6 28 69. I google them.

The first hits I get are dates. There was a Grateful Dead concert that night, in 1969, but I have a feeling that's not relevant. The next date, however, makes me gasp.

The Stonewall riots.

I know about the Stonewall riots because I know about history, and the gay civil rights movement, which I read about on my own, because they don't teach that stuff in school. LGBT people fought back against a police raid at a gay bar called the Stonewall Inn in New York City that night. That one event pretty much started the modern-day movement for gay rights and equality. Those people were heroes. And no one from my generation probably knows or cares. They're too busy taking pouty selfies for hookup apps.

The man on the phone said: *It all begins with a number....*

And he said something else, too:

That night. When it all began.

He must have been referring to Stonewall. Benoît was gay, obviously, but the guy on the phone was, too. It was the way he spoke to me: his tone, the way he called me "hun." A little bit flirty and a little bit judgy.

"We are the Swans," he said. And Benoît had a tattoo of a swan along with those numbers curving around it. It's a link, but I don't know what it means yet.

And I don't have a good feeling about it.

"Tell me what's going on," says Jackson.

I hand him back his phone, tell him about meeting Benoît.

He shakes his head at me. "Dude."

"I wound up in his room only because things didn't quite work out with Darren Cohen."

Jackson gives me a wide-eyed look.

"You didn't know about Darren?"

"No," he says, "but I guess it doesn't shock me."

"Anyway. I woke up and he was dead."

"Darren's dead?"

"No, the older guy. Benoît."

"Shit. What? How did he die? Was he really *that old*?"

"He was shot in the head! There was a bullet hole in the window. There was a laser sight crossing the room, trying to find me."

"That's so fucking scary! This just happened for real?"

"Like an hour ago, maybe a little more? What time is it even?"

Jackson checks his watch. "Around one-thirty. You walked into something bad?"

"No. That's the thing. It's like it walked into *me*."

I tell Jacks about the photos of me I found on Benoît's phone, the strange conversation with the voice on the phone, the cash in the suitcase, the murderous bellhop, how everyone started calling me Mr. Preston, the Stonewall riots.

Jackson just blinks at me, like, *Do I get a break before you delve into Season Two*?

I take the flash drive out of my pocket. "I got this from Benoît's laptop. We should probably see what's on it."

"All right, keep that shit in your pocket."

"And I need to charge my phone. I'm supposed to meet my parents tomorrow! And now the cops and these bad guys are all after me."

Jackson puts his hand on my shoulder. "Do you want to go to the police?"

I shake my head. "The Swan guy said they'd go after my family if I don't give them what—"

"I'm sure the police would protect your family, Aidy."

"How sure are you? They're watching my every move. I don't know how many of them there are. If it was you..."

He sighs, cracks his knuckles. "I don't know."

"I want to find out everything I can first. I'm afraid, man. This is heavy."

Jackson looks around. "All right, we should get you out of here now."

"Where?"

"Well, I'm staying with Leo at his cousin's place in Crown Heights."

"What? What place?"

"Some co-living startup called Kibbutzeteria. I said I'd crash with him tonight after Tats and I got into a fight."

"Dude, I didn't even know Leo's *in town*."

"Yeah, yeah he is. He just didn't have time to meet us for tea earlier. He's sorry."

I stare at a loose pattern of cigarette butts on the ground. "It's like you and Leo have your own thing going on without me."

Jackson sighs again. "Do you want to do this now?"

"Yes," I say, as the pot soothes my nerves, and stokes an appetite I'm rarely aware of, while churning my feelings of outrage. "Our relationship is important to me and I want pretzels."

"It's important to me, too."

"It's the only relationship in my life that's ever worked."

"No one is excluding you," says Jackson. "You get paranoid and obsessive."

"Is that what Leo says? Is that why he avoids me?"

"No one is avoiding you. You should probably not smoke pot right now."

"You have to admit you don't tell me shit."

"What? What don't I tell you?"

"Like, why are you even crashing with Leo tonight? What happened with Tats? Why don't you ever tell me shit?"

"Dude, *I DO*. Relax. There was no time. Shit's been getting weird with her for a while. I don't know. I just don't think I'm in love with her. I've been as far down this road with her as I can. I don't envision us moving forward from where we are. I want to see the world and experience different shit."

"You mean, like, more poontang."

I get a sharp look. "That word does not look or sound good coming out of those pillowy lips."

"Sorry."

"And her parents piss me off. There's all this pressure with them and they're kinda judgmental. Like I'm not good enough. I get the sense they think I'm a player."

"You are a little, though."

"They want me to commit. Like, *now*. They act like they're

all impressed with me, but keep asking about our plans for the future. And yeah, I get it, I guess. They don't want to see their baby get hurt. But what am I supposed to do, *propose*? I'm not even in college yet. It's too much, too soon. We want different things. We're in different places. I'm not ready."

"Yeah, but are you treating her well? She's home asleep and you're out partying."

"I told you shit got weird. I needed to get out for a while."

"Yeah, but—"

"Boy, get your ass up."

I stand up, brushing off my shorts. "Sorry."

"Seriously, I'm done. I told you to behave yourself. You didn't. Now the whole world's after you, you're dragging me into this shit, and you want to judge me for Tats?"

"I'm not judging. I like her."

He narrows his eyes. "My game is tight. How 'bout yours?"

I wipe my brow with the back of my hand. "I'm a mess. Obviously."

He shakes his head. "I'm still trying to understand this self-destructive side of you. I know where it comes from—"

"Do not bring up my brother right now," I say icily, through my teeth.

Jackson holds his hands out, defensively. "I wasn't. *Wasn't.* I was just going to say...I don't know how to respond or deal with you sometimes. Okay? You don't listen."

I stand there for a second, tapping my feet, taking in this whole night like a rainstorm pouring over me. "You really think I'm self-destructive?"

"There's that side to you, dude, you know there is."

The side of me that meets random middle-aged men in hotel rooms? Wipes fingerprints, steals ten grand from a crime scene? Chats with a stranger who wants to kill me about running from tornadoes in apocalyptic dreams?

"I think I am a lovely young man with a good head on my shoulders," I say primly, "all things considered."

"Okay, then." Jackson stands, pockets the vape pen. "I just think you should shut your ass up sometimes. Especially when someone's trying to help you. And look—no one excludes you because you like dick, and I know that's what you think sometimes. We're your best friends."

"I didn't think that. I don't! I mean I *do* like dick...a lot, yes, but that's not—"

"You do think it. I know you do. You got a persecution complex on top of everything else."

"Okay. Wow. How much are you charging me for this therapy session?"

"Not enough. There's no use going into all this now, though. There's obviously bigger fish to fry tonight. C'mon." He wraps his hand around my neck. "Let's ghost."

"I just hope you know how lucky you are," I tell him. "Everyone loves you and you get away with everything, there's never any consequences to—"

"I am a black boy in America. I do not get away with everything. I'm looking over my shoulder, too, more than you know—"

"Shit, I know, I know—"

"We all got problems," he says, whipping out his phone. "I ain't perfect."

"Are you sure about that?"

"Very."

There's no way out the back. We're kind of trapped. So I follow Jackson back inside the warehouse and onto the main dance floor, where things have gotten progressively weirder. This is not helped in any way by the fact that I'm now a little stoned. Jackson has his phone out, the Uber app pulsing. I overhear snippets of conversation.

A woman in a black Prada bucket hat points to a group of her friends: "Tick tock, motherfuckers, if you want to lose weight for fashion week, you better start *yesterday*."

A gay dude to a girl he's with: "All you *ever* do is talk about how much you hate Saoirse Ronan."

All other conversations get swept away as the music segues into a thunderous deluge of dance rock. The crowd seems bigger now: more druggy, pumped. Jackson brushes away thickets of bubbles that a guy dressed as a robot is blowing through a large wand. Through a bobbling bubble, I see one of the bikers, distorted and rainbowed, standing at the far corner of the dance floor. The other biker stands at the other side. They're clearly hoping to nab me as I leave. I pat my pocket. I bet they want that flash drive back.

I point them out to Jackson. He looks back at me and nods—he sees them, too.

But then we get lucky.

Some people dressed as zombies are wreaking havoc by

jumping onto the dance floor and "tagging" random dancers—slapping a thick red sticker with a biohazard symbol onto their backs. This throws everyone's rhythm off, and the crowd sways to the left after a zombie boy gets shoved.

And then a deer scampers through the warehouse.

A freakin' live deer.

People hoot and holler, not realizing they could probably get full-on gored by the panicked animal that some hipster fucktard just let in here.

Jackson grabs my shoulders and pushes me forward, and we follow the sprinting deer, leaving screams and chaos and spilled drinks in our wake. People race to open the front garage doors of the warehouse. The deer darts out into the night, its antlers framed by the dirty moon, the color of cereal milk, a perverted marriage of the urban and the pastoral, all wrong, something I think I'll always wonder if I really saw.

Jackson dips us into the crowd of partyers. Sweaty bodies jab into us, sharp elbows and knees, pushing against us, stepping on our feet. Everyone spills outside, desperate for the perfect Instagram shot of the deer bucking, terrified and confused, in the middle of the street, bringing traffic to a screeching halt.

Jackson guides me sharply to the right. We tumble into a black Chevy Suburban, which is waiting calmly by the curb, and speed off.

CHAPTER 6

Kibbutzeteria

We arrive at a sleepy-looking brownstone a few minutes later, after making sure we weren't followed. I don't hear motorcycles anywhere in the vicinity.

"Was there really a deer in there?" I ask Jackson quietly, as we step up to the door and the Chevy Suburban drives away. I look over my shoulder sixty times.

"There really was," he says, his phone out.

"So Leo's staying here?"

"This is the address he gave me. We should be safe here. There's security. Everything is accessed by an app, which I'm now trying to—"

The door clicks open.

"There we go," says Jacks, leading me inside. The lights flick on automatically. We walk past an indoor bike rack, completely full, in the foyer.

I have never been to a co-living start-up before. I'm not entirely sure what they are, but it's super-posh. Jackson explains they're like dorms for busy young professionals—people who work long hours on Wall Street or at Google or whatever, who want to live together, be around other people, and have everything taken care of for them.

There are hardwood floors, Moroccan shag rugs everywhere; the overall décor is modern but comfy, Swedish-functional, everything the color of oatmeal. Flat-screen TVs perched over a wooden banister inform people of packages waiting for them and provide a schedule of the week's activities. There's a movie night in a basement screening room, a meditation class in the third-floor flex room, cooking lessons in the downstairs chef's kitchen, a reading group taking place tomorrow in the backyard hot tubs. Dang.

We walk by a room filled with vintage pinball machines and another with mirrored walls, free weights stacked neatly on racks, a bunch of treadmills, sky-blue yoga mats, and purple and red exercise balls. Soft, trancelike music plays from a hidden sound system, and the lighting is all cool midnight colors.

Jackson snickers. "Leo told me the music and lighting are all on a timer," he says, "designed to shift with the daylight. For people who stay in and code all day and need an artificial sense of a day passing while they work."

"Really? That's so dope."

"Or totally unhealthy," he replies.

I feel sleepy all of a sudden. "How late is it?"

"Late," says Jackson. "A little after two."

Jackson turns a corner. We're facing a wall of frosted glass, and then I realize they're just tall cabinets. Jackson taps something into an app, unlocking two of them, revealing shelves full of snack foods, a fridge full of soda. Jackson tosses me a bottle of Curiosity Cola and a bag of pretzels. He points to his left with a grin, and I see a room with Ping-Pong tables and a full bar with ten different beers on tap.

"Can I move in? Like right now?"

"It's hard," says Jackson, swiping a bag of chips. "You have to apply for membership. It's pretty competitive—from what Leo told me, anyway."

"Makes sense."

"Let's find our boy." I follow Jackson to another staircase at the other end of the house. "He told me he was up here," he says, reading a text, "in the room at the end of the hall." We climb up carpeted stairs, walk down a long hallway. Everyone's clearly asleep—their doors, each with a nautical-style lantern out front and a brass number on the door, are closed, silent inside.

We stop in front of a door, next to a window that looks out onto a backyard. I see grills, tables with umbrellas, and the aforementioned hot tubs. Jackson types something into the app and the door clicks open. "And here we are," he says. We peek our heads into the room.

"Leo?" I whisper.

"Hey, man," says Jackson, as we move into the darkened room. "Wake up."

A shape stirs. I see the shape reach for its glasses.

The room isn't totally dark. Everything is blinking. Leo is the most wired individual on the planet; there are laptops and a gazillion other devices scattered around the room, charging. He clicks on a lamp beside the bed.

"Hi," he says, rubbing his eyes, and then when he sees me: "Aidy baby!" I come and sit next to him on the bed as he wipes his glasses on his shirt, puts them on. I rest my head on his shoulder, and he scratches at my scalp, ruffling my hair. "What are you bros doing?" says Leo.

"Sorry to wake you," says Jacks.

"No worries."

I look around the room. There are bunk beds sporting high-end, trendy, gray-striped bedding. Tech gear and video-game detritus is everywhere, lots and lots of manga, anime DVDs, and blind-box Japanese dolls, like a toy store in Tokyo crash-landed here. This is the room of someone who never wants to grow up.

I smile at Leo. His floppy hair, dyed neon-blue at the tips, looks even cuter all messy. I wonder if "suddenly awakened" could be a look in fashion, based on how well Leo rocks it. Those adorable eyes, reflecting kindness mixed with bafflement.

#UniveralCrushMaterial.

"My cousin Tye lives here," Leo explains. "Most of this stuff is his. He works for DigitalOcean. He's out of town for a week at an SSD cloud-server convention in Simi Valley, so he said I could crash and gave me access to all the amenities."

"Sweet," says Jackson, with a low whistle.

Leo turns to me. "I'm sorry I didn't get uptown. All this was kind of last minute. I was gonna head straight home to DC, but then I snagged a meeting at Goldman Sachs to be a summer analyst in investment management. They pay, like, fifteen grand for the summer."

I cover my face with my hands. "Jesus Christ."

"Everything okay?" says Leo.

"No. Everything is not okay," I say.

"What's going on?"

"Well, first off, he thinks we're abandoning him," says Jackson, leaning against a handsome desk made of blond wood.

"We aren't," says Leo, rubbing my arm. "We would never."

I point at Jackson. "He yelled at me."

Leo scowls at Jackson. "You yelled at my Aidy?"

"I did not yell!" Jackson yells.

"He did. Yelled."

"Aw," says Leo.

Sometimes they baby me a little. I allow it. It's cool.

"Oh, man," says Jackson, pacing. "Our little pet Aidy got into some trouble tonight. Do you want to tell him what's up, or should I?"

"What's happening?" says Leo.

"I need to charge my phone," I say. I hand my phone to Leo and he plugs it in. He could've probably just thrown it in the air and it would have landed on something in here that would have charged it. I stare at Leo's trombone, which he plays on occasion, safely gleaming in its open velvet-lined case as I explain the night's events.

Leo reacts by throwing his head back and laughing loudly. But when he sees we're not laughing with him, he frowns at us. "Wait, *what*?"

"Oh, yeah!" says Jackson. "Aidan is being hunted by a gang of very bad goons on motorbikes and the police maybe think he killed someone."

I bite my lower lip. "I've had better nights."

"Aidy, Aidy," says Leo. "What are we going to do with you?"

"What *are* we gonna do with him?" says Jackson.

"You have to go to the police," says Leo. "Let's call 911."

"We can't! They threatened my family if I don't get them this item."

Leo looks at Jackson. "But you don't have this item, or even know what it is."

"That's what we have to figure out," I say, my voice rising. "We're going to figure out what it is so I can give it to them."

Jackson leans in. "Dude."

I frown at him, mimicking his serious expression. *"Dude."*

"I know this is a lot. But you're not necessarily thinking clearly."

I slant my head sharply to one side. "I feel like I am. I got myself into this. I have to get myself out now."

"Aidan," says Jackson, lowering his voice, measuring his words: this is his authoritative tone, which he does sometimes. It can simultaneously irritate and titillate me, but I'm not having it right now.

"Jacks—"

He clasps his hands together. "You just don't want to freak out your family. I know why you do this."

"I'm getting a little sick of being analyzed."

"He's tired," says Leo, patting my back.

"You have to stop mothering him," says Jackson. "He's making bad decisions."

"I am not!"

"I'm not mothering him," says Leo. "But he is tired."

"And Darren Cohen's gay and closeted and cheating on Ashley," I add, softly, into Leo's ear.

"Really?" says Leo, pressing his head lightly against mine so I can feel the slight sandpapery crunch of his stubble. "How do you—"

"He was on DirtyPaws."

"Wow, that's...uh, unexpected." Leo makes a surprised face, then stage-whispers to Jackson: "Did you get him stoned? *He seems a little stoned.*"

Jackson sighs, and rubs his face.

"I'm good," I say. "All good."

"You are too worried about freaking out your parents," says Jacks.

"You know how high-strung they are. I have to keep everything stable. THAT IS LITERALLY MY JOB IN LIFE."

Jackson: "You can't constantly be in the position of trying to protect *them*."

"Right." I sit up, taking charge. "I need to find out who's coming after me, and who this Preston is these people think I am. We need to see what's on the flash drive I nabbed from that hotel room."

The night is coming into sharper focus now. The shock is

wearing off, the pot is leaving my bloodstream, my adrenaline levels are stabilizing. I have to make decisions.

I don't know for sure if the police are really looking for me. I don't know for sure if they saw my face clearly enough or know who I am, since my identity was in flux over there at the stupid Mandarin Oriental. I can obviously crash here with Leo and Jacks, but I have to meet my parents tomorrow. There cannot be any deviation from that plan or they will die from hysteria—that is a thing that will happen. And I have only my wallet and phone without any ID on me. So shit.

The rest of my stuff is back at the hotel, and I'm wondering if it's safe to go back there. I even handed my keycard in to the desk lady! Why did I do that?

I don't know what the hell I'm going to tell my parents, if I should tell them anything at all. We're supposed to leave directly for the airport after dinner to see my death-rayed aunt—so there will be questions if I am not packed, checked out, and holding my bags when I get to the restaurant.

"I don't want to get my parents involved in this," I announce, making at least one firm decision, rubbing my forehead. "They don't deal with things well, *as you know*. Particularly pertaining to me. I cannot deal with a shitstorm from them right now."

"Well, you may not have a choice," says Jackson.

Jackson and Leo sit on either side of me.

I show them the photos on my phone—I got some pretty decent shots of the bullet hole in the window, the broken glass on the carpet, and poor Benoît lying in bed—first the tattoo on his arm, then a tight shot of blood pouring out the side of his head. When I get to this particular photo, both Leo and Jackson wince and lean back, like we're watching a horror movie.

It's only then I realize how fucked up what happened really was, now that the shock has worn off and I'm seeing it from a sort of distance.

Jackson looks at me and his face softens. "I'm sorry that happened and you had to see that. I've been too hard on you tonight. My bad. Are you okay?"

"It's okay. And yeah."

"The guy on the phone said '*We are the Swans*'?" asks Leo, his arms wrapped around my shoulders.

"Yep."

"And then there's a swan tattoo on the dead guy," he adds.

"Those numbers correspond with the date of the Stonewall riots."

"But what does that have to do with anything?" says Jackson.

"I don't know yet." I reach for my phone. Now that it's back on and partially charged, I see a series of text messages from an unknown number.

The first text is the shushing-face emoji.

Oh, shit.

But it's too late. Jacks and Leo are looking right at it.

The next text is a photo of my parents. I know where it's from. For two seconds my mom had a Facebook account, didn't know how to use it, and posted only this one photo of them, which is from a wedding they were at in Boston or something. (I swear, sometimes I think my mom isn't so much a person as a living mass of forgotten passwords and failed CAPTCHA tests.)

The next text says:

An Army of Lovers Cannot Lose.

And that's it.

"Don't text back," says Leo. "Don't do anything."

I shakily put the phone facedown on my lap like it might bite me. "It's the Swans. They know who my parents are."

They also know my phone number. I was talking to them on Benoît's phone. How the hell did they get my phone number? That is so freaky.

"Let's just stay calm," says Jackson.

"I'm calm." I take a breath.

"Police?" says Jackson, desperate to do this, holding up his phone.

I shake my head. "Let's look at what's on the flash drive."

Yeah, so, what we find on the flash drive is in no way comforting *at all.*

There are five folders. In one of them are more photos of me. I can't begin to describe how creepy it is seeing photos of myself on a dead guy's flash drive. In the second folder, marked *Maldrone,* there are snippets of computer code. Leo thinks it's some kind of malware.

The third folder, labeled *DroneSpecs,* has PDF files of government specs for military attack drones. The MQ-9 Reaper, the RQ-4B Global Hawk, the MQ-1B Predator, and the RQ-170 Sentinel.

The fourth folder is labeled *SkyJack.*

Leo scans the contents, his coder's eyes sparkling as he ingests its meaning, a flush of understanding washing over his cute genius face. "Oh, shit."

"What?" Jackson and I both say.

"This folder contains the source code Samy Kamkar created for SkyJack."

"You have to talk to me like I'm a three-year-old," I say.

"So basically, just talk to him like you usually do," says Jackson.

"Okay," says Leo. "Kamkar is a total badass hacker. He created the Samy worm, which brought MySpace to its knees in like 2005. Then he went legit. A few years ago he created the software and hardware specs anyone could use to build a Parrot drone that could hijack *other* Parrot drones wirelessly, creating an army of zombie drones at the mercy of its controller."

"That can happen for real?" says Jackson.

"Kamkar proved it was possible. He released the source code publicly. You just needed a Raspberry Pi circuit board, wireless transmitters, and a quadcopter of your own."

"Yeah, who doesn't have all that?" I say.

"It was innocuous, though."

"Then what does it mean?" I say. "Why is it on there?"

"I don't know yet... let's see." Leo clicks open the last folder, titled *Swan Phase 3*.

While he's reading through it, I wonder: *What the hell is Swan Phase 1? Or 2?*

"This is all loose data about weak encryption between military attack drones and their controller modules," says Leo, reading the screen, "and how the GPS on drones can be manipulated, and their communication links jammed. This isn't good."

"Why?" I say, my voice weak.

"The Kamkar stuff, this stuff, the Maldrone stuff. It feels like an assignment for a black hat."

"A what?"

"A hacker who does bad things."

"Oh."

"A white hat is a hacker who does good, helpful, playful things," says Leo.

I frown. "Playful?"

"The white hats' intent isn't malicious," says Leo. "They have ethics. My guess is whoever Mr. Preston is—whoever they think *you* are—is a black hat who was supposed to deliver them some pretty sophisticated malware that would enable them to hack military attack drones. Which is why they were gonna pay big bucks for the code."

I point at the flash drive. "So this is sort of like the manual of what they wanted?"

"Exactly," says Leo. "They were most likely awaiting a product, in the form of source code. E-mail wouldn't be secure enough. They were probably expecting to receive a separate flash drive from you."

"They know who I am. So they obviously know I'm not a hacker named Mr. Preston." I have no idea what any of this has to do with me. But at least they think I'm someone smarter than I am. I'm almost flattered someone saw my pale, goofy face and thought: *Here's a guy who can hack military drones.*

"Aidan," says Jackson, "they thought you killed Benoît, right?"

I nod, slowly.

"Well. If they didn't kill him, and *you* didn't kill him..."

"Yeah, I don't know who killed him. That remains an open question."

"It's a little too open. There's someone else at work here. Another party."

"A third party," Leo agrees.

"They're the ones who killed Benoît, and are obviously manipulating information, fudging your identity, tricking the Swans into thinking you're someone else," says Jackson.

"Yeah. Benoît was expecting someone else. I didn't realize that he was asking me for *the item,* a flash drive or whatever. I thought he was talking about sex."

Jackson and Leo just blink at me.

"Seriously?" says Leo.

"Uh, I wasn't really thinking with my brain. It was a DirtyPaws hookup."

Rolling his eyes, Jackson turns to Leo. "What do we know about hacking military attack drones?"

"I'm not even sure you *can* hack them," says Leo. "I can't imagine they'd be vulnerable in that way. But they were betting some dark-web hacker genius could figure out a way to do it. And then someone stepped up to the plate."

"Mr. Preston," I say.

"Yep," says Leo.

"And they think I'm him." I still can't get over that. "But that name is so obviously fake. It's like a villain in a dinner-party murder-mystery game."

"Nobody would use their real names...or expect anyone to use their real names in this line of work," says Leo.

Jackson is scouring all the local news outlets and their Twitter feeds, his phone in front of his face, and says there is nothing posted (yet) about a murder at the Mandarin Oriental.

"Do you think it's safe to go back to the hotel?" I ask.

Leo and Jackson both shake their heads.

"I have all my shit there. Laptop. Luggage. A cool book I was reading..."

"I don't think you should leave this house," says Leo.

"...my iPad. My Kiehl's Facial Fuel Energizing Face Wash. Also, they have my IDs. I need to get those back. And I can't stay here forever. And I don't want to get you guys in trouble or involve you in all this, so..."

"He's giving you clues," says Leo, looking at his phone, frowning.

"Who?" I ask.

"The guy on the phone. The Swan or whatever. He's leaving a trail of bread crumbs for you." Leo looks up at me. "Why do you think he would do that?"

That's a good question, because he seemed pretty sure I was lying to him about not being Preston. If he's cluing me in about who *they* are, then maybe he believes me.

"He's testing me," I say. "Seeing if I'm one of them or not. There was a weird connection. He said he identified with...my pain."

"How would he know about all that?" says Jackson, curtly. "Intimate details about your life?"

"I don't know," I say, getting goose bumps. "It was freaky."

Jackson looks over at Leo. "What bread crumbs?"

"Well, there was the Stonewall stuff," Leo says to me. "But he just did it again, fed you a piece of information about who they are."

I rub my eyes, not wanting to look at my phone again. "A bunch of lovers?"

"An Army of Lovers Cannot Lose," Leo corrects. "Do you know what that's from? I'm reading about it right now."

We all gather round, reading off Leo's phone.

The phrase is taken from a leaflet, written anonymously, that was distributed at a gay pride march in New York in 1990. Back then gay men were dying from AIDS and the government was doing nothing about it. Meanwhile, anti-gay activists were going around saying *Homosexuality is a disease, and AIDS is the cure.*

Gay people were being beaten in the streets, shunted off to the margins of society, watching their friends die, attending funeral after funeral, never knowing if they'd be next.

The leaflet says fear is the greatest motivator.

It talks about terrorizing oppressors into retreat.

About *rising up.*

I realize for the first time, reading this, that all these right-wing assholes are actually *scared* of gay people. All nonprocreative behavior threatens them. Birth control. Abortions. Any alternatives to the hetero-norm nuclear family. So they felt they needed to wage a war. Deny gay people their equal rights. Not treat them as human beings deserving of dignity and respect.

Shit, they're *still* doing it...

There's another Army of Lovers line: "*We are an army of lovers because it is we who know what love is.*" It's saying gay people know more about love than anyone else because they've risked so much to have it: prejudice, bashings, bullying, banishment, disease, death.

I keep reading. Here's where I start to get even more upset:

The leaflet talks about gay people being bullied by society into being silent, into hiding their rage with drugs, alcohol, suicide, conformity, and overachievement while repeatedly being told by straight people *TO STOP OVERREACTING. STAY INVISIBLE.*

I've never been a particularly political person. Some kids at my school are. But something corrosive is rising up in my chest. I can taste it.

It's never been easy being gay—it's not easy now...because things are regressing after years of progress. I can't deny that; no one can deny that.

"*Rights are not given, they are taken by force if necessary...*"

"*Straight people will not do this voluntarily and so they must be forced into it. Straights must be frightened into it.* Terrorized *into it...*"

I look up from the leaflet.

Holy shit. The Swans are terrorists.

They want to hack government drones and *kill people.*

And for some reason they're waiting to see if I'm one of them.

Leo and Jackson are watching me.

I sit back on Leo's bed, clasping my hands in my lap. "We are not calling the police."

"Aidy," says Leo, "this is possibly *terrorism.*"

"We don't know that for sure," I say, uncertainly. "We don't know anything about what this is."

"We kind of do," says Leo.

"Bad people are coming after you," says Jackson. "We know that. The Swans. Whoever shot that guy in the hotel room. You fell into a spider web of shit here. Tell me why you don't want to call the police?"

"Because the Swans threatened my family—"

"Yeah, if you didn't deliver the flash drive, which you don't have anyway."

"I can reason with that guy I talked to on the phone."

"How do you know that?" says Jackson, raising an eyebrow.

Because I just have a feeling. There was a mysterious link between us. "If I don't go to the police, he'll see—"

"What? That you're one of them?" asks Leo.

"Aidan," says Jackson, his eyes narrowing, "are you sympathizing with them? The Swans?"

"No!" I protest. But...*am I*? Just a little? No. They threatened me, and my family. I mean it was a little vague. But still, it was a threat. They're obviously evil.

But maybe...also justified?

"I mucked up a crime scene," I say. "I took all that cash. After I woke up with a dead body next to me! The Swans could make it seem like I killed Benoît. And the police may not even know who I am yet, and I'd just be incriminating myself. Unnecessarily."

"I can pretty much guarantee if they don't know who you are yet, they will very soon," says Jackson. "You left your ID. And fingerprints. There are security cams all over that hotel. You did everything short of making a YouTube video."

"I just—"

"This is really about protecting your own ass," says Jackson.

I jump up. "YO! This didn't happen to you! And the police may not believe me. Ever consider that? And yeah, I'm scared, dude."

"Aidan, listen," Jackson starts to say, in a softer tone, but I cut him off.

"And don't give me that bullshit about making bad decisions, because my decisions weren't that bad, okay? No riskier than the shit you guys do. This could have happened to you. This could have happened to anyone. My aunt caught on fire. That could have happened to someone else's aunt. You know? *Right?*"

My poor Aunt Meredith. She's never had it easy. Twice divorced, bad investments, mood disorders; she seems to just have bad fucking luck. I wonder if you can inherit that. All she did was go to a Vegas casino and try to get away from her unhappiness, her dashed dreams, and then she nearly gets burned alive by the sun? Fate is so random and cruel.

And that kid Drew, who died in an avalanche, skiing in the Alps. Why did we make fun of that? That's so awful. I can't imagine what that must have been like, realizing an avalanche was coming right for him, then being swallowed up.

Some by fire and some by ice...

And some by walking into a hotel room...

Homosexuality is the disease and AIDS is the cure...

"Who are these Swans anyway?" I say. "Just some pathetic

losers trying to wage a war no one will ever know or care about. They haven't done anything except try—*unsuccessfully*—to get some stupid malware."

But even as I say this, I know it was hardly a party prank—someone got killed.

And by who?

There's a long silence.

"All right. It's really late," says Jackson, "and I have an early interview. So I think we should crash, get some rest, and reassess in the morning."

So we do. And I have crazy-deep sleep, my brain trying to shield me from the nightmares waiting to emerge, bloated with whacked-out images of all the terrible things that happened to me tonight. And *could* happen to me tomorrow.

Instead of all the politics and the radicalism and the history and all that fervor and pain, my brain focuses in on what it wants to cradle the most.

So, of course, I have this early-morning dream, short and gauzy, where I'm in bed with Tom again, and we're laughing, my head on his naked chest. Morning sunlight pours through the windows, as it did. And it feels so real, like we're back together again, that when I wake up—realizing it was just a dream, and that I'm really lying in a bunk bed in Brooklyn as a possible fugitive from justice, chased by helmeted creeps on bikes—tears gloss my eyes.

I sit up and see the time. I slept late. Jackson's already back from his interview. He's still wearing his suit and tie, and of course he looks amazing. There's a TV on and Leo and Jackson are glued to it, sitting on their respective beds across the room from me.

"What happened?" I rub my eyes. "Are they reporting a murder at the hotel?"

Leo looks at me, shakes his head.

CNN is in frantic Breaking News mode. They clearly don't have the time or interest to cover some dead guy found in a five-star hotel.

They're way too busy focusing on three small-scale terror attacks that all happened this morning while I slept.

CHAPTER 7

The Swans

Here's what's blaring on CNN:

At approximately 8:08 this morning, Dale Ashford—the governor of Florida—died during routine surgery. His drug-infusion pump had been hacked, delivering a fatal overdose of medication. Ashford had recently issued an executive order revoking newly enacted protections for LGBT state workers.

At 8:49 a.m., Wallace Norvett, the governor of Kansas, dropped dead on a golf course. It is now believed that his implanted cardiac Bluetooth defibrillator was hacked, causing a fatal arrhythmia. Governor Norvett opposed LGBT anti-discrimination laws, and rallied Congress not to accept homosexuals as a true minority. He had argued that government funds should be diverted from caring for people with HIV and AIDS into conversion-therapy programs. He apparently had managed to keep his heart condition a secret (also, he was cheating on his wife).

And at 9:10 a.m., North Carolina Republican Representative Grady Leader—a vocal sponsor of anti-LGBT legislation that crashed his state's economy due to a boycott—was involved in an actual crash: a fatal highway collision. It was the result, they now say, of his Chevy Impala's OnStar navigation system being hacked, locking his brakes while he was going eighty.

The feds connected the dots fast: coordinated attacks, a "fixation" on a method (what they're calling "cyber-warfare"), and victims with outspoken anti-gay beliefs. This immediately drove the media into a big-ass frenzy, labeling the three deaths "terrorism" because at precisely the time of death of each victim, an image of a swan was simultaneously tweeted from the hacked accounts of all three victims.

They show the image on the screen, and yeah, it's the same menacing-looking swan graphic as Benoît's tattoo. No numbers, though.

What was that thing I said last night?

Just some pathetic losers trying to wage a war no one will ever know or care about.

They just took out two governors and a congressman.

This is some seriously sinister shit.

And yet, there's a voice in the back of my mind saying: *Good for them.* Part of me wants to applaud.

The media clearly have no idea what any of this means. And

it makes me wonder if we know more than they do about what might be coming next.

Was this Phase 1?

Jackson says we should all go to breakfast.

His interview went well this morning. Like something involving Jackson *wouldn't* go well. He's pleased with himself. But he still looks worried.

I can envision Jackson and Leo taking this out of my hands now, doing something they think is for "my own good." I watch, out of the corner of my eye, Jackson staring at his phone, looking at me, and staring at his phone again, sighing, lips pursed.

Leo hands me my very own blue Egyptian cotton towel so I can take a shower. I nab a spare phone charger from Leo, grab Benoît's flash drive, turn the shower on, let the bathroom steam up, and sneak downstairs. That cash I swiped from the hotel room is still stuffed into my shorts. I slept with it on me. Quickly and quietly, I slip out of the house. I just can't let this drag on where Jackson and Leo might be seen as my accomplices, get into trouble, or be put in harm's way because of me.

I'm on my own here. I always was.

Brooklyn looks positively charming in the daylight, leafy and serene. I have no idea where I'm going. I think I'll head into Manhattan, go back to the hotel, retrieve my keycard, and then decide about calling the cops. If they're already there, looking for me, I might be safer in their hands. But maybe they're not. Yet.

I try to figure out the trains on Google Maps. But I get only one block down before two thick-necked men, one of them holding a silver pistol that glints in the sun, step forcefully onto the sidewalk and cut me off.

Bizarrely, looking at them triggers a pleasant memory.

I never got along with other kids my age. I used to spend time at my neighbors' house. They lived across the street—an elderly couple with grown kids who had moved away ages ago. They'd make me iced tea, and we'd chat. One day they led me into their overstuffed attic. They had piles of Hardy Boys books, the vintage ones from the 1960s with the blue covers and the spooky-yet-campy mystery titles. "Take as many as you want," they told me, "they're just gathering dust here." So I took them all.

These two dudes remind me right away of the Hardy Boys on those covers, with their navy V-neck sweaters and white-collared shirts underneath.

If the Hardy Boys were beefy, scowly, and packed heat.

The gun is thrust hard into my lower abdomen. That'll leave a bruise.

"Mr. Preston," the armed one says, throatily, and I know immediately these aren't the police.

My heart instantly starts pounding. "Never heard of him," I reply.

They lead me toward a cherry-colored Chevy Tahoe idling in the middle of the street. "Get in," the guy with the gun says.

"I don't get into cars with strangers, sorry."

They both frisk me, fast and rough.

Then Hardy Boy without a Gun opens the rear door, grabs my head, and shoves me inside. He opens the driver's side and takes the wheel as Hardy Boy with a Gun gets in the passenger side. As soon as the Tahoe screeches away, Hardy Boy without a Gun turns around and snatches the phone out of my hands.

"I just charged that."

"You won't be needing it," he says.

Hardy Boy with a Gun, to his credit, doesn't point his weapon at me as we speed off. But he gives me a look over his shoulder, like: *Don't give me a reason to.* They both wear gloves. I don't like that.

"Did we meet last night? Were you the guys in the club? Hey, nice work. Sorry we couldn't hang out longer. That was fun, though."

I always get chatty when I'm terrified.

They don't answer. We go over a bridge, then onto a highway. I try to memorize our exact route, but that's hard because I barely know New York and we're going fast. The doors are locked. Believe me, I tried that.

I lean back. The leather seats are smooth and cool.

My palms are sweaty. I'm trying to remain calm. I did not expect things to accelerate so fast, or quite like this. Three people are dead today because of these guys; they are obviously serious and mean business. And they're good at what they do.

And I feel ambivalent. I would never condone murder, but I can relate to their anger. Why shouldn't we fight back against these homophobes? The blood of every gay kid who commits suicide thinking they'll never be loved in this world is on their hands. And aren't they all pro-life and shit?

I might only survive if I show the Swans the side of myself that agrees with them, even admires what they're doing. Which might be a challenge, truly convincing them, because I'm not exactly a terrorist.

I lean forward, put my head in my hands to quell my rising fear, and then sit back again, with a loud sniff, and say: "Listen, I'm supposed to meet my parents later today, my whole family, in fact, for dinner. Everyone's going to be pretty worried if I'm not there. We have a flight to catch."

No one says anything. The car picks up even more speed.

"To Nevada..." I add. "My aunt was burned by the Hotel Death Ray. Maybe you heard about that? Awful. Well. She'll be upset if I'm not there."

Through her haze of pain meds, I doubt she'll even notice if I'm there. Once, for my thirteenth birthday, she sent me Ethan Hawke's first novel. My parents must've told her I like to read or some shit. It was such a WTF gift I realized she just didn't know me at all. And why should she? We never see her. She thought she was getting me something cool. But instead she gave me *The Hottest State*.

It wasn't even that bad. I wound up reading his other book, too.

If I survive this, I should reach out to Aunt Meredith, try to be in her life a little more. What a weird resolution. Okay. Who cares? I'll do it.

The Hardy Boys are quiet, staring at the road ahead.

I'm pretty sure I'm going to be murdered.

These are terrorists who think I betrayed them. But everything is out of my hands at this point. There's nothing more I can do. The previous twenty-four hours of nonstop traumatic crap have now come to this crushing head, so I can almost let go a little.

"So was that you guys today?" I say, keeping my tone light. "On the news. Killing those homophobes? Nicely done."

Hardy Boy with a Gun shifts in his seat. But neither one answers me. I look out my window. We're heading out of the city. I wonder if this will be my last few hours on the planet. Well, I had a solid run. Not a long one, but there were some good times, I guess.

After a while, I see a road sign indicating we're heading toward Long Island, then another sign that says we're entering the Merrick Gables, whatever that is.

We're in some sort of picturesque suburban enclave now. Stucco homes, Mediterranean style. This isn't the first place I'd pick for a terrorist group to congregate, but what do I know about their real estate needs?

After what I estimate is forty-five minutes from when we left Brooklyn, the Tahoe pulls into a long driveway. The house, also in that chic Spanish style—white with orange roof tiles—is set far back from the street, buried under intense landscaping: lots of low-hanging trees that seem to want to eat the house up.

My door is pulled open, my seat belt snapped off. I'm plucked out of the car and led by the back of the neck toward the front door. One of the Hardy Boys (the blonder one I'm calling Joe, the darker-haired one I'm calling Frank) knocks on the door. Someone opens it, but I can't see who it is. Then I'm led inside, down a carpeted hall, into a library, where I'm pushed down into a leather chair draped with a soft Aztec blanket.

"Wait here," says Hardy Boy Joe. "Stay in that chair."

They close the door behind them as they leave.

I hop right up, run over to the door, but it's locked. There are floor-to-ceiling windows framed in dark wood, but outside I see only leaves tickling the glass, like we're in the middle of a jungle. Antique lamps—one of which is on a drafting table made of blue glass, littered with various papers and stacks of high-end art magazines—cast the room in sepia light.

In the distance, suburban sounds I recognize: leaf blowers, buzzing bees, chirping birds. It's as if I've been yanked through a portal back into my own childhood, but in a backward sort of way, from the other side of a frayed curtain, so everything feels wrong.

I hear the sound of a motorcycle getting closer.

Expensive-looking photography books line the wooden bookshelves, along with books on philosophy and a few novels that look like rare editions. There are drawings and photographs framed in glass of moody boys with bangs and bedroom eyes on the bookshelves and on the floor leaning up against the walls, which are covered with patterned wallpaper. Closer up I see the pattern is twisty vines and grapes in faded greens, violets, mustard yellows.

I think about breaking one of the windows, but the glass looks pretty thick.

I don't even see a pen anywhere. The only thing I find is a butterfly paper clip at the edge of the table. I unbend it and furiously scratch the tip back and forth across the metal edge of the table until it's warped and snaggy. I put it in my pocket just as the door is flung open.

"I said: *stay in that chair,*" Hardy Boy Joe bellows. He grabs me by my hair, hard, and throws me back into the chair, whiplashing me.

"Ow!" I say. "That hurt, you *pecker.*"

"Easy, easy," says a muffled voice from behind him, out in the hallway. A voice I recognize right away. "He's in here?"

"Yeah," Hardy Boy Joe fumes. He glares down at me, flexing his hands, then stomps out of the room. "Where you wanted him."

A slim man of about medium height enters the room. He is dressed entirely in black leather. His jacket is zipped up to the neck, and he's wearing one of those motorcycle helmets with a mirrored green visor.

Standing against the wallpaper, which makes kaleidoscopic shapes in my eyes, there's something disconcerting about the way he just stares at me, his gloved hands at his sides, unmoving. He lifts up the visor, exposing a patch of his face—clean-cut with cloudy, jade-green eyes.

"Do you have it on you?" he asks.

"Do I have what on me?"

"Let's not play any more games, Mr. Preston."

"You must know by now I'm not this Mr. Preston."

He shrugs. "What should I do, ask for ID? You're a runaway teenage cyber-warrior who uses a multitude of them."

I am? Fuck, that sounds kind of awesome.

"Your identity is always in flux," he adds.

I cough into the crook of my arm. "Well, it is now."

"That's the downside of working with *mercenaries,*" he hisses, but more to himself. "You took the money, I assume?"

"I took some of it," I admit. "No choice, dude. You called the cops. I was on the run. I'm not a hacker. I don't know how to hack drones."

There are voices outside and inside the house, footsteps on wooden floors. There are lots of other people in this house, I realize.

He gazes out the window. "And if you're not Mr. Preston, how would you know what we were after?" he says, striped by light and shadow.

"I looked at the contents of the flash drive Benoît had on his laptop."

He nods. "Shrewd of you. May I have that back?"

I take the flash drive out of my pocket. He moves a little closer, arm outstretched, and I place the flash drive in his leather-gloved palm.

"I want to go home now. I'm supposed to have dinner with my parents."

He cups the flash drive in his palm gingerly, as if estimating its weight, before saying anything. "Tell me about them."

"My parents?"

He nods.

I breathe slowly through my nose. I want my voice to sound stable, so I don't give away my escalating terror. "Why?"

"Because I want to know all about you."

"But why?" I repeat, cautiously. "You've threatened my life, you threatened their lives, you kidnapped me..."

"I just needed to get you here so we could have a little talk. Mission accomplished."

I don't believe him. I open my mouth without speaking, but only for a second. "Would you hurt them?" My voice squeaks and bends. I'm having trouble maintaining composure.

After a tiny pause: "That depends."

"On?"

"You had a brother?"

I get a nice jolt right there. This is the second time he's done that to me.

I swallow, and nod.

"I'm sorry," he says. He sounds sincere.

"How do you know these things about me?"

"It's a gift."

I run my tongue along my lower teeth, considering that, trying to make sense of this. "Are you going to let me go home?"

"There is something bruised about you. That interests me. Your *wounds*."

I shift uncomfortably in my seat.

"You don't see yourself that way?" he asks, curious.

"I don't see myself as anything."

"A cipher, then. Someone with a mercenary's morals. Sell to the highest bidder. You didn't even know—or care—who we were."

I shake my head vigorously. "You obviously aren't as gifted as you think you are if you still think I'm a mercenary cyberwarrior named Preston." I laugh a little. "Give me a break."

He takes a step toward me and sits on the edge of the desk.

"How did he die?"

It's called dilated cardiomyopathy, or DCM. It's a type of enlargement of the heart that can cause sudden death with absolutely no symptoms. Young people can have it. My brother collapsed in the middle of his high school basketball game. He was fifteen. I was eleven. It can be congenital, which is the real reason my mom freaked out over my EKG.

To think I'm older than him now, older than my *older brother*, who was always there first, guiding the way for me, weirds me out so much. His name was Neil. And he was a great guy, and a perfect older brother—sweet, gentle, kind, sensitive, just all good things, and I miss him every day.

It sucks so hard that I lost him, that our family lost him, that the world lost him, because I think genuine sweetness is such a rare, underrated virtue, and Neil had that in spades. I'm not as sweet as he was. But I think losing him is why I can be snarky sometimes. I'm just masking pain.

I'm fine admitting that. It's the truth.

It also sucks because I'm muddy on the last time I ever spoke to him.

I wasn't at that game where he died on the court. I had something else that morning. I wish I had said something supportive at least, something loving and kind, because you never know, obviously. That it'll be the last time.

I have a sister, too. Her name is Nicole (I call her Nicks, after Stevie) but she's way older than me—twenty-eight now. We were never all that close. And she tends to be a little...high-strung.

It runs in the family.

After Neil died, two things happened: I stopped being afraid of things. I wasn't exactly reckless, not like that. I didn't do hard drugs or take up parasailing. But death meant less to me. I guess I figured if something awful happened and I did die, then at least I could see Neil again.

The other thing that happened was a perceptible shift with my parents. I was briefly in therapy about this, we all were, *blah blah,* but that was a waste of everybody's time, 'cause nobody can bring Neil back. What happened with my parents was harsh, yet I get it.

With my sister out of the house, I think they saw me as just another Potential Tragedy. If something dramatic (like my heart, or my burned-up aunt) happens, my mom will totally unspool from her shell and freak on me for sure. But, overall, my parents became detached. I think that's a big reason they had no problem sending me to Witloff, with not too many questions asked. I think the general attitude was: let's get this Potential Tragedy out of our faces.

When I came out to my parents at thirteen, they weren't ho-hum about it, nor were they particularly accepting. I mean, I hear stories about kids who come out to their parents and a cake gets baked, there's a party, they go to PFLAG events, all this gippity-goppity gay shit. With my family it was the type of conversation where someone has to sit on the bottom step of a staircase. They were pretty stolid, fists pressed to foreheads, nodding furiously but remaining silent, like they had expected something along these lines.

A day later I get a handwritten letter on my dad's stationery. The medical letterhead just made it seem that much more frosty and official.

In that letter was my dad's Darwinian deconstruction of how homosexuality is pretty much an unnatural state of being in the continuum of human evolution. "Human beings are engineered to reproduce," he argued. "What's the purpose of sperm?" he mused. Because if there's one thing you want your dad to bring up, it's definitely *sperm.*

He stopped short of calling me a total aberration, but he condemned the "hedonistic culture of gays," which propagates HIV, he said, and asked if I "really wanted to play with fire."

You hear about the biblical shit. How the Bible dictates that homosexuality is a sin. I think you can laugh that stuff off for the most part. Or at least I can, but I'm not religious; never was. What I got, instead, was this bullshit *scientific treatise* on how I'm basically a human error—from my own father—which was so much more chilling. Mostly because he asked questions I couldn't really answer yet and presented his points thoughtfully, even if they were totally wack. He ended the letter saying: "Of course we love and accept you no matter what."

No matter what. That was the part that really got me.

I get that my dad hasn't been totally right in the head since Neil, and fine, whatever. But he shouldn't have projected his own fears and ignorance onto me. And no one has all the answers. *No one.*

I realize I'm talking about Neil, fully and freely, which I never do. I am telling this man, who may or may not be murdering me in the next few minutes, shit I *never* talk about.

I'm legit impressed. "How did you get me to do that?"

"I simply asked," he replies. "Maybe you just needed someone to listen, Aidan."

I sit back, my eyes fluttering. "You do know my real name."

"Of course," he answers, blithely. "But that's just another name."

Not really. It's mine.

He's never going to believe I'm not some mercenary homicidal black-hat cyber-warrior. He clearly needs to cling to this narrative that I'm some kind of lost boy who went over to the dark side, someone he can save, or make use of. Or just dispose of without feeling much about it.

"Aidan, Aidan, Aidan," he hums, relishing the sound of my name.

I think of my mother knocking on my door.

I'd never heard her crying like that before. Deep, deep sobs. "Aidan... Aidan, baby, something's happened... *Aidan*!"

"You hold on to so much," he says. "You figured out so early how unfair and brutal the world really is. What does that do to a boy?"

I stare at him. I say nothing.

"It feels good talking about him, doesn't it? Almost like you can bring him back in brief little flashes."

It's like he can see into the darkest parts of me, like seeing through onyx. He gets that side of me, the side of me everyone pretends isn't there, or softens with euphemistic language like: *Makes bad decisions; plays with fire; can be self-destructive; heedless; impulsive; gets too attached; gets obsessive...*

He doesn't just see it, though. It thrills him. I can tell.

I have to get him to trust me.

"I didn't kill Benoît."

His eyes are smoky, fascinated, unblinking. "Then who did?"

"A third party," I say, echoing what Leo and Jacks were saying. "I just fell into this."

I sense hesitation, his interest piqued. His eyes are on me, searching. "Aidan," he says almost gently, "you know who we are now... where we're based. I have to protect our cause. That's my priority. You understand that."

I try to swallow but I can't. "So what do you want?"

"Knowing who we are, and what we do... would you want us to stop?" he asks.

I grip both my arms. "Stop what? Killing homophobes?"

After a moment, he nods slowly.

The world would be better off without people who hate gay people. But what the Swans are doing is illegal and vicious. It's murder.

However... maybe sometimes that's how you have to make real change: fight wars. Wage revolutions. *Rise up.*

Yeah, but these people are terrorists—and terrorists always see themselves fighting some stupid invisible war.

It's not that invisible, though. It's hardly stupid. We *are* under siege.

And truthfully? I'm glad those homophobes are dead.

Even though... I don't condone murder.

I can't have it both ways, though. I get that.

But... pushing gay kids to suicide by encouraging society and their own families to reject them? Isn't that a form of murder?

The easy, lazy answer is *yes,* I want this all to stop. The harder answer is no, I want to see what they can accomplish—because I'm intrigued. And because the Swans seem disturbingly good at splitting me in two, triggering a dormant part of myself I've never been in touch with—this desire to fight back against injustice, hypocrisy, and the cruelty of the world. They see some kind of rage in me. But it's not just that.

They see *potential.*

"I won't go to the police," I tell him.

He seems disappointed. "That's not what I asked."

"No," I reply, sounding more confident than I expected; I have to survive the present circumstances. "I don't think you should stop." There we go. Better.

I can't tell if he's satisfied by my answer. I can't tell if he believes me.

He pulls the visor of his helmet back down. I can see my squirming reflection. I look so small, lost, insignificant.

Without another word, he tosses the flash drive in the air, catches it, and leaves the room, shutting the door behind him.

Two minutes later, Hardy Boy Joe comes in and pulls me out of the chair. I try to wriggle out of his grip, but it's iron tight—when he's not solving local mysteries involving haunted garages and missing clocks, Hardy Boy Joe clearly spends time with a well-paid trainer.

"What's happening?" I ask. The panic is so fast, a liquid almost, filling my throat.

"He says you can keep the money," he growls, leading me out of the room, holding me by the scruff of my neck.

I feel like I didn't hear him correctly. "What? *Why?*"

Did I actually convince the biker dude I'm one of them?

He shoves me down a long hallway: parquet floors, more framed photos on the walls, splashed with afternoon sun, tall windows on the other side, overlooking a courtyard with a pool. There are people out there.

At the other end of the hallway, another man turns a corner, stops, and stares at us. It takes me a second, but then I recognize him:

It's the homicidal-looking bellhop from the Mandarin Oriental.

He's wearing white cotton trousers that look lost in time, like when you see old photos of a young Marlon Brando in front of his house in Hollywood. He's shirtless and totally ripped, with a white towel around his neck. His long blond hair is unkempt and he's a day or so unshaven, which makes him look even more like a scheming soap star. You could slice cucumbers on his jawline.

"Do you want a tour?" Blond Bellhop asks me. His voice is ominously deep and husky and doesn't go with his sneering face.

I have a PTSD reaction to seeing him again. I instantly start to shake. My stomach cramps. Every part of my body wants to run, but I know I should hold my ground and stay very calm. "Not really," I respond, breezily—too breezily, maybe.

"I'm sure you want to see the pool," he says.

I shake my head. My pulse is racing at a speed where I wonder if I may collapse. "I'm good," I say, stiffly. I feel like if I attempt to walk or move my brain won't know how to fulfill the action.

Blond Bellhop comes toward us.

Hardy Boy Joe loosens his grip on the back of my neck and pushes me toward him. Blond Bellhop, grinning in his oily way, swings his arm around my shoulders and thrusts open one of the glass doors. He guides me out into the courtyard. I try to free myself from his grip, but his arms are super strong, his grip viselike. The pool, surrounded by potted plants and flowers, is narrow. Low-hanging trees create a canopy over the sapphire-blue water. The calm, sylvan setting throws me.

Like frightened birds, about seven or eight boys sit up from bronze-colored lounge chairs where they were sunning themselves. They're all a bit waify, generically cute, pouty, most of them with auburn hair, probably a couple of years older than me. They all wear identical sunglasses—tinted green—and white bathing suits in a vintage style, like Blond Bellhop's billowy pants.

At first I can't put my finger on what instantly weirds me out about them. But then I get it. I look just like them—like we all showed up for the same casting call. Something about the synchronicity of their movements, their outfits, everything, is also really off-putting. Blond Bellhop merely has to look at them and grunt, and they all scatter. Magazines flutter down. Bare feet whisper off. Glass doors open and slam.

I can't escape Bellhop's grip. All my mental alarm bells are ringing. I need to shake him off, and get in a position where I can kick, punch, scratch.

"So this is the pool," says Blond Bellhop, his tone detached, but his hold tightening like a python.

"Cool," I respond, looking around for an escape, "it's very n—"

In one sudden motion, he whirls me around and grabs me by the throat, lifting me off my feet.

My hands immediately wrap around his and start trying to pry his fingers loose, but the fucker is so strong. I shout out, but then I can't make another sound. He's full-on choking me, his eyes an empty glare. I slam my fists against his chest, his chin, which has zero effect. He doesn't recoil at all.

He's on drugs, I think.

He gets me down to the ground, flat on my back, hands still wrapped around my throat. I can't even kick him; all his weight is pressed down on me.

He starts sliding me into the pool. The top of my head grazes the surface. Then my head is all the way under, and then my neck and chest, his hands firmly clamped around my throat, squeezing hard. I thrash, desperate, but his hold is like iron.

Holy shit. I'm really going to die here. This psycho is going to drown me.

But I'm not quite ready to accept this. I'm not resigned yet. My parents *will not grieve another son.*

I see Blond Bellhop's red, furious face, fluttering and distorted through the clear skim of the surface. Everything gets darker and bluer as he pushes me deeper down. Sound becomes a heady echoing swish, my world a frenzied spray of bubbles petering out as I slowly lose a grip on my own consciousness.

Then it's like I leave my own body, and I'm observing everything from afar. I can problem-solve my current murdering like it's happening to someone else.

My wallet falls out of my pocket, dropping away, and then the iPhone charger, a thin white snake slithering into the depths. The currency strap on my stolen cash opens, releasing all the bills. But both my hands are still free.

And I nabbed something from that room.

I reach into my pockets, scraping around in them like mad, because I can't remember which one I put it in. But then I find it, and manage to free the unraveled paper clip. I stab the end of the paper clip deep into Bellhop's wrist and drag it down with all my might, opening up his wrist like a zippered pouch. A scarlet flag is unfurled before my eyes, rocketing off into angry tendrils. I feel the salty warmth of his blood fill the pool, and my mouth. His grip on my throat slackens and I free myself.

We reverse.

He falls into the water with a loud splash; I climb out, gasping for breath. I roll onto the hard cement beside the pool and stand up, heaving, coughing loudly, spitting up water, my throat scratchy, throbbing.

Oh my God, Oh my God, Oh my God...

I almost drowned. My breathing is like a stalled car trying to start again. My throat feels crushed, damaged.

Blond Bellhop is thrashing around in the pool like a broken toy, gasping and choking, but then he stops, just like that, floating facedown, spread-eagled, as jets of blood spurting from his arm turn the pool a ruddy, uncomfortable purple.

Bloodstained hundred-dollar bills float to the top, surrounding his motionless body.

I spot a graveled path and a little wooden gate. An exit.

I tear down the path. I unlatch and open the gate, then run along the side of the house until I'm out front. The Tahoe is still sitting in the driveway. There's a familiar café racer motorcycle parked behind it now. I run as fast as I can.

Just keep running, I tell myself. *Get as far away as you can.*

It's a sunny day, unseasonably warm. I run by pleasant, quiet houses, gardeners dutifully tending lawns and shrubs. I see moms in Subaru Outbacks, loaded up with groceries bursting out of paper bags. I see a few little kids on bicycles, pedaling in groups; basketball hoops set up on driveways, toys left on lawns.

I am sopping wet, my hair a crazy mess. My whole neck is throbbing. I'm spitting and sputtering. I have to stop, twice, by someone's freshly mowed lawn to dry-heave onto it. I have no phone, no wallet or ID. At this point it's pretty much a matter of time before someone calls the police on me. But I keep going. I'm alive, and that feels like a miracle. Like a precious second chance I don't ever want to mess up.

I hit a busier road. There's a stately school, brick, with lots of windows, surrounded by pine trees. There's a crossing guard getting out of her car, about to begin her duties. I regain as much composure as I possibly can as I ask her to point me in the direction of the nearest train station.

And she does. Chugging a cup of coffee, she takes little notice of my current state. It turns out I'm not that far from the train station—my first lucky break of the day.

Or my second if you count the paper clip: Death by Office Depot.

The Long Island Railroad will take me to Penn Station. The Babylon line.

It's just—*I have no freakin' money on me anymore.* But I keep going, walking at a brisk pace, following the crossing guard's directions until I see the station. There's a Manhattan-bound train—yes, thank God—pulling in just as I get there.

I run up the stairs at a breakneck pace and practically fling myself through the open doors. And I'm in. The train pulls out of the station, taking its sweet time. I watch Merrick recede as the train lumbers along the glistening tracks.

CHAPTER 8

Shiloh

People are staring.

I don't know what I look like, but based on people's faces it can't be good. I've been wearing these clothes since last night, and they're stuck to my skin. I'm still dripping. My sopping underwear is chafing my inner thighs so badly I've developed an unfortunate limp to go with the rest of this madness.

I see the conductor punching people's tickets. I race from car to car, as I try to outpace him. I finally reach a half-empty car toward the back of the train. I find an empty two-seater and plop myself down.

I just have to get back to the city. That's all I have to do.

The seat squishes against my wet butt. I lean forward, my cold, heavy hair hanging down. I put my head between my knees, trying to calm down. I look up briefly and notice a middle-aged woman with dyed red hair sitting across from me, looking concerned, lips parted as if wanting to say something, her attention diverted from her crossword.

The train makes its next stop. More people get on.

At some point the conductor is going to reach me. I have no ticket, no cash, he will probably call the police, and then this will all come to its natural horrible conclusion. I have no plan, absolutely no idea what to do.

"Excuse me, is anyone sitting next to you?"

"What?" I say, looking up.

I blink, and think: Why is this gorgeous guy, basically Tom Daley's twin, asking to sit next to me? He's dressed really well: slim-cut jacket (camel-colored, badass move), thin white button-down shirt (opened to the second button), matching pants (well-tailored), and plum-colored loafers without socks.

I slide in, taking the window seat. He takes the aisle seat, blocking me from people's stares. There are other empty seats in this car. I wonder why he decided to sit next to me. "You look like you've had a rough day," he says, smiling.

He has a great freakin' smile.

"I fell in a pool," I mutter.

"Saw you and thought you might want this." He removes his AirPods, pockets his phone in his jacket, opens a leather messenger bag on his lap, and removes a small folded towel with a wink.

"You're giving me a towel?"

"It looks that way."

"Do you regularly walk around with a towel on you?"

"I play tennis. Just back from a match at a friend's place."

"Wouldn't you have a gym bag, then?"

"Hey, don't look a gift horse in the mouth."

"I don't trust gifts. Or horses."

"I can rescind my offer," he says, dangling the towel, his tone gentle, teasing. "I mix up the contents of my various bags. I forget things all the time. I just left all my tennis clothes at my friend's house in my other bag, along with my racket. I was rushing to make the train. And now my friend's off to Miami, so it looks like I'll be taking up golf. I may seem put-together but, trust me, secretly I'm a total slob."

"You're a secret slob?"

"Don't pretend that's not a thing."

"Did you win your match?"

"I did not," he says, with a sigh.

What an adorable prepster. I take the towel and dry off my hair and neck. I sop water from my drenched shirt and shorts. "This was unexpected. Thank you."

"Took one look at you and thought: there's someone who needs a friend."

I hand the towel back to him. "Are you in some kind of religious organization?"

He laughs. "Also, you're pretty cute."

Oh shit. *Now? Seriously?*

"I'm Shiloh," he says, extending his hand. I shake it.

"Aidan." My heart does a little gymnastics competition in my chest.

"I'm on spring break from Duke," he says.

Duke. Of course it's Duke.

"I'm a junior," he adds. "Headed back to the city now. Dinner with my parents."

"I'm on spring break from Dartmouth," I lie. "And, yeah, same. Dinner. Parents."

"Very nice. I have some friends at Dartmouth. Do you know Jefferson Collier?"

Oh, here we go with the name game. "No. I have no friends. I keep to myself."

He laughs again. He has a great laugh. "I doubt that's true."

"It is. I'm not very social."

"I bet you choose your friends wisely. I'm sure it takes a lot to win your trust."

"That might be the case, yes. But I doubt we know the same people."

"You seem pretty sure of that," he says, amused. "Dartmouth, right? Anyway. You seem like a fine chap."

Chap? What year does Pretty Boy Floyd think he's in?

"I am." I wipe my forehead with the back of my hand.

He nods, looks off. I'm terrified I went too far and the conversation will be over, along with the totally-unexpected-but-not-entirely-unpleasant flirting. Now he thinks I'm some kind of social misfit who doesn't have any friends. God, why did I say that? I don't know how to fix this. My head isn't clear. I just killed someone and I'm running from terrorists, *gimme a break*.

After only a second or two, though, he breaks the silence:

"Have you noticed when you're heading to dinner with your parents you tend to be extremely frazzled?"

"Totally."

"Spastic almost. Forgetting things right and left."

"Especially with *my* parents. They tend to twist my stomach into knots."

And now, of course, with a sudden unpleasant jolt, I think of my family. Are they in actual danger? And what am I supposed to do if they are?

They won't listen to me. They never hear me.

"Oh, I'm sure that's true for everyone," he says.

"Yeah. But probably more so for me."

They'll just panic, blindly panic, because that's what they do best.

"And why is that?" he asks.

"I guess there's just a lot of drama," I say, glossing over *all that,* eyes darting to the entrance of the car, where the fastest conductor of all time has just entered. "But considering how fine a chap you think I am, and I can't argue there, maybe you wouldn't mind giving me a hand here."

He turns to me. "I assume that's not literal."

"Not yet."

"Will this require more than just a towel?"

"I think so," I say, eyeing the conductor, who is already half-way down the car.

"Tickets, please!"

"See," I tell Shiloh, "I had a bit of an accident... as you already gleaned..."

"I'll bet you lost your wallet. Didn't you?"

I nod.

He leans in. I can smell the ghost of well-chosen shaving cream and athletic deodorant, all mint and citrus. "Who are they?"

"Who?"

"Who's after you?" he asks me.

I laugh, my voice froggy. "It's complicated."

"Try me."

"Tickets!" says the conductor, standing right over us. Shiloh calmly hands the conductor his ticket. The conductor punches it. "Tickets!" says the conductor, looking right at me. Shiloh takes this moment to mess with me a little, grinning and shrugging, but then he turns back to the conductor.

"I'll get his ticket, thanks."

Shiloh hands the conductor a twenty. The conductor gives me a curious look, makes change, hands it to Shiloh, and punches my ticket. And then that's over and the conductor moves on to the next car. "Tickets!" I hear him call.

We roll along in silence. I close and open my eyes, exhaling.

"You have bruises on your throat," says Shiloh, quietly. "And there's some blood on your shirt."

My hand instinctively goes to my throat. It's tender there, and I wince. I look down at my shirt. There are splatters of blood on my arms and stomach. "Thank you for helping," I say.

"How will you explain all this to your parents?"

"I plan to clean myself up at least."

"Where are you staying in the city?" he asks.

"The Mandarin Oriental."

He whistles. "Sucks for you, huh? I'm not far. My parents live uptown."

I swivel around to face him, making the seat squeak. "Look, you've been great, and maybe you can give me your address so I can pay you back for the ticket—in fact, please do—but I'd rather not get you involved in my life right now."

"Well, I already feel involved. Now I actually feel responsible for you."

"Well, you're not."

"I can only look at those sweet, wide eyes of yours and know you couldn't have done anything that bad."

"You don't know me."

"I'm an excellent judge of character."

"Well, maybe not this time."

"*Every* time. And I like adventure. I lead a fairly boring life."

"You're awesome—total husband material—but sorry, man, your timing sucks."

The train makes another stop. More people get on. We're not far from Penn Station, only a few more stops. But we're not moving; we seem to be stalled here. Then, out the window, I see the cops. They're pouring out of two patrol cars, heading quickly up the steps to the station, toward the train. They're about to board. Shiloh leans over my shoulder and sees them, too. "Hmmm. Maybe I *did* misjudge you."

"Oh, *shit,*" I whisper, slinking down in my seat.

"Are they here for you?" says Shiloh. He looks almost impressed.

"I don't know."

"Get up," he says.

"What?"

"Get. Up."

I obey, getting to my feet, sliding past Shiloh, who stands, clamps a hand down on my shoulder, and leads me out of our car and into the next. Shiloh pounds once on the bathroom; when no one answers, he opens it and shoves me inside, whispering, "Don't say anything, keep the door locked, and don't open it until I knock four times."

"Okay."

The bathroom is cramped and vile; it smells like piss and fumes and Purell. I try to offset panic, leaning over the tiny dripping sink, taking deep, controlled breaths. I hear commotion outside.

The conductor says something to Shiloh.

"Yes," he says. "He ran off the train just as we pulled in..."

Oh, my God, they really are looking for me.

"Toward the front, I think?"

Another voice, maybe a cop.

"No," says Shiloh. The bathroom handle jiggles. "It's busted. I've knocked and knocked. I've been trying to pee the whole ride since Freeport, so pretty sure no one's inside. Seriously, my bladder is about to burst!" He laughs, loudly.

I put a fist to my mouth so no one can hear me breathe.

More muffled voices.

"Yeah, I didn't see where."

The voices recede. Footsteps come and go. The train makes noises.

After what seems like freakin' forever, we start to move again.

No one knocks on the bathroom door. I don't unlock it or peek outside or anything. I count three more stops, then the train begins its final slowdown. As it screeches to a stop, and before I have even a second to wonder if Shiloh has bailed on me, which he certainly has every right to do, there are four loud knocks.

I unlock and open the door. Shiloh is standing there, a wry smile, his messenger bag slung over his shoulder.

"Out. Stay with me. Keep your head down."

We pile out of the train quickly, and squeeze up a jam-packed escalator until we reach the main level. Shiloh keeps us well blended in the crowds of commuters, as we keep moving. There are cops all around, but it's Penn Station, so maybe there are always cops around. I can't tell if there are more of them than usual, or if they're actively looking for me.

It doesn't matter. Shiloh knows Penn Station well. He gets us through it fast, weaving us in and out of clumps of people, then out and into a cab.

"Mandarin Oriental Hotel," he tells the driver, then leans back against the seat. "Catch your breath," he tells me, as we pull into Seventh Avenue traffic. "When you get to your room, take a hot bath; you were sopping wet on that air-conditioned train for the whole ride."

"Uh. Yes, sir."

Except I don't have my keycard, my phone, or any kind of ID on me, so a few more challenges probably await before I can get all giggly in a bubble bath.

"They were looking for me?" I say in a low voice.

"Mmhmm," says Shiloh.

"Did they say why?"

"Just wanted to know what happened to the kid I was sitting next to. I think someone on the train called, thought you were hurt."

I hope that's all it was.

"I can't believe that bathroom thing worked," I say.

"I have an honest, convincing face."

"I would have described your face a bit differently."

"You want to tell me what's going on here?"

"First, I want to know why you're helping me out like this."

"I'm not sure," says Shiloh. "There's just something about you."

"No dice. I'm not that cute."

"Oh, it's more than that," he says, craning his neck to scour the traffic. "Can you make a left here and get us onto Sixth," he directs the driver, leaning over the seat, "and let's take Sixth up, thanks."

"What time is it?"

"It's almost three," says Shiloh.

"What time is your dinner?"

"Oh, not for a while," he says. "I just wanted to get back to the city. Yours?"

"Five."

"That's kind of early."

"My sister has kids. And we have a flight to catch."

"So you're an uncle."

"I am."

"Uncle Aidan," he says. It does have a nice ring when you say it out loud.

My nephew, Sam, is three and my niece, Annabelle, is five

and a half. I can't ever remember either of their birthdays, but they're cute as hell.

"What about you?" I ask.

"Only child," he replies. "No siblings."

"Yeah, I know what an *only child* means."

I don't know why, but when he says *only child* I think of Neil and I get sad again. I've been sad about Neil ever since I talked about him earlier to Motorcycle Helmet Terrorist. I feel manipulated. That was a bit of psychological warfare right there.

"Maybe it's that," he says, looking at me.

"What?"

"The way you suddenly get sad like that."

I swipe lightly at my eyes. "I didn't know I did."

"Your face." He's suave enough not to point directly at me when he says that.

Ten minutes later, we pull up in front of the Mandarin Oriental. A bellhop (not the murderous one I just killed, obviously, but now I have PTSD whenever I see one, and I can probably forget about room service for the rest of my life) opens the door of the cab. I step out onto the street. It's muggy out, the sky pigeon-gray.

Shiloh pays the driver and hops out as well. He's tall. I just realized that now, for some reason. I stare at the entrance to the hotel. I turn to him. "I don't know you at all, obviously, or why you did any of that, but thank you."

His mouth curls up at the corners. "So what's next?"

"I'm going to go back to my room," I tell him, not that confidently.

"It's that face of yours," he says.

"What about it?"

"It can't lie."

I tap my feet, anxiously. "What is my stupid face saying now?"

He laughs a little. "You just look a little nervous."

"Yeah." I don't know what I'm doing. Coming back to the Mandarin Oriental, *the scene of the crime,* might be the dumbest thing on earth. But I have nowhere else to go right now, and if the police are eventually going to find me, maybe I can at least change clothes first. I really don't know. I'm not in this line of work.

"If you wanted to escort me inside," I find myself saying, "I wouldn't say no."

"Let's do it," says Shiloh.

Whoever's looking for me, or might be coming after me, probably won't expect to see me with a companion. That might delay my arrest or potential murdering. *Maybe.*

"The lobby is actually on the mezzanine level," I explain, softly, in the elevator.

"I've been here once or twice before." Shiloh's smile is refreshingly reassuring, in the manner of an old-fashioned movie star after a car chase that went particularly well. "I love their tea service. And the view, of course."

"I'm hoping there won't be an issue," I say. "But I lost my ID and my keycard. So I'm hoping...I can get all that back...from the desk."

He leans into me, brushing his shoulder against mine, which

makes my stomach jump a little. "You *are* really staying here, aren't you?" he says.

"Well." I laugh a little. "I was."

He gives me a slightly amused, slightly concerned smile. I can't imagine what he must think I got myself into.

The elevator opens. I make a beeline for the front desk. The lounge is packed, but the lobby isn't too crowded, only a small line of people checking in. My heart is beating so fast. I'm relieved I don't immediately get jumped by a bunch of police officers, their handcuffs out, or dudes wearing motorcycle helmets. But then:

"AIDAN!"

I whirl around at the sound of my name.

Tatiana bounds toward me from the lounge. A harried waiter runs after her, holding a check and a pen. "Miss! Miss! You forgot to sign."

"Oh, sorry," she says, turning, quickly signing the check, then coming toward me. She is clearly in a state.

"Tats?"

"I've been here... waiting for you," she says. I can see she's been crying, but she still looks amazing in this cute summery striped top and matching navy-blue skirt ensemble. "I'm sorry. I didn't want to overdo it and show up at your room or anything." She looks at Shiloh. "Now I feel foolish."

Shiloh steps forward, hand outstretched. "Shiloh."

Tatiana shakes his hand. "I'm what's left of Tatiana," she says with a small laugh, fighting back a sob.

"Nice to meet you," says Shiloh. "What's left of you sure is pretty."

She shoots me a look, like, *Who's the charmer?* and nods at him, holding out one hand as if hailing a cab, thanking him for the compliment without words.

"Tats. Are you okay? Were you...drinking tea here by yourself?"

She looks back at the lounge, hoisting her purse higher on her shoulder, like she may have forgotten something. "Lame, right?"

"No, not at all."

She dabs at the corners of her eyes and nods. "I'm really sorry. I thought Jackson might be with you. I couldn't reach you. He won't answer my calls or texts."

"I lost my phone."

"We had a fight," she says.

I feign surprise. "Oh, no."

"Spare me. You know full well. You and Jackson were at that ridiculous warehouse party in Bushwick last night. He posted pics of it all over Instagram. He tagged you in all of them."

I stare at her. "Jacks posted images from last night on Instagram and tagged me?"

What is wrong with him?

She nods. "Look, I don't want to get in the middle of your friendship. I don't want to cause drama. Although that's totally what I'm doing, isn't it?" She laughs to herself, blowing her nose with a wrinkled brown Starbucks napkin. "I'm in love with him. And I think it's over. I'm afraid it's over. I don't think he wants to be with me anymore."

"I don't know if that's true," I say, balling my hands into fists, knowing precisely it's completely true.

"It's my fault. I put too much pressure on him," she says, for some reason addressing this to Shiloh. "That was wrong of me. I guess I was always afraid of losing him, him going off to college, things changing...and who can do the long-distance thing forev—"

"You're both going to be in Cambridge," I interject.

But it doesn't seem like she's heard me. "I just wanted more than he could give, and I wound up chasing him away...not that I haven't done that before, and then my stupid parents, I..." she looks at me, frowns, blinks back tears, and takes a step back, her ugly crying warping into total bewilderment. "*What the hell happened to you?*"

"I got into some trouble."

Tatiana shakes off her heartbreak like an old quilt so she can focus on me. She dabs at her lips with the napkin, straightens her skirt, and takes me in with newly clear eyes. "Aidan? Are you okay?"

"He's okay," says Shiloh.

"What happened?" she asks Shiloh.

"Oh, I really don't know," he responds. "He won't tell me."

"Who are you?" she asks him.

"We met on the train," I tell her.

"What train?" she asks me, looking back and forth from me to Shiloh.

I clear my throat. "A lot's happened. The hotel took my keycard and my ID and I need that back. First off."

"You don't have your keycard?"

"No."

Tats straightens her shoulders regally, her *this shit wouldn't fly in Singapore so give me some space* attitude ready to annihilate whoever gets in her way.

Tatiana and Shiloh march me to the check-in desk.

"Yes, this is absolutely unacceptable," says Tatiana, her perfectly modulated tone of voice suffused with just the right amount of dismay, to the meek-looking blond guy with bad skin who asks what he can do for us. *"This,"* she gestures at me, like I'm a snorting creature made out of disparate body parts by a mad scientist in a small Swiss village, "is a guest of this hotel. *Of this hotel, okay*?"

"Yes?" The check-in dude looks afraid. "Is something wrong?"

Tatiana makes a show of looking all around. "Is this the Mandarin Oriental? This is the Mandarin Oriental, right? Because please tell me I didn't just pay fifty bucks for a bunch of stale scones at the Radisson."

He bristles at the word *Radisson*. It's amazing.

"This is the Mandarin Oriental, ma'am," he replies hotly.

Tatiana does this violent-nodding thing. "He needs his keycard. *His keycard*."

"Well, of course," the guy says, confused and startled. "What's your name, sir?"

I lean in and speak politely. "Aidan. Jamison."

He looks at his screen. "We're so sorry, Mr. Jamison, there must have been a mix-up on our part. We have this waiting for you." He reaches behind his desk and hands me an envelope. I rip it open: inside is my keycard and my two IDs. I almost cry.

This is at least one wrong thing that just righted itself. I'm so amped up I accidentally drop everything onto the floor. Shiloh bends down, picks everything up, and hands it all to me.

"What was the source of this mix-up?" Tatiana asks the desk clerk, hands on her hips. She's overdoing her outrage by a mile, but I love her for it.

"I'm not certain. It seems there was a computer glitch and Mr. Jamison's information was briefly mixed up with another guest's."

"Which guest?" I ask.

The guy holds up a finger. "Actually," he says, "we have a message for you . . . from the other guest." He hands me a folded piece of paper.

"From who?" I ask.

"A . . . Mr. Preston," says the check-in guy.

Every time I hear that name now, my heart skips five beats.

My hand closes over the piece of paper. "And where is this Mr. Preston now?"

He consults his computer screen. "Looks like he checked out this morning."

I frown. "This morning?"

"Correct."

"Do you know his full name? Any forwarding address?"

"It looks like it's all been wiped from our system."

Tatiana opens her mouth to say something else, but I cut her off. "Okay, thanks."

"You're welcome, sir. Please let us know if you need anything else."

"Oh, I will," I say, stepping away from the desk, motioning to Tatiana and Shiloh to follow me toward the elevators and up to my room.

I open the door to my room, cautiously, expecting anything.

My room is made up, but apart from that everything is just as I left it. My luggage is untouched. My laptop is on the desk. My iPad is on a chair by the window. I instinctively look for my wallet and phone, then remember those were lost back at Swan Headquarters.

So much has changed since I was last in this room, lying in bed, and I would do anything to get my life back the way it was before I met Benoît. A couple of swipes on my phone and now I'm living in a different reality.

Tatiana throws her purse down on the bed and opens the curtains. "The world is going mad," she says. "Have you seen the news? Cyber-warfare. Three people dead." She sighs, looks at her nails. "I mean, the world is better off without them, but still..."

Yeah, that's the conclusion I came to as well, but it doesn't really matter anymore. The Swans see me as their enemy now. I am in the way of their cause. A cause that part of me respects and supports.

All this is so complicated. I just wanted a spring break. Watch YouTube, listen to a lot of Taylor, maybe have some good sex, visit my burned aunt...

"Aidan, baby, something's happened..."

A Christmas card being shoved under my bedroom door.

"You're not my goddamn brother..."

"Ugh," I say, holding my head, in response to the rush of awful memories.

Tatiana doesn't notice my fresh heaping of distress; she's shaking her head, lost in her indignation: "...and I just cannot fathom a five-star hotel in New York mixing up information, losing people's keycards! If this was in Singapore—"

"Okay, Tats," I say, suddenly exhausted.

Shiloh is looking at me more closely, frowning slightly, lingering by the door, adorably unsure where to place himself in the room.

"You can come in," I tell him, with a laugh, waving him inside, and he smiles, shyly, and sits down on the chair by the desk.

"Are you okay?" he asks me, gently.

"Yeah, why?"

"You look a little...I don't know...pale."

"He's just stressed out," Tatiana explains.

"I don't have a lot of time," I tell them. "I have to meet my parents for dinner."

"Not like that," says Tatiana. "What happened to your throat? Are those bruises?"

"I was strangled. And then almost drowned. More like simultaneously."

There's a brief pause. I tap my knuckles against my forehead while they both stare at me.

"You were...?" she says, her head sliding to one side.

I sit heavily on the bed and try to quickly explain the sequence of events: from when I first met Benoît, being on the run last night, meeting up with Jacks, escaping the warehouse party, crashing at Kibbutzeteria, being kidnapped this morning, then nearly being murdered in the Merrick Gables slightly after lunchtime.

There's another, longer pause.

"Are you serious?" says Shiloh.

"We have to call the police," says Tats, starting to dig through her bag.

"I don't want to do that! If they're not looking for me, I don't want to draw attention to myself. I may have broken a few laws."

I mean, now I actually *did* kill someone, so...

"Don't you think it's strange," says Tats, waving her phone around, "that they're *not* looking for you?"

"Right now I think everything is strange."

She points at the TV, which isn't on. "Do you think... are you telling me you think you're involved with *the terrorist attacks that made international news today*?"

"I don't know."

She looks at me like I'm insane. "Are you even safe here?"

I hold out my hands. "I don't know. But I have to meet my parents. I have to talk to them. I need to do it in person. I worry about them having heart attacks over me or something. I worry about that *a lot*. They've been through so much shit, and there's no room to deviate from any of their plans. We are having dinner. I have to be on time. That is happening and is non-negotiable."

"What does the note say?" says Shiloh.

Right—the note from Mr. Preston himself. I forgot I had it in my hand.

It's handwritten on hotel stationery. Neat block writing in black ink:

> SORRY FOR THE MIX-UP. THEY'LL NEVER LEAVE YOU ALONE UNTIL THEY GET THE ITEM. LET'S MEET AND WORK THIS OUT. IT'S THE ONLY WAY TO END THIS.
>
> —MR. PRESTON

There's a phone number written at the bottom of the paper.

"Uh. We should call the number, I guess," I say, not feeling good about any of this. My stomach is in knots. "But I lost my phone. Should I use the room phone?"

"Ugh, they'll charge you a fortune," says Tats.

Shiloh stands up, taking out his phone. "I'll handle this for you. Is that okay?"

"Yeah, okay." I'm too freaked out and exhausted to argue, but also I can't stomach the idea of talking to any more pernicious strangers on phones right now. No more veiled threats, weird riddles, dropped hints, or psychological probing.

Shiloh grabs a piece of paper and pen from the bedside table, motions to the bathroom. "May I use your bathroom?" he asks me.

"Yeah. Go ahead."

"Thanks." Shiloh goes into the bathroom and closes the door. I hear his voice, muffled from behind the door, then the sound of the sink running.

Tatiana sits on the bed, gestures at the bathroom with her head. I still can't get over how quickly she regained her composure; not twenty minutes ago she was an emotional mess. "What's the deal with that cutie pie?" she asks me.

"I don't know. He helped me escape from the train. Just sort of swooped in."

"You always like them older?"

"Well, last night was..." I stop and look at her. "Wait. Did Jackson tell you?"

She looks caught. "Tell me... what?"

I tap my foot. *"About my past?"*

She presses two fingers to her lips.

"He did, didn't he?"

Tatiana crosses her legs and slips off one of her high heels, clearing her throat. "He may have told me something about... that you were involved with someone..."

"He wasn't supposed to talk about that. It was a *secret.*"

"You're his best friend," she says. "And I was his girlfriend. There's crossover. He probably shouldn't have told me, you're right, but he worries about you."

"Why does he worry about me?"

She laughs a little. "I guess he thinks you get yourself into trouble."

I'm not having any of that. "I feel like trouble tends to find me."

"In some cases, though, you've gone looking for it."

"Tats, this isn't entirely my fault—"

"I'm not saying it is—"

"But, yeah, I see what you mean, I get it."

Shiloh returns from the bathroom, pocketing his phone. "Why did you need to go in there to talk on the phone?" I ask him.

He shrugs. "I had to pee. I wasn't lying about that on the train. I can multitask."

"So did you reach this Mr. Preston?" Tats asks him.

He nods. "I did."

Tats and I both sit up straight, all cars.

Shiloh holds up the piece of paper he was writing on and slides the pen behind his ear. "Well, I told him I was you." He looks at me. "He was curt. He gave me directions to a location. As well as info on a bus you're supposed to take to get there. And he said no matter what: *come alone*."

CHAPTER 9

Dinner

Mr. Preston—Jesus, that stupid name—wants me to meet him at the visitor center of Mohawk State Park, in upstate New York, tomorrow at noon. He said he would know me by sight. I'm supposed to take a 6:15 a.m. bus from the Port Authority Bus Terminal, which will take me directly to the location. The trip is five and a half hours. The state park has hiking trails that wind around the Adirondacks and Lake George. Apparently it's really beautiful there.

Tats is looking at me incredulously. "You're not really thinking of—"

"I'm going."

"Have you lost your mind?"

"Do I have a choice? If he can give me the flash drive the

terrorists think I owe them...then maybe this will end, like he says. They're trying to kill me. They almost succeeded once." My hand involuntarily goes to my throat. "They'll try again. They're good at finding me. Only problem is, I'm supposed to go to Nevada with my family today. I have to find a way to get out of g—"

"Aidan. *Aidan.* Listen to me," says Tats, standing, her arms outstretched. "They're obviously trying to get you alone and isolated."

"Maybe it's just a secure spot for Preston to give me this item."

Tats isn't having it, plus I have my own doubts that this makes sense. But I don't know what the hell else to do.

"Listen," she says. "You've been through a lot, you're not thinking clearly. *Listen.* You will be up there, in an unfamiliar, faraway location, without your phone or your wallet. You don't even know if this Preston person exists!"

"I know."

"You don't know any of these people, or their intentions, except we know they're terrorists, or affiliated with terrorists. Honey. You don't know if they will try to kill you up there. You don't know if they will *kill you anyway* once they receive this flash drive that for some mysterious reason they think you have, which you don't. We literally just had a conversation about how you tend to get yourself into trouble. Maybe make a different decision this time?"

"What's the alternative?"

"You must—*you have to*—call the police!"

I'm nodding. "You're right. This is nuts." I scratch at my scalp. "Shit..."

"I concur," says Shiloh. "I don't think you have a choice anymore."

I turn to Tats. "What time is it?"

She tells me.

"I gotta get ready for dinner!"

"Aidan!" she cries.

"Just wait here! PLEASE!"

I grab some fresh clothes, run into the bathroom, and take the fastest shower of my life. (After this day, it still manages to be the most satisfying, though.) I throw on a pair of skinny black jeans and a white polo shirt. I'm forced to do a douche pop with the shirt collar to hide the bruises on my neck.

When I come out of the bathroom, Shiloh is looking out the window, hands clasped behind his back, and Tats is checking her phone. She gives me a long look: "Honey. I have to get home. I have a family thing. I'm so sorry."

I kiss her on both cheeks. "Okay. Thank you. Sorry for all this."

"Aidan. You're not going to be stupid. Right?"

"I already am stupid."

She lightly slaps my cheek. "No. You're not." Her tone turns a bit more serious. "It's time to grow up, Aidan. Face your parents. Tell them what's going on. They'll survive. And they'll support you. They have to. And then call the police." She points to my laptop. "I'm going to FaceTime you later. And you better be in this room, heading to bed, not heading to any state park."

She looks at Shiloh. "Take care of him. *Please.*"

He smiles at her. "I'll try. It was very nice meeting you."

"Aidan," she says. "Text Jackson. Okay?"

"Yeah."

Tats looks at me, then back at Shiloh. She grabs her purse, heads to the door. She pauses for a second, hand gripping the door handle, looking down at her shoes. I know she feels helpless and she hates it. She also feels guilty, I think, about leaving me to an uncertain fate, knowing I probably won't follow any of her advice, and thinking I'm going to get myself killed.

I'll bet she's going to warn Jackson and tell him everything. But they're not speaking, so I don't know what will happen then.

Tats gives me one last look over her shoulder, then makes her exit, leaving a pleasant scent in her wake—sugar and roses, something like that.

I turn to Shiloh and extend my hand. Every time my eyes focus anew on his face, everything inside me gets all mushy. It's kind of embarrassing and ridiculous.

"Thank you. For everything."

He shakes my hand. "You're welcome. What are you going to do?"

"I don't know yet." I give him a charged look. "I wish I could stay here with you, to be honest." My eyes roam to the bed.

His mouth gets a little tight. "Well. That's not the way the cards are playing out."

"Yeah, I know. Sucks."

"Plus," he says, moving in, taking my face in his hands and giving me the lightest of kisses on the side of my jaw, "I saw your ID when everything tumbled out on the lobby floor. I didn't really think you went to Dartmouth, Witloff boy."

My face must turn a million different colors.

"Yeah," he says, nodding at me in a disappointed sort of way that makes my chest tense up. I still feel that kiss. It's doing things to me.

I close my eyes. "I'm sorry. I was running from bad guys."

He smiles softly at me and turns away.

Okay, wow. I get this terrific lump in my throat because here I am in the middle of this huge mess. And out of nowhere, so *randomly,* this guardian-angel hottie just appears and genuinely seems to care about me (or the little about me that he knows). That was selfless and kind, and I probably didn't make a great impression, lying to him, in the middle of an already whacked-out drama he had nothing to do with. And still, he never quit trying to help me. And that doesn't really make any sense, does it? None of this does...

"I see some thoughts marinating in that head of yours," says Shiloh.

"I'm just not sure about you, man."

"You're suspicious."

I am a little, but that seems almost rude. "Wouldn't you be? As much as I want to believe everything about you, it's all a little too perfect, a little too pat. You dropping down from the heavens like that." I want to be honest, but I don't want to push him away, either.

"I didn't drop from the heavens. I told you: I saw someone

who looked like they could use a friend. I think you need to have more faith in people. Despite everything."

I don't say anything.

"You want my advice?" he says.

"Sure."

"Listen to your friend. You have a family. Tell them everything. Let them help you. Call the police." He pats me on the shoulder. "No one else can do that for you. Or should. You have to grow up a little."

Ouch. *What is with everyone telling me this today?*

The pat on the shoulder feels like a rejection. A patronizing one. "I'm not a little kid," I tell him, kind of petulantly, and then I feel embarrassed for getting upset.

"You didn't want to tell me who you were," he says. "I'm a stranger. I get it. But I'm curious"—his eyes wander over to the bed and then back to me—"if things had gone down a different path, given all the flirting going on...if you would have ever told me you were in high school."

"Honestly, probably not."

He nods, opens his wallet. "You need some cash for a cab?"

Jesus. Fuck. I take the money. I can't look him in the eye.

He takes out his phone. "What's your number?"

I tell him. When he texts me, I hear the *ding* on my iPad and I remember that I still have it. There's that, at least. I can access my texts again. I'm not cut off anymore.

"Now you have me."

It's almost cruel the way he says that.

"Text me if you need help," he says. "If you're in trouble. Don't hesitate."

"I won't."

There's a tiny pause where we just kind of look at each other.

"Kiss me again," I command.

Shiloh steps forward, cups my chin, and kisses me lightly on the lips. It's the softest kiss I've ever had, charged with so many different emotions, and I feel it through my entire spine like it came with little electrodes.

It's so short.

Shiloh steps back, with a deep exhale. "Good-bye, Aidan. Be smart. Be safe. Take care of yourself."

I'm literally swooning. I have to press my feet into the floor to stabilize myself. "Yeah, you, too."

And then he leaves.

There's a pummeling of loneliness right then. I have this impulse to go after him, tackle him, apologize. But I can't—it's too late. This sucks so hard. It is possible he's right—that paranoia clouded me and fear muddled my mind. Shiloh might be a genuinely kind, compassionate person; someone I would've liked to get to know. Seeing his text on my iPad (**Shiloh, hi**) makes me feel even worse. There are also a slew of texts from Jackson and Leo: worried, asking where I am, and then kind of pissed at me for running off. I can't deal with them right now.

I quickly pack my bags. I stuff my laptop and my iPad into my backpack and fling it over my shoulder. I roll my two suitcases out the door.

But I really don't like the last text I saw from Jacks: **Dude. Have you seen the news?**

And from Leo: **Turn on the news. Dude! Call us!**

But I can't, because I don't want to be late. My family hates it when I'm late.

And I already decided I'm going to Nevada with them.

Screw the goddamn Swans.

Despite my backpack weighing me down, despite dragging two suitcases behind me, I decide to take the subway down because Shiloh gave me way more cash than I expected, and I figure I should probably conserve some of it. Because who knows?

I'm stuffed in tight with all my shit on the crowded train. But I take solace in the mini-mobs of rush-hour commuters, with their books and Kindles and headphones playing muffled hip-hop, Candy Crush spangled across their phone screens. The more crowded it gets, the more I can wrap myself in their lives for a little while, squeezed out of danger, forgetting the madness of my own.

I'm ejected into a busy intersection of the West Village, all turned around, and make my way down a quieter street with town houses and pretty little shops, my suitcases kind of deafening as I roll them down the sidewalk.

The restaurant, Bella Fegato, is subterranean, hidden between a posh-looking toy store and a brand new building of sleek, glassy lofts.

A tall, elegant woman in a black dress greets me from behind the host stand as soon as I burst through the doors. I spot my family at a corner table in the back and make a beeline for them after dropping my suitcases with the coat-check girl. My mom's hair, in a sort of modern bob thing, is blonder than ever.

My stomach knots up right away. Typical.

The restaurant is rustic seaside Italian, purposely roughened up. It's like they want you to feel you've been drifting on a raft for days and finally washed up on the shores of Tuscany, yearning for fusilli. The place is empty, given the early hour. All the waiters are refilling everyone's water glasses, hovering, as my family ignores the menus spread out in front of them.

"Aidan!" my mother calls when she sees me, reaching out with her hands.

"Hello, hello," I say, leaning in for a kiss from her, which lands awkwardly on the side of my nose. "Sorry I'm a little late."

"How did the echo test go?" she asks.

"Oh, it was amazing."

"Aidy, *what did they say*?"

"The technicians aren't allowed to say anything," I explain, "until a doctor interprets the results. But the woman said I had nothing to worry about."

My mom claps her hands to her mouth, then addresses my father, who has my giggling nephew on his lap, bouncing him up and down. "They said he doesn't have anything to worry about!" she tells him.

"What?" My dad's hearing is not what it was.

"Doesn't. Have. Anything. To. Worry. About!" She pounds her chest. "His heart!"

"Oh?"

"Okay," I say, "that's not confirmed. I have to see the doctor."

"Of course," says my mom. "But still, she wouldn't have said that!"

My eyes flit to the empty chair that Neil would have been in. That happens every time we go out to dinner. Sometimes I see him smiling at me, the Ghost of Christmas Never. But I don't right now. There's just an empty chair in an Italian restaurant with lots of bleached wood.

My dad hands my nephew over to my sister. He leans forward, hugs me, and pats my head. "Nice to see you, you look good," he says, like I'm an old man who he plays chess with every other week in a park somewhere.

I swing around the table and hug Nicks, who isn't wearing makeup and looks more tired than ever, almost like it's a competition—*who can look the most exhausted?*—and my brother-in-law, Rick, the only one who ever directly acknowledges my being gay, always asking if I've "found a nice dude yet." He wears a maroon V-neck shirt meant to show off the tattoo looped under his collarbone: Chinese lettering he thinks is ultra-sexy and super mysterious. "It's Rumi!" he says proudly to anyone who asks.

Except Rumi is Persian. So. Anyway. Let's not go there.

"Did you see the Klimts?" says my mom.

"Hi, Pixie!" I kiss Annabelle on the cheek and pinch her nose. She's sitting in her own chair playing with the menu, her ice-blond hair in a neat ponytail, and she smiles up at me. Her dimples kill me. She says, "Uncle Aidan!" in this delighted sort of way, kicking her feet.

"The Klimts!" my mom shrieks. "At the Neue?"

"And you!" I say to Sam, now sitting on Rick's lap, having been handed over by my sister so she can attend to what's left of her martini. "Look how big you are," I say, kissing his forehead, pressing the back of my hand to his cheek.

"Hi," he says quietly, unsure, like I may whisk him off and sell him into slavery. Sam probably doesn't remember me. It has been a while.

"I'm Aidan," I tell him. "Your uncle Aidan."

"You're away in ssh-kool," he says, touching the edge of my ear.

"That's right! I'm Uncle Aidan and I'm away at school."

"The Klimts!" my mom shouts. She's already had a glass of wine. Maybe two. There's a smear of lipstick on her teeth.

"Holy shit, Mom," I say, my fists pressed to my ears, finally sitting down, grabbing my napkin and throwing it onto my lap, freeing all the silverware. "No, I didn't get a chance."

"Why? Why not? You had all day."

"How was the hotel?" asks my dad, looking at the menu.

I put down my backpack, my iPad stuffed in, next to my chair. "Fine."

"You had all day," says my mom, looking around, then turning and making a tickling motion at Annabelle. "I see you!"

"What is your thing with me seeing the Klimts?"

She turns back to me, napkin pressed to her lips. "Nothing. I just figured. You were in the city. I know you haven't been there. Why not see—"

"I need a glass of wine," I tell her.

"Waiter!" she hollers, but he's right there, so he nearly jumps out of his skin.

I shake my head at Nicks. She laughs at me, rolling her eyes. "How is school?" she asks me, reaching over and plucking a fork out of Sam's grabby hands. "No, sweetie," she tells him, "that will hurt you."

"It's fine. It's school."

"You look off," she says, squinting, letting Rick deal with Sam.

"I want an egg," says Annabelle.

I press my tongue against my upper teeth. "Off?"

"Yeah," says my sister. "Is everything all right?"

My mom's picked up on this now. "What is it? What's the matter?" she says, looking at me, then at Nicks. Then, to the waiter, gesturing at me: "He needs wine." The waiter silently points at the wine list.

I look around. *Where are we?* Italian place. Tuscan. Fine.

"Uh. Glass of Sangiovese?" I ask the waiter. He nods and runs off.

"What is it now?" My dad.

I lean forward. "It's okay. I just lost..."

"What!" says my mom, hands out. "*What did you lose?*"

"My wallet."

"Oh, my God," she says, sighing into her lap, "Aidan, how did you manage—"

"Just cancel the credit cards. Don't freak."

"What is it?" My dad again.

"We have to cancel the credit cards!" she shouts at him.

"Why?"

"Aidan lost his wallet!"

"Jesus." He sighs. "His wallet now?"

"Egg!" says Annabelle.

"You want an egg?" Rick says to her, giving her a peck on the cheek. She nods and laughs. "All right." He turns to me and grins. "Find a nice dude yet?"

Oh, Rick—you have no idea.

"They'll give her an egg," my dad says to Rick. "Why not? They have eggs here."

"You're not answering your phone," my mom tells me.

"I tried calling you, too," my sister adds.

"Did you bring your bags?" my mom asks. "Did you check out of the hotel yet?"

"They check you out automatically, in the morning. My bags are with me."

"Well, we're not going!" says my mom, announcing this to the whole restaurant. "The trip is canceled."

I sit back. "What? What do you mean? Why?"

"Because my *fucking* sister" (she always whispers any curse words while simultaneously overenunciating them) "left the hospital. Left Nevada!"

Oh, shit. We're not going. I'm not going.

"She's in Atlantic City," says my mom, seething. "At another goddamn casino, all bandaged up like an Egyptian mummy, gambling. *More gambling!*"

"I still don't understand why she would have left Nevada if she knew we were coming," says Nicks.

"Well, she didn't know. It was supposed to be a surprise!"

"Jesus, Mom," says Nicks, finishing her drink. "You were going to just surprise her? Some planning might help if flying is involved, especially with the kids."

"I spoke to the airline. We'll get a partial refund."

"Okay, great," says Nicks, rolling her eyes. "Just no surprises next time. Hopefully a sinkhole won't open up under this other casino, given Aunt Meredith's luck."

"We tried to call you," my mom tells me.

"You knew about all this?" I ask Nicks. She nods through the swirling fog of her fatigue. "So how come you're here, then?"

"To see you, goofball. We already had the restaurant reservation. So...why not?" She shrugs. "I needed to get out of Beacon."

Nicks and Rick live in the Hudson Valley, about an hour and a half north of New York City. Nicks runs some celebrity-stalking blog called Peek-A-Boo that's always in danger of collapsing under an endless array of lawsuits, and Rick owns a string of restaurants ("farm-to-table bullshit," says my dad) around their town of Beacon. He used to live in North Brooklyn, so he's trying to bring Brooklyn artisanal dining even farther north. All his restaurants are named like: Corn & Compass, Crab & Freckle, Tripe & Tempest.

"We already checked you back into the hotel," says my mom. "The Mandarin. We got you another room. So after dinner, just go back. Your sister can drive you back uptown so you don't have to drag your suitcases all around the city."

"We have the car seats," says Nicks, looking worried.

"We can manage," Rick tells her, reassuring.

"They have these things called cabs!" my dad announces.

My mom guzzles some wine. "Your father and I are going to Atlantic City on our own to visit Meredith, see if she needs anything, talk her into getting help. Clearly she has an addiction! She shouldn't have left the hospital. The woman has burns on forty percent of her body! I don't want to inconvenience you kids. You both deserve a break. We'll be gone two days. We'll pick you up from the hotel on our way back. Enjoy the city. For God's sake, see the Klimts!"

"*What is your obsession with Gustav fucking Klimt!*"

"Aidan, calm down," says my dad. "Jesus."

"He's an amazing Austrian artist!" my mother yells back. "*The Woman in Gold*. My God. Aren't you interested as a human being living on this planet?"

"I dragged all my luggage down here!"

"Well, try answering your phone, then! We pay enough for that plan!" She suddenly pushes her chair back, loudly. "And what's this now?" she says, rooting around in her purse, which is hanging off the back of her chair. "Someone's calling me."

"What's going on?" says my dad.

"Someone's calling me!" she repeats, louder. "I hear it vibrating! Don't you hear that?"

"I don't hear it," says my dad. "We need to order." He motions to a waiter.

She pulls out her phone and frowns at the screen. "It's you!" she screams at me.

I'm currently biting my nails to bits. "What?"

"You're calling me!"

She turns the phone around to face me. I see my name and a dorky pic of myself—*why the hell did she pick that photo?*—playing a cartoonish-looking Seymour in an eighth-grade production of *Little Shop of Horrors.*

Rick laughs. "Uh-oh. Butt dial!"

And my hands do go to my pockets, instinctually, before I remember—I don't have my phone on me. It's at Swan Headquarters.

The Swans are calling my mother.

I grab the phone out of her hands and decline the call.

"Where's your phone?" says Nicks.

I shoot her a sharp look; she shoots me a look back like "*What?*" but it's too late.

"Aidan, where is your phone?" says my mom, hands clasped in front of her face.

I think about a volcano about to erupt. Mount Vesuvius. People buried under ash. "I lost it, okay? It's lost!"

A brief, almost fragile hiss of oxygen, like an airlock about to open in a jettisoning spacecraft. And then:

"*WHAT????!!!*"

Everyone yelling at once:

"YOUR WALLET AND YOUR PHONE!" my mom screeches, arms raised.

"I AM NOT PAYING FOR ANOTHER TWELVE-HUNDRED-DOLLAR PHONE!" my father explicitly informs a frightened passing busboy.

"They're not twelve hundred dollars!" I yell back. He always inflates things.

"So who is calling me?" demands my mom.

"Um."

"Are you dealing drugs?"

"Yes, I'm dealing drugs, Mom. I'm the Scarface of Witloff Academy."

"Everyone, relax," my sister says.

"Give the kid a break," adds Rick.

This was a bad idea. But escaping to Nevada with my family seemed like such a shiny, wonderful option about an hour ago.

"What is happening with you?" says my mom. Then, leaning forward and lowering her voice to emphasize the point that she no longer knows who I am: *"What is happening with you?"*

My father smacks the table. "Enough! We'll deal with this later."

But my mom isn't done. "I just don't understand what's..." she trails off.

It's chilling how everyone gets so quiet all of a sudden.

"Aidan?" says my mom, her voice strained, hushed. But her eyes aren't on me; they're somewhere behind and above me. So I turn around.

On the TV over the restaurant bar, my face is on the screen.

My face is on CNN.

"Aidan?" my mom says again.

PERSON OF INTEREST SOUGHT IN CYBER-TERROR ATTACKS

That's what it says under my photo. That photo of me looks familiar. Then I remember where I saw it: it's an enlarged shot of me...one of the pics I saw on Benoît's phone. I turn back to my mother, pressing my fingers into my temples. "You need to be calm right now so I can think."

Tears are in her eyes as she reaches for me. "Honey. Did you join ISIS?"

Her phone on my lap starts vibrating again. It's me. I'm calling her.

"Aidan!" she cries. *"Are you radicalized?"*

I grab my backpack and my mom's phone and run out of the restaurant, nearly crashing into a young couple chasing after their little kid. "Sorry!" I shout at them. I answer the phone, moving away from the restaurant, down the street, crouching behind a parked car so none of my family can come after me. "Who is this?" I hiss.

"I want to play a song for you," says a very familiar voice.

"What?"

And then he plays it, as if holding the phone up to a stereo speaker.

I know the song because I love Motown. Martha and the Vandellas: *"Nowhere to run to, baby, nowhere to hide..."*

"Great," I say, as the music fades. "Do you have any OutKast?"

"Also appropriate."

"You hacked into my phone? The FBI can't even do that."

"I'll wind your watch, boy. You don't know who you're dealing with."

"I'm beginning to get an idea." I remember how fast they found my phone number. They started texting me only hours after I left Benoît's phone in the hotel room.

"I figured dialing *Mom* might get me a direct line to you."

"Where is this all leading, man?"

"You took two from me," he says.

"I took *one*. And that was because he tried to kill me. I have the bruises to prove it."

There's a pause. "And if I told you I didn't authorize that?"

"I wouldn't believe you."

"It's true. I didn't. You can never trust a bellhop these days."

"You're hilarious."

"On the one hand, I did warn you: my priority is to our cause, and you've become a liability. On the other hand, I'm not entirely cold-blooded. Nor am I irrational. What we do unfortunately attracts some unstable people."

"Maybe you should consider another line of work, then. I just walked by a Sabon store that's hiring. I bet you'd be good with soap."

He hums at me lightly, a bee before a sting. "You know what they say..."

"I don't."

"The best assassins, spies, terrorists, mercenaries, whatever... are the ones who love nothing but their mission. They have no loved ones."

My jaw clenches. "I'm not enjoying these threats to my family."

"Are you going to warn them, Aidan?"

"Do I need to?"

"I know you'd do anything to spare them the added strife."

You know what? Fuck this guy and his highfalutin language. His *cause*. His *mission*. Give me a goddamn break. And he is both cold-blooded AND irrational, which makes him a little bit of a liar, too.

I hate liars.

"If you know enough about me to find my family, you must know I'm not the black-hat hacker assassin you think I am," I say.

"Can't be certain of anything. There's too much white noise now."

"What does that mean?"

"Maybe you are who you say you are. Maybe not. Maybe you're the best black hat we managed to unearth. Maybe you're just a pitiful kid with bad luck—"

"It's the second thing, and I also have a bad *heart*—"

"How did you kill him? In the pool?"

"Paper clip I found in your office."

"You're going to tell me you haven't had any training?"

"I haven't. I was fighting for my life." But shit, I know how this looks.

"Here's my offer. You ready?"

"Ready steady."

"You get us that source code, and if you can't—if you don't have it, if you're just a sad little heartsick schoolboy who was in the wrong place at the wrong time—then you come join our cause. Sorry, my friend. Fate is fate. Those are your two options."

"There's no third option?"

"No third option. I saw something in your eyes, Aidan, and I'm never wrong."

I want to ask him what he saw, but I know he's going to tell me anyway.

"You'd fit in so well with us," he adds. "You're *perfect*."

I think of all those boys by the pool.

Why did they all look like me?

This isn't just about a selfless cause that any empathetic soldier can join. This guy is a terrorist and he has followers. The Swans are a cult. And I'd be the newest member.

"I can get it for you," I say.

"Oh, what's that?" he says, his voice louder, clearer, closer to the phone now.

"I can get you the... *item*." I lower my voice. "The source code."

"I'm so pleased to hear it."

"But then I'm out. We're done. Deal?"

Mr. Preston, whoever he is, had better come through with the flash drive. Even though I have a bad, desperate feeling about this whole plan.

Probably because it's bad and desperate.

"Deal," he says. "We have more in common than you know."

"Are you actually saying these things, or are you reading off the closed captioning for *The Dark Knight*?"

"I, too, loved someone who took their own life."

I freeze. I hate, *hate* when someone uses that term, like life is something that can simply be snatched back, as if it were stolen all along.

"You need to start forgiving yourself," he says. The hint of kindness in his voice throws me, a jar of acid spiked with honey.

My nostrils flare. "I will get you the item."

"What a treat. We'll find you, then, when the time is right."

He hangs up.

I stand up, shivering, even though it's warm out, so warm. My world has become an impossible whirlwind—nothing stable, nothing nailed down.

I see my sister approaching at a steady, rapid gait down the street. She's puffing on a cigarette. When she sees me, she waves her arms, speeds up, hobbling in her high heels, then grabs my arms, and pulls me back down behind the car. "They're looking for you," she says.

"Yeah. I saw."

"I mean: Mom, Dad, everyone. Also, we ordered appetizers. Hysterically."

"Hysterical appetizers."

"Is there any other kind?"

"You smoke?"

"I started again," she says, peering over the car, then ducks back down.

"I didn't know you ever smoked."

"It's a stressful time. Rick and I are having some problems. He thinks I'm sleeping with Colby, my spin instructor." She throws her dark hair over her shoulder.

My lips slide together unevenly like two logs passing each other on a white-water rapid. "Are you?"

She takes a long drag. "Things didn't get that far," she says.

I don't really know my sister. I don't know her life. But then again, who knows what she's thinking about me right now?

"Nicks. You, the kids, Mom and Dad—everyone might be in danger. And I have no idea what to tell you to do."

I feel so fucking helpless and responsible.

She takes this in. "Okay. I'll deal with it."

I squint. "How?"

"I don't know," she says, staring at a woman walking by, clearly admiring her Lululemon attire.

I snap my fingers. "Focus."

She whips her head toward me. "I am."

"I have to go," I tell her. "Now."

"Aidan. There's a manhunt for you. They're linking you to a murder at the Mandarin Oriental. That's what they're saying on the news."

I cover my face with one shaky hand. *So they are looking for me.* But I was just at that stupid hotel. No one was looking for me an hour ago. There was no *manhunt*. Nothing makes sense right now.

"They haven't said your name. No one's released your name. But your face is everywhere. That sweet face!" She fights off a flood of emotion. "What's going on?"

"Wrong place, wrong time, and then it just got worse. Spun out of control. I made a few bad decisions early on, but I didn't deserve where they all led."

"Jesus," she says, "it's just like the Great British Baking Show."

I close and open my eyes. "Right. JUST LIKE THAT."

She takes another puff, then throws the smoldering remainder of her cig over her shoulder. "We'll get you a lawyer."

"It's bigger than that now."

She peers up at me. "What happened to your throat?"

I fix my collar. "Strangled."

She claps her hand to her chest. "Where do you think you're going to go?"

"To fix this."

She starts to cry. "I'm sorry we were never there for you..."

"Oh, God, Nicks, not now. *Please.*"

She puts her hand on my shoulder. "No, I mean it. I was older. Neil died. You were on your own. That wasn't right. And yet still...we're all apart! Scattered!"

I put my hand on her shoulder, too. "Thank you. But I'm not some drug addict who just knocked over a liquor store. I literally just stumbled into something—"

"I don't ask about your life. Do you...have you found...a *partner*?"

I laugh, snotty and garbled, into the crook of my elbow. My sister has chosen this moment, of all the moments of our lifetimes, to try to get closer to me. I love it.

"I want you to know the kids better!" she cries. *"My babies!"*

"Nicks. I need cash. I need your credit cards, too."

She pulls herself together, sniffs, digs through her wallet, hands me a bunch of twenties and an American Express Gold card. "If you use the card, they'll trace it," she tells me.

"Yeah. But. Just in case."

"Oh, my God, Aidan, are you really on the run from—"

"Do you have, um..." My fingers make shapes in the air. "Like, a hat? Sunglasses?"

"I don't have a hat. I have these..." She pulls a pair of large round sunglasses from her purse and hands them to me. I put them on.

"How do I look wearing these?"

"Like Jackie O went blind."

I hand them back. I hear my name being called down the street. "Shit."

"Aidan. Are you sure you're all right?"

"Obviously, I'm not. But I need you to trust me that I'm not a terrorist."

"I do." Her face looks so pained. "I've just been reflecting on everything lately, everything that happened before tonight, and I just..."

"What?"

"I took the kids to the planetarium, Whoopi Goldberg was narrating this thing about the solar system, and I realized how small we all are—"

"Oh, God, okay."

"And do you think I need Botox?"

"...Fucking WHAT?"

"Just...the light in the restaurant...I saw my reflection... around my mouth..."

She makes a claw-like shape with her hand around her mouth where the Botox would go.

I kiss her on the cheek. "You look beautiful. Really. It was great to see you and the kids."

"I mean, I'm not twenty-two anymore..."

I juggle my mom's phone. "Should I give this back to Mom?"

She pops a mint to cover the smell of the cigarette. "Keep it. You may need it."

"Can they track me down easier if I have it? The signals or something?"

Neither of us knows the answer to that.

I give the phone back to Nicks. I'm not thinking clearly, but all my mom will do is endlessly call that phone trying to reach me, leaving blustery forty-five-second voice mails (talk about terrorism!). Also, I don't remember anyone's numbers anyway, so it's not like I can call or text anyone using my mom's stupid phone that she barely even knows how to use herself.

I remind Nicks that I left my luggage at the coat check, give her a giant hug, and then I'm off.

CHAPTER 10

Mohawk State Park

I fling myself in front of a cab and climb inside. "Port Authority Bus Terminal, please." As the cab pulls away, I think about my face being splashed all over cable news.

I think about Shiloh and his amazing smile, his coy, unexpected kindness. His mysteriousness. I get upset all over again.

I think about Tom. And that last day we had.

He said we could swim for a bit, but he wasn't happy about it. He wasn't happy I was even there. A frown cratered his face like a fault line when he saw me at his door. A distance had been swelling between us, and now there was this.

It was late afternoon when the sky turned a rancid green and the rain came, slapping everything. Lightning slashed over the treetops. When the storm was over, the smell of electricity was in the air. Everything was puddled, dripping, and the sun had made its final escape for the day.

Everyone was gone, of course. My parents were at something. Shane was elsewhere. His mom was out of town. Tom and I were alone during the storm, just watching the pool get pelted. I thought of meteors falling and striking Earth.

I realized Tom didn't want me to come inside the house with him.

Truthfully, I messed up, maybe.

He had already told me to stop coming, told me to stop knocking on their front door when I knew he was home alone. But I didn't listen. I kept thinking he was going to change his mind.

Thing is, we had already started breaking some of our own rules, like meeting at different times; he even came over to my house once to get me. I wasn't mowing his lawn much anymore. We were getting brazen. Then this coldness began to creep in from the edges, out of nowhere. And I knew what was coming. He told right me then and there, after the rain let up, that it was over for good.

No more, he said. *No more.*

Half his face was illuminated by a slice of amber light pouring out of a window, spilling across the soaked lawn. He looked pained and worried, like maybe I wouldn't understand.

There was always this torment in him I didn't know what to do with. Him just saying it, finally—that we were done—didn't come as any kind of relief. It was the opposite. It was a gut punch. I suddenly knew what a broken heart meant.

He stood his ground, calm and contained. He explained that he had so much more to lose than me, that he had to think of his family. He said he didn't want anyone to get hurt over this. And I actually laughed at that.

I asked him if he loved me. And he didn't answer. He just looked away.

I lost it. I really lost it then.

I'll never forget the meaty sound of my fists beating against his wet chest as droplets of water were flung off my hair. He had to grab my fists in midair. I either slipped or he threw me to the ground to stop me.

I told him I could ruin him. I told him I could wreck his fucking life.

He told me his life was already in ruins.

That's what he said: *Already in ruins*.

He looked so beaten down and pathetic that I didn't know if I truly hated him or just felt sorrier for him than I have for anyone ever. It was a wild moment. Confusing as hell. Everything about him (and us) was confusing to me.

Over the past several weeks, he had been the one needing constant reassurance. He would lay his head on my chest while I told him, over and over, that everything was going to be okay, stroking his arms, his hair. I had become the wise one, the protective one, even though I was never sure what I was protecting him from. Of course I probably knew, deep down. Just like I knew this day would come.

Tom looked out at the dark pool, the inflatable toys making sad shapes in the misty night, huddled in one corner, as if not wanting to overhear. Wisps of steam rose from the surface like tongues. And then he turned and walked inside the house, leaving me there, covered in mud and wet grass, sobbing on my side, fetal with pain.

In the immediate aftermath, I didn't try to make contact. I feigned a bad cold (I had, in fact, caught one) and missed three days of school. I didn't try to get revenge on him for hurting me. I stayed in bed. I told no one.

The only thing I truly regretted was that I had threatened him, made him more fearful, made him feel even more miserable, defeated, and alone.

I didn't know being in love is a kind of prolonged ache. I didn't even know I was in love with him. I realized only when it was gone, extracted from me like a rotten tooth.

When I get to 42nd Street, I buy a baseball cap and a pair of sunglasses at the first souvenir place I see. I'm sure I look weird wearing sunglasses at night, but whatever.

I avoid cops with dogs as I buy a bus ticket ($55.75!) at the Port Authority Bus Terminal. I use cash for everything. I take out my iPad. The Wi-Fi is weak all over the terminal, but I manage to find a lone spot where I can text Jackson and Leo.

I tell them I'm okay, that I'm on my way upstate. I tell them to talk to Tats if they want to know more. I give Leo all my passwords. I tell him my phone has been stolen and hacked. I need him to disable everything, change all my passwords, so no one can get info on me from e-mails, texts, voice mails, or whatever's on my phone. Although I'm sure it's already too late and that's totally pointless.

Now I just have eleven hours to kill.

I duck into a Pixar movie at one of the big theaters off Times Square (don't enjoy, totally distracted), then fall asleep in a corner table at a Starbucks, right near the bathroom, reading *Age of Wonder*. That was stupid. My hat and sunglasses slipped off. I could have been spotted. My backpack could have been stolen. I got lucky. A manager wakes me up, but he does it gently, and leaves me alone when he sees I'm not a drugged-out street kid.

Speaking of, McDonald's is quite a scene late at night. I watch, fascinated, chomping a Big Mac, as prostitutes mingle with tourists clutching Playbills. Scary-looking people pound on the door of the one working restroom, desperate to get in.

A tweaking club kid, wearing a backward baseball cap with gold lettering scripted across, angrily complains to the cashier that he didn't receive a cherry on top of his ice cream sundae. "But fine, that's whatever," he says, waving her off, walking away. Then he stops in the middle of the dining room, lowers his head, and begins to sob.

I wish I could chill back at the Mandarin Oriental, but that's obviously not an option. I avoid the news. I don't want to see my name in a headline crawl. I don't want to see a photo of myself on a ginormous Times Square screen. But that becomes impossible to avoid, and I catch a screaming piece of breaking news. I can't help looking. Crowds slow, heads crane up.

Instinctively, I pull the cap tighter over my face.

There's been another attack.

Heartland Baptist Church, known for their hateful attacks on the LGBTQ community, was picketing the funeral of a gay teen—a recent victim of a school shooting—in Garville, Kansas. A swarm of drones descended on the crowd, throwing people off balance and scattering the homophobes. At that point "a small assault team of snipers," well-hidden on various scattered rooftops, picked off the picketers, effectively wiping out most of the church's membership since there were only like forty of them. It was well-choreographed—like a ballet.

Picked off the picketers. That has a ring to it.

I can almost hear the Swans laughing.

The shooters all got away. The drones flew off. When I see the image of the swan that was tweeted from Heartland Baptist Church's hacked account, I slowly back away and run down a side street filled with packed restaurants and bars.

I get back to Port Authority early and wait, avoiding any more crowds.

I purposefully grab a window seat toward the back of the bus so fewer people will pass by. An old woman sits next to me. She's grandmotherly but unsmiling, eating peanuts from a small crumpled paper bag and throwing the shells on the floor. She smells a little like cats and old cheese.

I'm feeling that unnerving combination of fear, dread, and admiration that the Swans elicit in me. Things are definitely escalating.

And how are they doing all this so effectively?

I don't let go of my backpack. I keep it firmly on my lap. I recline my seat back so I can just zone out. I charge my iPad.

There's Wi-Fi on the bus. Leo texts back. He tells me the new password for my e-mail. He walks me through how to remotely lock and wipe my iPhone using the Find My iPhone app on the iPad. I do it right away.

Jackson texts, asking where I'm going. I tell him. He asks how Tats is. I tell him he should ask her himself.

Jackson tells me all the cable-news outlets are connecting Benoît's murder at the Mandarin Oriental with the coordinated cyberattacks, and now the attack on Heartland Baptist Church, which has apparently sent the religious right into hysterics. My face is still all over the news as a "person of interest," but the authorities don't seem to have released my name just yet. I don't know why.

I hate texting on an iPad, but I'll do it for Jacks.

JACKSON: Ur famous bro.

ME: U mean infamous.

JACKSON: Like the game, lol.

ME: :P

JACKSON: WHY did you run from Kibbutzeteria?

ME: I didn't want to drag you guys into this

JACKSON: was that rlly it tho?

ME: also worried u were gonna call the cops

JACKSON: yo why don't u trust me I am ur best friend

ME: bc you WERE gonna call the cops

JACKSON: u have trust issues

ME: you were tho

JACKSON: I mean that would have been best thing don't ya think?

ME: Not how I wanted to handle things. I need to make decisions for myself and ur not respecting my ability to do that.

JACKSON: I get that but HOLY HELL u r going through a lot rn. I wanted to help!

ME: Respect, but sometimes you treat me like a helpless kid and I hate that. I can help myself.

JACKSON: I want to say 1 thing don't get mad.

I lean back against the seat and sigh loudly.

JACKSON: I think sometimes you do risky shit, make irrational decisions so u can make things right retroactively.

Ugh. He may not be so off base about that.

JACKSON: Nothing will get solved that way.

ME: k

JACKSON: I'm legit scared this is the last time I'm ever going to talk to u.

I close my eyes for a second, then decide to tell Jackson something I've always wanted to say.

ME: In case I don't see u again . . . uhhh . . . I think for a short while back in freshman yr part of me was a little bit in love with u.

There's an extended pause. Those animated dots, starting and restarting. Jackson deciding how to respond to this.

JACKSON: I'm flattered. srsly. Never knew. Part of u falls in love with everyone tho, right? Least for a while?

ME: yeah maybe. Just the peeps I care about tho.

JACKSON: There's a v. thin line bet friendship and that other stuff, the romantic stuff u know.

I smile at that. Jackson will be a great therapist one day. He'll be a great anything one day.

ME: yep.

JACKSON: If I went that way Id totally run away with u. You'd be my bae!

ME: LOL. Thx.

JACKSON: What ur doing rn is totally nuts.

ME: It's my only option to stop this shit. If I can get them this item, it stops.

JACKSON: Except if it doesn't.

ME: No other options.

Jackson and I digress a bit into a rapper we both like who just dropped a new album. It's a nostalgic yearning for the normal friendship we used to have, when we'd talk about music and watch movies—when I wasn't a fugitive, a suspected terrorist, and a murderer.

ME: Love 3rd track.

JACKSON: That shit slaps, man.

ME: k, I should get some sleep.

JACKSON: Word. Love u. Do not let yourself be isolated or go with anyone alone.

ME: Love ya 2. I will survive this. Singing to u: I will surviiiiive, hey, hey!

JACKSON: LMAO. Ur so gay.

ME: ttyl.

I lower my cap over my face and manage to sleep for most of

the ride. I don't leave the bus during any of the pit stops. I use the bathroom only once, and I take my backpack with me. I wake up just as we're nearing the state park. I watch the thin line of horizon out the window ignite into a neon blue. Coupled with the steady roar of the bus engine, things seem almost mundane, maybe even hopeful.

I'm very aware I could be walking into a trap. Maybe this was the stupidest thing, coming here. But the Swans left me no choice. I do not want to join their evil "organization," even if part of me does want to root them on a little bit, but only from afar.

I don't understand what Preston's motivation is. Why have me travel all the way to the Adirondacks to meet him? What is he going to want in return?

Trap, trap, trap: my brain, on repeat, rattling around that word.

The more I think about it, the more nervous I get, because he was so insistent on me coming alone, and so scant on details. But there's a chance he's someone who can help me. And I need someone on my side right now.

As we reach our final destination, Leo texts me.

He reminds me I can use the Find My iPhone app to see where my phone is at this very moment. I didn't bother before. I assumed it was still in the Merrick Gables.

Leo says check anyway.

It's not.

There's a gray dot, meaning it's offline, but it shows the last known location. It's close by.

My phone seems to have followed me to the Adirondacks.

I don't know if that's a glitch in the app. But if it isn't a glitch,

I don't know what it means. And I sure as hell don't know what to do about it now.

We disembark. The visitor center won't open for another forty-five minutes, but apparently they serve an early breakfast in their main cafeteria. That's good, because I'm famished. But now I have even more time to kill, and no more Wi-Fi.

The visitor center looks like a bunch of interconnected wooden cabins with exposed beams on a sprawling campsite. The triangular rooftops are the color of oxidized pennies. Coming from the city, and being asleep for most of the ride up, everything feels so open all of a sudden, like someone unbuttoned the world. The sky is cerulean clear. I see the lake sparkling in the distance, reflecting the morning sun. Mounds of mossy-looking mountains rise all around us.

I step away from the crowd that's getting off the bus, slinging my backpack over my shoulder, keeping to myself, eyes peeled for anything out of the ordinary: anyone who seems to be looking at me, or have any interest in me whatsoever. But no one does.

Most of the people coming off our bus, and the two that arrive next, are in chatty groups: couples and families and old friends, people with serious backpacking gear, waving maps and guides around. People who look like they know exactly what kind of kayak paddle to buy at a sporting goods store. I'm the only one traveling alone.

Because who the hell goes to the freakin' Adirondacks by themselves?

The one thing that comforts me is that this place is pretty busy. There are crowds of people here, so if someone wanted to harm me, this is not the place to pick. This is definitely more the place to meet clandestinely, make some kind of handoff. I'm not surrounded by Heartland Baptist Church members, and I doubt the Swans want to kill innocent people.

But, again, *why here*? And why was my iPhone heading here, too?

Maybe Preston is or was a Swan? Maybe the Swans found out about this meeting and are going to facilitate the handoff. Or try to kill me.

If it's the second thing, it doesn't matter—if they want me dead, they'll get me eventually. They're good at finding their marks. I might as well see if what Preston said is true. I can't get what he said in that note out of my head:

They'll never leave you alone until they get the item. Let's meet and work this out. It's the only way to end this.

I'm praying that's true.

I sit on a rock, off the parking lot, swatting bugs off my arms, and watch people until the visitor center opens. Hungry hikers stream in to get their hearty breakfasts. I head in with them, never taking off my cap or my sunglasses, my fingers nervously twirling the strap on my backpack, prepared for anything.

I think the best thing to do is act like a normal tourist. So I load my tray up with hunks of scrambled eggs and disc-shaped sausages and hash browns and mini cups of orange juice and ciabatta rolls like I'm Bear Grylls. This is probably the most food I've ever held in my hands in my entire life. I'm not exactly a mountain man.

I pay the cashier and take my tray to the bustling dining area in the back of the visitor center, which overlooks the lake. The walls are all glass, the large windows at the top swung open to let in the breeze coming off the water.

To buy time I eat slowly, so I'm not sitting by myself, hunched over an empty tray. My eyes are everywhere, looking for whoever I think this Mr. Preston is. But everyone here is talking to someone else. There is no lone man wearing a raincoat and fedora, holding a briefcase. There is Wi-Fi, though. And it works.

I have texts from Leo and Jackson, asking for an update, and five from my sister, asking me if I'm alive. But I don't respond to anyone just yet. I think I need to be off the grid in case the police are trying to find me; they may be monitoring the phones of my family and friends. Silence is smart right now.

Says me, Veteran Fugitive.

The Find My iPhone app doesn't provide me with any new updates. My phone is still offline, its approximate last location the same, not that far from here. I scan the cafeteria—still no one who could be Mr. Preston.

I open my iPad and dip into my Tumblr, just to keep myself occupied. I haven't been on it since I uploaded those photos at the Mandarin Oriental, when I first got back to my room. I love the series of the woman with the eye patch holding the orange Hermès bag. I took my customary burst of photos, following her trajectory across the lounge. But now I see something I hadn't before.

When she passes by my table, on her other side is a man holding a camera. The man is aiming the camera right at me. He's standing on the upper tier of the lounge, leaning against the wall. He's pretending to take pics of the view, but his lens is clearly on me. I never noticed Benoît, standing no more than a hundred feet away from me, snapping the photos of me that I'd later find on his phone, and on that flash drive in his laptop.

There's one last pic in the bunch, as "Lady with Hermès" walks out of my frame. In the photo the man has lowered the camera from his face. He's looking away, about to make a break for it. My stomach lurches.

The man isn't Benoît.

It's Shiloh.

I stare at the photo for so long that I don't pay enough attention to the voice in my head saying: *Moron, Shiloh is the one who sent you here. No one else spoke to Mr. Preston on the phone. Only he did. In the bathroom of your hotel room. So you couldn't hear a word.*

But I can't stop staring at the photo. So at first I ignore the buzzing sounds above me. And the sudden rise of laughter, the clicks of smartphone cameras. I don't actually look up from my iPad until a mom grabs her kid right in front of me and says, excitedly: "Look, honey, look at the drones!"

And then that's all I hear—just that one word.

Drones.

I drop my iPad and look up. Through the open glass windows, someone has expertly piloted what people around me are excitedly calling "two top-of-the-line DJI drones" right into the middle of the cafeteria. Everyone is laughing, pointing with forks.

"Best aerial shots you can get!" a guy says, except I'm not focused on the cameras on the two sleek silver drones. I'm worried about the small canisters they're carrying.

"I'm expecting a package!" a woman says, and everyone around her laughs. She should take her routine on the road.

These clearly aren't hacked military drones, but they're still drones. And after the attack in Kansas, it's the fixation on an idea—a method of attack—that scares me enough to take action.

I stand up. "Everyone get out," I say. But I say it hesitantly, under my breath, and no one hears me. So I do the opposite of what I've been trying to do for the last fifteen hours: I call attention to myself. I push my tray away (into some poor woman's lap, actually), stand up on the table, and start waving my arms around like mad.

"EVERYONE GET OUT!" I scream. "IT'S AN ATTACK! GET OUT NOW!"

That's pretty much all it takes. Everyone looks at me, looks at the drones, jumps up, and scatters. Trays drop. Silverware clatters. People begin to scream and rush out. But it's too late. There's a hissing noise, and the room fills with smoke.

It's a thick white smoke that instantly makes my eyes burn like mad.

Tear gas.

The screaming gets louder. There's a stampede. I drop to the floor, under the table, to avoid being trampled. Backpacks and other gear are abandoned. People's shit gets strewn everywhere. I see a pair of swimming goggles peeking out of an open, upturned backpack. I rip off my sunglasses and snap on the goggles. I grab a red bandanna out of another backpack and wrap it around my mouth, although that doesn't help much. I can hardly breathe at all.

I hear glass breaking. I look up. People are smashing out the windows. The drones calmly buzz around the cavernous, high-ceilinged room, still smoking. The tear gas is unreal. It makes every single thing on my face hurt. I hear shouts, then someone is dragging me out from under the table.

It's a state trooper.

"C'mon, kid," he says, standing me up, a bandanna wrapped around his nose and mouth, "let's get you out of here." He grabs my shoulders, about to spin me around, but then his head suddenly thrusts forward in a very unnatural way, accompanied by a spray of blood that gets me right in the face.

There's an arrowhead sticking out of his throat.

At first I can't believe my eyes, that what I'm seeing is real, but the state trooper falls into me and I can't support his weight, so I have to maneuver around him in order not to get crushed. He falls forward, collapsing to the ground, dead.

Fear and shock fight for control of my body so I just wind up feeling very cold, my brain shielding me from this reality while trying to make sense of it all, taking in every little detail.

The arrow is made of carbon, with neon-green fletching. It went clean through. It's a hunting arrow. Most likely shot from a crossbow. Most likely meant for me. This was a trap.

Of course it was. I'm so fucking stupid.

They're out there, in the woods, trying to kill me.

Of course they are, they're *terrorists:* they have no problem killing innocent bystanders. So there goes that theory.

The fresh air from all the broken windows is weakening the effects of the tear gas from the drones. There are loud gunshots. More state troopers have rushed in. They're shooting at the drones. A couple of their shots miss, shattering more windows. The broken glass all over the floor is probably just as dangerous as the tear gas. I crouch down beside the dead state trooper, and roll him onto his side. I unholster his gun (I think it's a Glock) and shove it in the waistband of my jeans.

Another neon-green arrow whizzes by, embedding itself in a nearby wall.

Holy shit.

The other state troopers aren't seeing the arrows. I shout at them, but they can't hear me; they're busy taking down the drones, rushing people out of the visitor center.

I dig around in people's abandoned backpacks, pulling out T-shirts and hoodies and shorts, stuff shoved way down into bags that isn't contaminated by the tear gas. Then I stand up, keeping my head down, and run out as fast as I can, along with everyone else the state troopers are quickly ushering out of the building.

Outside, it's chaos: people are vomiting, coughing, crying, and grasping each other. More police cars, sirens wailing, skid to a stop in front of the visitor center. Two ambulances pull up as well, joining a third that's already here.

I'm not safe here. I'm not safe surrounded by people, by the police, by an entire army even. Those arrows will find me.

Nowhere to run to, baby, nowhere to hide...

I move away from the crowd, wiping the blood off my face. I rip off my shirt and pull on a fresh T-shirt. I put a gray hoodie on over it. I take off my jeans and put on a pair of cargo shorts that just manage to fit, a minor miracle, since usually everything is too big on me. I transfer the gun. I still have no phone, and I just lost my iPad and my backpack (with my laptop inside). I pull off the swimming goggles. My eyes weren't affected. My throat is burning, though. I need water.

I need to get out of the open. I think about running over to the police, but it's insanity—they're still getting people out, tending to the wounded; they might not be able to protect me in time, and any pause could be too late. So I run toward the woods surrounding the visitor center, heading right for the sun-splotched trails. As soon as I do, another arrow flies into a 1950s-style wooden sign with yellow lettering, welcoming me to the Mohawk State Park trails. It misses me by a hair.

Those bastards—those sneaky, lying bastards.

I can't see where they are. I can't see who's shooting arrows at me.

I race through the trails in a zigzag pattern, taking cover behind the bigger trees whenever I can. I'm on a stony path that cuts through the woods. I try to get higher up to see more of my surroundings. As I do, the glistening lake emerges from beyond the trees. I'm already sweaty, dehydrated, totally out of breath.

On the path directly below mine, I hear a rustling, and in the corner of my eye I see a flash of green that's brighter than anything else in the forest. I hide behind an oak tree, and peer down. There's a man wearing a black windbreaker, loading a crossbow with one of those evil green arrows. He's creeping through the forest.

I take the Glock out of my shorts.

He crouches, moving stealthily, until he's behind a tree, right under me.

I breathe through my nose. I can do this. This is my only chance.

It's me or him.

I move out from behind the tree and aim the gun. *"Pssst! Katniss!"*

He emerges, lightning fast, and whirls around, his crossbow already aimed. But I'm quicker. I fire the gun, and through the explosion of smoke I see him go flying back into the woods. He hits the ground hard and doesn't move again.

My ears are ringing and I wobble for a second. I wish I could say I've never fired a gun before. I hate them. But when I was a kid, I went hunting with my survivalist uncle (in the North Maine woods) and he taught me how to fire a gun, along with a lot of other crap. I know a little about crossbows, too. I didn't enjoy hunting, and I'll never do it again, but at least I had that experience. Only something as ugly and horrible as this would make that knowledge useful again. Bile fills the back of my throat.

I don't know if there are more of them. So I keep running.

I fly through the trails, eventually making my way out of the woods and onto the lakeshore. There are people here, and my presence probably endangers them. It's warm for this time of year, so people are on kayaks, Jet Skis, pontoons; parents and kids are walking along the edge of the water. I think about that poor state trooper.

Was all of this my fault? Because I showed up here?

I stuff the gun into my shorts. I look around, panting, trying to get my bearings. There's a beach nearby. I see lifeguards and people swimming.

I make my way to the beach, trying to get as far away from the visitor center (and where I was) as possible, in case terrorists armed with crossbows are still coming after me. I try to steer clear of people, but it's still early—not as crowded as it probably will be later on. I go up a sandy hill, past the parking lot, onto a road, and that's where I spot a motel.

Three police cars, lights and sirens going, zoom past me as I cross the road.

The Mohawk Candlelight Lodge is doing that "quaint" thing—it looks like a converted house with canary-yellow siding and green shutters. Mountains loom over it, ribboned by swirls of fog the sun hasn't burned off yet. Two stories of rooms face a half-empty parking lot: white lattice balcony, white picket fence surrounding a pool off to the side of the motel next to a white lattice gazebo covered with ivy. There are cottages on the other side of the parking lot that look like mini versions of the motel.

I walk into the office. The lace curtains over the windows behind the desk soften the light, making everything look rural and dreamy. A heavyset red-headed woman wearing a green MOHAWK CANDLELIGHT LODGE T-shirt and khaki shorts emerges from an office behind the desk. When she sees me, she gives me a funny look. She takes her seat in front of a computer screen littered with pink Post-it notes.

"How can I help you?" she says, her round, pale face tired, with a patina of oil around her chin. "Are you with your parents?"

"I need you to call the police," I tell her. "I was in—"

She claps her hands to the sides of her face. "Oh, my God, were you in that attack over at the visitor center? We just heard about that! Oh, sweetheart, look at you!" She rushes over to a mini fridge and hands me a bottle of water, which I greedily snatch and drink down so fast she just stares and hands me another one.

"Thank you so much," I tell her.

"Do you need an ambulance? I think I can radio...did you get help over there?"

"I'm okay," I tell her. "The water helped, thanks."

"Did you know our phones are down?" she says.

I press my palm against my cheek. "How would I know that?"

"Landlines aren't working, and everyone's just getting a busy signal on their cells. Must have something to do with the attack; we're a small town, the system must be overloaded, the towers or something, I don't—"

"Are there...um, many other motels around here?"

"We're the closest one to the visitor center. There's also Mohican Village Resort about five miles west—nice place, different price point. Depends what you're looking for."

I'm trying to assess how safe I am here; apparently I didn't manage to get all that far from the visitor center, or even the state park. I was probably running in circles. That was real cunning of me. I nod at her. "Um. Can I get a room, please?"

"Room or cottage?"

"Room."

She taps at her keyboard. "Actually, we don't have any cottages available at the moment, so it would have to be a room. How many are you?"

"It's, uh, just me."

"You have a credit card, sweetie?"

I slide my sister's Amex over to her.

"I can put you in room 104, on the downstairs level. One king-size bed. Continental breakfast included. How many nights? You said it's just you, right?" She glances at the credit card, then at me, frowning. "Are you Nicole Jamison-Towne?"

"My sister."

"Do you have ID on you, sweetie?"

I don't want her to know my name. Just in case. "Uh. No. It got lost."

"Well," she says, giving me a *sorry* look and handing back the card.

I wave it back. "No, look, please just run the card. I'm with my family."

"I thought you said you were alone?"

"I mean I'm alone *right now.* My family was taken to the local hospital."

She gasps. "Oh, sweetie! Are they—"

"Everyone's okay. They just have chemical burns. Um. Their

skin. And their eyes, too." I sigh. "I really don't know about their eyes, actually. I think they'll be okay. I hope. They told me to just go and find the nearest motel, take whatever room available, and they would meet me here later. I ran through the woods, along a beach, to get here *and I really need to take a shower.* My skin is burning. You have no idea."

"My God, of course. I'll go ahead and set you up in room 104 because this is an emergency, and we should all do what we can to help! But when they get here, please tell them to check in with me right away. I'm Lorna. I need ID for the credit card."

"Of course I will. Thank you, Lorna."

"How are you going to find them?" she asks.

"Uh, I'll just call my mom's cell from the room—"

"The phones are down!"

"I'll walk over to the hospital, then. Or hitchhike?"

"Do you need a lift? We can give you a lift over there. I'll ask Jack, our maintenance man; he has a pickup. Which hospital are they at? Seven Winds? Fountain Falls? Eagle Springs?"

God, these fucking names. "Uh, I'm not sure. I think I should clean myself up and wait for cell service to be restored. I'll just keep calling my mom's phone until she answers, and I'll tell her where I am. I'll figure it out."

"Okay. Do you want a bigger room?"

"Not right now. I just really need to—"

"Of course, of course. Just let me know how else I can help."

She slides me the room key. I let her keep Nicole's credit card.

CHAPTER 11

Digital Dust

The room is no-frills basic, with a view of the parking lot. It's a measure of just how far I've fallen during my spring break that I started off at the Mandarin Oriental and wound up at the Mohawk Candlelight Lodge. I feel naked without my wallet, my phone, my iPad, my freakin' laptop, and everything else in my backpack. This really sucks. I don't have my book. Even my Burt's Bees Lip Balm is gone.

I close the curtains and lock the door. I rip off my clothes and take a very long shower. I flush out my eyes. I drink a lot of water from the bathroom sink. Thanks also to my survivalist uncle (probably stocking up on freeze-dried food as we speak), I know to iron all the clothes to get any residual traces of tear gas out of them.

I didn't even realize I was wearing a woman's pink T-shirt (proclaiming she donated at a blood bank in Jupiter, Florida) and an extra-large hoodie that says Syracuse University. The cargo shorts are so baggy and pockety that I can't even deal. They probably belong to the son of a duck hunter who wears them at monster truck shows. But I get dressed. I keep seeing the Glock lying on the bed, next to the pillow, and wonder whose life I'm living right now. I pick up the phone—still dead, no signal.

Parts of my body keep feeling numb and tingly, and then it goes away. I feel nauseated and then that goes away, too. I have flashy spots in my eyes. I don't think any of this is from the tear gas. I think it's the shock. I shot a man—the second person I've killed in two days. And then someone else, a state trooper, died because of me. I'm trying to shove these facts into the back of my mind but they keep rising to the surface. I'm just trying not to totally lose it here.

I need a plan. But instead, I take a nap, the Glock not far from my grasp.

I wake a few hours later, after hearing the roar of a motorcycle that I'm not sure is real or was steeped into my tangled, dreamless sleep. I slept longer than I meant to. I open the curtains and look outside. It's afternoon now, and my stomach is grumbling. The sun has shifted in the sky; the clouds drift over the mountains, speckling them with shadows. It looks like a movie backdrop. I wonder how long I have left in this room before Lorna comes calling.

I see someone walking past my room, across the parking lot toward the row of cottages. He has a very familiar gait.

Shiloh.

Stylish as hell, he's wearing a light-pink shirt under a perfectly pressed blue-and-white seersucker jacket with cream-colored slacks. He enters one of the cottages, number 7, closing the door behind him.

What. The. Fuck.

I wish I could check the Find My iPhone App again, but I no longer have my iPad. Then I remember something I should have remembered a lot earlier, if I hadn't been busy running.

There's someone else at work here. Another party, Jackson had said.

A third party, Leo had agreed.

They're the ones who killed Benoît. Are they the ones orchestrating this little jaunt to the Adirondacks? Is Shiloh a part of that? Or is he one of the Swans?

Or simply a cute kid from Duke who wants to help me?

Yeah, right. *Who just happened to show up here...*

I stand with my back against the door, grinding my fists into the sides of my head.

"God! Jesus!" I sputter to myself, stamping my foot.

I don't know what to do next. I don't even know how I feel: angry and betrayed, heartbroken. Totally fucking confused. Wondering how much of my life will forever be altered by these events. I pick up the phone. There's a dial tone now. But I don't know who to call...what would I tell the police at this point?

A lot, a voice in my head says.

They think you're behind it all, says another voice. *Keep running.*

But I can't run forever. No one can run forever. And now that the phones are working again, Lorna is going to expect my injured family to return. Otherwise she might call the cops. I stuff the Glock in the pocket of my shorts (the pockets are that deep, yes), grab my keys, and walk across the parking lot.

The sun moves behind the clouds as I approach cottage number 7 and knock on the door.

After a moment, Shiloh comes to the door. He's taken off his seersucker jacket. He rubs his face once, like he was asleep, his eyes a little glassy. He looks surprised at first when he sees me, then breaks into this wide grin. "Aidan!"

He seems genuinely happy (even relieved?) to see me. This throws me off. I was expecting a different reaction—surprise with traces of guilt, resignation about being caught, something even darker and cold-blooded, I don't know.

"You're okay. Thank God." He grabs me and gives me a tight hug, but I wriggle away from him. "Sorry," he says, looking a little startled by my reaction.

"What are you doing here, Shiloh?"

He looks over my shoulder. "Look, just...come in."

He holds open the door for me. After a moment's hesitation, keeping one hand in my pocket, on the gun, I walk inside his room.

I look around his cottage. There's a single suitcase, still packed, on the floor. The room is drab as hell: frayed orange carpeting, faded flowered wallpaper, two twin-sized beds made up with workmanlike baby-blue cotton blankets. The windows let in only selective rays of dead, dust-particled light.

"What are you doing here?" I repeat my question, a little sharper this time.

"Getting you out of here."

"You came all the way to the Adirondacks for me?"

Oh, man, how I wish I could believe it.

"I don't think you realize the danger you're in right now," he says.

"Oh, I realize it. People are dead because of me. You and I barely know each other. And you come all this way."

"Aidan—"

"This," I say, my voice rising, gesturing to him, and then to the room around us, "doesn't make sense. Neither does the fact that you were at the Mandarin Oriental, photographing me *a day before we actually met.*"

Shiloh holds up his hands defensively. "Hold on, now."

"Don't deny it. I have photographic proof."

"Where?"

"My Tumblr. I was taking photos. I saw you."

"Show me."

"Show you? *Fuck* you. I lost all my devices. *How am I supposed to show you?*"

"You saw me on your Tumblr. You're sure?"

"I saw you photographing me. Don't even."

"Aidan. Why would I be at the Mandarin Oriental photographing you?"

"I don't know. *Because you're one of them?* It never made sense that you just appeared out of nowhere, trying to help me like that. I knew it! No one does that."

"You've been under an enormous amount of stress and strain. Don't you think it's possible you saw something that wasn't accurate? Something you only *thought you saw* because you've been driven to irrational fear and paranoia by shock, by all the insanity that's transpired over these last few days. It's understandable—"

"I do not think it's possible," I snarl. "I saw your face. YOUR FACE."

"You can't for a moment believe in human kindness?"

"Not this again, dude. Seriously, I—"

"That someone would do something to help you because they felt a connection with you?"

"I don't know you. I don't know who you are, or who you could be working for...*any of that.* You're a stranger...a stranger who sent me here. I know that. You led me into a trap!"

"You're so sure it was me on your Tumblr, taking photos of you at the Mandarin Oriental, that you're willing to turn your back on the only friend you might have right now?"

"You're not my friend. I just said that...*I don't know you.*"

But the more he says it, worming into my head with his insistence, looking at me with his trusting eyes, his beautiful mouth turning down into a crumple of melancholia, the more he manages to plant a seed of doubt. It's a seed of doubt I want very much, because I'd love nothing more than to believe him; that he's my white knight, my guardian angel.

So I start wondering if it was actually Shiloh I saw in that photo, or if he's right and my senses *were* dulled or tricked by everything that's happened, and I really *am* in a state of slow-burning shock. That's entirely possible, I suppose. But I can't go on and on wondering about it right now because something not good is happening in my chest.

It's gotten really tight.

"Are you all right?" says Shiloh.

"I'm...having a little trouble breathing," I say, clenching my fists.

He holds out his hands. "Okay. Just take it easy."

"I have a heart condition," I tell him.

"What kind of heart condition?"

"They think it might be enlarged. It's how my brother died."

"Your brother died? Oh Aidan, I didn't know that. I'm so sorry."

Now, the tightness becomes pain—a pretty sharp pain, emanating from the center of my chest. "Shit."

"What's happening?" says Shiloh.

"I may...be having a heart attack. I don't know."

"Okay. Calm down. Let me get you a glass of water."

Shiloh runs into the bathroom. I hear water running. I bend over, grabbing my knees. There's that coldness again. It freaks me out. So I stand up and open a closet, thinking I'll just grab a blanket or maybe his seersucker jacket. But when I open the closet it's empty except for one thing, sitting on the top shelf, which is exactly my height.

A motorcycle helmet with an iridescent visor.

And it's funny because the first thing I see is my own

reflection, once again, fossilized in a silvery sea of electric green. I see the wounded look on my face; probably very similar to the one I gave Tom at the end there. And then I see Shiloh in the reflection, from behind, slowly coming toward me, with something in his hand that doesn't look like a glass of water.

I whirl around and aim the Glock right at his chest.

He doesn't expect the gun, not at all. He jumps back.

"I have your phone," he says, startled, displaying it in his palm.

I left my phone at the Swans' headquarters. This explains Find My iPhone tracking it to the Adirondacks with me.

"What are you doing with my phone, man?"

"Put the gun down."

I shake my head. "Nuh-uh."

"Where did you get the gun?"

"Where did you get my phone?"

"I have your phone because I want to give it back to you. I came up here to help you. Please believe that."

"You're a liar." I feel my face contort into muscular rivulets of spectacular rage. I keep the gun trained on him even as I begin to shake, and I have to use both hands to keep it steady. My heart is thumping in a way that doesn't feel right, angry and stuttering. It feels like I'm breathing through a straw that's getting thinner and thinner.

"Aidan," he says, "you're not going to shoot me."

"How sure are you?" Tears slide out of my eyes.

"Why don't we trade? You give me the gun. I'll give you your phone back..."

"How dumb do you think I am?"

"The magazine. I meant just the magazine. We can't stand here forever in a standoff."

"I can just shoot you, then."

"That's not who you are, Aidan."

"You don't know who I am." I start to laugh. "*I* don't even know who I am anymore." And man, is that true.

There's a resigned sort of sadness about him that isn't making sense to me. But I'm too dizzy to think clearly anymore—about him, or anything. My head feels light and strange, as if it may lift off my shoulders and burst like a balloon.

"We should get you help. You don't look good."

"Stay back."

"Please." He looks desperate, pleading.

I lower the gun, just a little, because everything in my body hurts, throbs, especially my chest and my throat. Shiloh takes this opportunity, quickly steps forward, and takes the gun from me. I'm too weak to stop him. I already feel half dead, disoriented, like nothing really matters anymore anyway.

Shiloh leads me over to one of the beds, his palm against the back of my neck. I lie on my side, gasping for breath, totally paralyzed. I don't know what's going to happen next. I'm all out of chapters.

He turns me over, onto my back, puts my phone in my hand, presses my thumb against the screen to unlock it, and dials 911. He puts the phone on speaker. As it rings, and before I hear "*911, what's your emergency?*" Shiloh pockets the gun and quickly leaves the room.

The emergency lights flashing through the front windows are a relief. I want to drink those rapidly pulsing reds and blues. I can finally stop running now. Lorna opens the door, keys in her hand, leading the paramedics and a bunch of police officers into the dim cottage. But there are no handcuffs, no guns drawn.

Two police officers lift me off the bed and escort me out.

Given that there are about six hundred police vehicles and a SWAT team in the parking lot and blockading the road surrounding the motel, I'm going to assume they're not just responding to a seventeen-year-old kid with heart palpitations.

As I'm led into an ambulance, I hear the *rat-a-tat* of helicopters.

The EMTs have questions about allergies. I have none. So they give me an aspirin to chew and put a nitroglycerin tablet under my tongue. An oxygen mask is pressed over my face. The ambulance speeds off, sirens going *weee-wooo-weee-wooo.*

Then it's several hours of seeing only what's above me: the ceiling of the ambulance, fluorescent lights swishing by as I'm rolled down various hospital hallways, an examination room with monitors, bright lights, bland mint-colored walls.

They take my temperature and my blood pressure. A freezing-cold stethoscope is pressed against me. Electrodes are placed on my chest. I'm hooked up to stuff: an EKG machine. An IV. My blood pressure is taken. There are blood tests, various other imaging tests. I have to answer a lot of questions about what the pain felt like, medications I'm on, allergies (again), and my family history (ugh). Stuff like that.

Eventually a cardiologist comes in and tells me he thinks I'm in shock and I just had a bad panic attack. "From what I'm seeing on the echo," he says, "your heart isn't enlarged. That's what your family cardiologist is going to tell you, anyway. I understand the concerns given your brother's death, but those EKG tests are frequently inaccurate. There was no indication of myocardial infarction. Your heart is healthy."

I close my eyes and exhale. That is a relief—a huge one. But because of the shock thing, they want me to rest in the hospital, possibly overnight. And they want to know who to contact. But I don't want my family involved right now.

I get into it with them about that, sitting up in my hospital bed, wearing one of those revealing thin blue robes, but then a man comes in and tells the nurse he'll take it from here. He smiles at me, handing me a prescription for anti-anxiety pills from one of the doctors. "I don't need that," I tell him, pushing it away.

"Are you sure? You do seem pretty anxious."

"Who are you?" He's clearly not a doctor. He's wearing a blue suit and tie.

"My name is Dan Schwartz. I'm an agent with the FBI." He drops the prescription in my lap. "You'll need to fill that here in the hospital."

"Am I under arrest?"

"Not exactly."

"What does *not exactly* mean?"

"It means if we were going to place you under arrest, we would've already."

"I'm not a terrorist."

"Oh, we know that," he says.

"I don't understand."

But as soon as I say that, I think: *Kaboom. Here's our third party.*

He smiles, shoves his hands in his pockets. "You seem kinda pissed." He looks a little like my eighth-grade science teacher—a slightly-geeky-sort-of-handsome youngish Jewish dude with thick wavy brown hair.

"This was probably the most expensive panic attack of all time," I tell him. "I feel like an idiot."

"You didn't know it was just a panic attack. You've had quite a week, Aidan. Don't beat yourself up. Do me a favor?"

"Are you owed one?"

"Spend the night here. Let them observe you, do their thing. In the morning I'll come pick you up. We'll get pancakes. How does that sound?"

"It sounds weird."

"Pancakes?"

"No. Pancakes sound good. Just the situation itself."

"Yes, well, you're not in a world anymore where anything is going to sound less than fully and completely weird."

"Fair enough."

"I appreciate your cooperation. Part of your staying here tonight is for your own protection, so..." He leans over me, and whispers right into my ear: "Maybe...*maybe*...we can get Uncle Sam to pick up the check for the hospital stay. No promises, though."

"And leave my parents out of it?"

"For now. But we'll give them a call, at least—let them know you're safe."

I narrow my eyes. "Then I'll see you in the morning, I guess."

"Good." Agent Schwartz saunters over to the door. "Oh, by the way"—he half turns back to me, pointing lazily—"where did you get the Glock?"

"At the visitor center...during the attack. A state trooper was killed right in front of me...with a crossbow. I took his weapon."

He presses his lips together and nods, like he's impressed. "His name was Damien Coster. He had three kids. Seems like he was a good man."

"I'm sorry to hear that."

"Yeah, we were, too."

"Do you know where my phone is?"

"One of our guys may have it. It was recovered from the motel room. I'll get it back to you stat."

I frown, licking my dry, crinkled lips. "Okay."

And with that Schwartz slaps on a pair of cheap sunglasses, opens the door, and leaves me to my thoughts, which are many and varied, and mostly too exhausting to unravel right now. So I close my eyes and sleep for a really long time.

I have swampy, fiery dreams. Everything feels heavy and threatening.

My house is on fire. But the flames are cold and listless, and they take their time to burn through everything. There are cloudy funnels of embers and sparks. I keep forgetting what to do, who I'm supposed to save. I wander in dizzying circles.

I go into my brother's room. Neil is sitting there on the edge of his bed, a PlayStation controller in his lap. But he's just staring at the TV screen, motionless, his face glowing with stagnant light. When he sees me he smiles, but it's a sad smile, through black smoke. The smoke gets denser around him, and when it consumes him, snuffing out his face completely, I know it's too late.

I walk into another room and find Tom staring out the window. His neck is empurpled with mottled bruises. When he sees me he just shakes his head like he's disappointed in me. I shout at him to get out, to get out of the house, but he doesn't move. And then the smoke consumes him, too.

I wander into my own room. It looks like it did years and years ago, when Neil was still alive and I was a little kid. Shiloh is there, sitting at my old Ikea desk, flipping through a Witloff Academy brochure. I yell at him, too, to get out of the house. He throws down the brochure and rushes out with me, grabbing my hand. But in the hallway, suffocated by swirling smoke, I realize he's not holding my hand anymore. He's gone.

I know in other rooms I will find my parents, Jackson, Leo, my sister and her kids, and all of them will refuse to follow me out, or get lost trying. And I can't deal with the pain of that, the loss. So I just keep running, trying to get out of the house, but the smoke is thicker now, inky black and menacing, and it's flickering inside, like it's not just smoke but storm clouds, too, bottled-up lightning inside them, uncorking its bolts.

The state trooper, an arrow sticking out of his throat, emerges from the smoke and points me in a direction. I run, but it's just a dead end, a cobwebby brick wall. So I keep running through an impossibly vast space. I run into Benoît, a bullet hole in the side of his head, blood dripping down his face. He smiles and points me in a different direction, but it's another dead end, another brick wall. I pound the wall in fury.

And then, in total Dream Logic, deranged Blond Bellhop is drowning me again, but it's Tom's pool, not the pool in the Merrick Gables. Then the bellhop morphs into Tom and his face is twisted and murderous, just like the bellhop's was. But I can't bring myself to hurt Tom. So I let him drown me, even though his wrists, both of them, start to bleed. Then my vision goes swirly, into darkness.

I get discharged around nine a.m., after a lot of paperwork. I fill the prescription for the anti-anxiety meds. I pocket the amber bottle with the round yellow pills, but I don't take any of them. The rattling of the bottle is comfort enough—for now.

There is a tight ring of stone-faced police officers standing in the hospital lobby, all of them looking at me like I'm an alien. They part in half, in this biblical way, as Agent Schwartz emerges through the throng with a wave, wearing pretty much the same suit as yesterday. He leads me outside to a silver Toyota Camry idling in the emergency lane in front of the sliding-glass entranceway, next to an ambulance.

Schwartz quickly looks around us, in the manner of an investigator, and opens the back door of the car for me. As I get inside, he takes the passenger seat. A woman in a navy-blue pantsuit sits behind the wheel.

"I told you to circle!" Schwartz tells her, making a circling gesture, as we pull out.

"I circled. Then I came back," she replies.

"This is Agent Monica Hernandez," says Schwartz, gesturing at her with his thumb, leaning his elbow against the passenger window. "Seat belts, please."

"Hi, Aidan," says Hernandez, turning around. She has a wide smile. For some reason I think: *She's a mom.* "Nice to finally meet you. How are you feeling?"

"Like I'd love some answers."

"We'll get some pancakes first," says Schwartz. "As promised. We're in from DC. But I heard about a good place around here."

I notice, out the back window, two other Camrys tailing us, as well as two police cruisers, lights off, farther behind them. "What's your specialty at the FBI?" I ask the agents, still staring out the back window.

"Cyber Division," says Hernandez.

"Counter-terrorism Division," says Schwartz.

"Oh," I say.

We go to a place called Billy's Pancake House where the waitresses wear frilly dresses with bows on the back, and brown bottles of different flavored syrups are clustered together on the tables. We're shown to a booth by a window that looks out on a highway; they're doing construction work out there. There's something so mundane about this place, and the crawling, helpless traffic being redirected around orange cones outside, that it's almost soothing. I stare, mesmerized, at the bright-yellow vests of the construction workers as they mill around, laughing, languidly holding traffic signs.

I get the Lumberjack Special, which is a short stack of pancakes with scrambled eggs and bacon. The food reminds me of the breakfast I had at the visitor center before the drone attack, so my appetite dissipates, then comes back in waves; the pancakes are just okay, nothing all that great, really.

We eat in silence for a bit, and when I slow down, only a quarter finished, Schwartz points at my plate with his fork. "Not hungry?"

"Not really."

Schwartz looks at Hernandez, then wipes his mouth with a napkin and sits back. "You're not in any trouble with the authorities, Aidan. I'm sorry to be the one to tell you this, but we pretty much caused everything that's happened to you."

I clank my fork down on my plate, sit back against the booth, and wait for him to go on.

"It's called the Digital Dust program," says Hernandez.

"It's an experimental program CTD devised a few years ago to combat homegrown terror," says Schwartz.

I blink, slowly.

"We'd like to get you on a flight back to New York City at, oh..." Schwartz checks his watch. "2200 hours. Would that work?"

I nod.

"We've been watching the Swans for some time," says Hernandez, in a light, placating tone of voice. Someone cast these two perfectly. Schwartz is the dad—the guy with the cold, hard facts. Hernandez is meant to soften that with a more maternal vibe. "As I'm sure you figured out already, they are a terror organization, targeting those they perceive to have a public, anti-gay agenda," she says.

"They want to hack military drones," I inform them, coolly.

"Yeah, we know about that," says Schwartz. He wipes his mouth again, even though it's already pretty clean. "Here's the thing: When you've been in counter-terrorism for a long time, you come to accept that there's going to be certain concessions. It's a different world we're in now. Sometimes it comes down to cold, hard risk assessment. Trade-offs."

There's a dead, knotted feeling inside me, devoid of light and love, cooling my blood. I grind my teeth.

"The Swans have a certain type they favor," he says.

Of course they do. I think of fallen angels. I think of Darren Cohen, lost in that huge, soft bed.

"Their members tend to have a specific physical look, and a certain kind of background: they tend to be...troubled young individuals."

I think of the pouty boy-clones by the pool in the Merrick Gables house.

I saw something in your eyes, Aidan, and I'm never wrong.

Hernandez clears her throat. "The Digital Dust program uses a computer algorithm that processes keywords and images across a solar system of digital output—tweets, e-mails, text messages. But also Instagram, Tumblr, Twitter, Kik, Snapchat..."

"Jesus," I say.

"All that leaves a footprint, which the NSA can track. Digital Dust cobbles together a fictionalized persona using actual data with photographic backup."

When I speak, my voice is flat and removed. "Why not just have someone go undercover?"

"Not easy to do, but we already have an agent on the inside," says Schwartz.

"Then what's the problem?"

"We needed a fictive decoy," he replies.

I don't like the sound of this.

He continues: "To lure the Swans out of hiding, acquire evidence, and learn what their plans were, as our agent inside continued to gather more intel. We coerced the suspect—who you knew as Benoît—to provide that necessary intel. A plan was in place designed specifically so Benoît would need to match the type of malware they were looking for with the source code that would be provided in the exchange."

I watch my own fingers *tap tap tap* the table. "That's the flash drive Benoît had?"

"Correct. We needed to convince the Swans they had found their gem. They already have teams of young hackers in place, spread out in a vast underground global network. But they've been looking for that special one."

"A troubled, gay, black-hat cutie pie who can design malware to hack military drones?"

They nod, slowly.

It makes a certain kind of sense, but I can't quite believe what they're saying anyway. "And I was your *fictive decoy*?"

They both sit back with an eerie synchronicity, like I blew a giant gust of air at them. And then they nod again.

"So...all this happened to me because of what your agent inside and your Digital Dust program told you they were looking for?"

"Now that the Swans have caught the world's attention," says Schwartz, not really addressing my question, "they want to up their game."

"The sniper attack in Kansas was pretty upped."

"They want to take things further. By hacking military drones, they're sending a clear message: every government building where someone denies a gay couple a marriage license—*we will hit.* Every small-town bakery that refuses to bake a gay couple a wedding cake—*we will hit.*"

Hernandez frowns at me slightly. "You're smiling, Aidan."

"Was I?" Honestly, I hadn't realized.

Schwartz and Hernandez glance at each other.

I lean across the table. "Are they any more unethical than you guys?"

Hernandez sips her coffee, eyes trained on me.

Schwartz clasps and unclasps his hands. He looks like he wants to say a bunch of different things, but decides against all of them. "Well, they're terrorists. Are you sympathetic, Aidan?"

"I'm not *not* sympathetic. Look who they're attacking." My gaze keeps flitting around the restaurant, to other people's pancakes, other people's lives.

"I have a gay son," says Schwartz.

Hernandez gives him a sharp look.

"Is he cute and single?" I ask without smiling.

"The reason the Swans knew what you looked like," Hernandez cuts in, "is because Digital Dust flagged your image, as well as your background, from the cloud of digital data the algorithm was scanning."

I think about PRISM, the surveillance program Edward Snowden exposed that sifted through people's internet communications. This sounds suspiciously similar, equally covert, and way more pernicious.

"Then we took more surveillance photos and fed them to the Swans so they would know precisely who to look for," Hernandez continues. "Once we chose you as our virtual decoy, we knew you would be at the Mandarin Oriental that day, so we set that as the drop-off point."

"And we arranged a rendezvous for that evening," says Schwartz.

"Pretending to be me?"

"Yes. And we were going to move in, arrest Benoît, who was a senior operative in the Swans, and recover the flash drive with their plans on it. Get that evidence."

I give him a nasty grin. "You didn't bank on DirtyPaws."

"We didn't know the target would initiate contact with you first, no."

I almost laugh. "Your suspect wanted a side of dick with his malware."

"Before we had time to make the arrest, it was too late."

"You were attracted to each other," says Hernandez. "The Digital Dust program worked *too well.*"

"You walked right into our sting," says Schwartz.

"The thing is," says Hernandez, "Digital Dust was designed to cobble together virtual identities—but when it tagged you, we looked closely and realized we had an opportunity on our hands that we couldn't pass up."

I glare at her. "I'm not a brilliant amoral hacker bent on revenge."

"Your physical type was part of the equation. But it was your personal history that really interested us. Because we knew it would interest the Swans."

She literally takes my hands in hers like we're in a prayer group or something.

"Your brother's death," says Hernandez. "Your failed relationship with the father of a disabled friend. The tech genius stuff we could fake. But what we couldn't fake is an actual troubled soul with a checkered past."

I push her hands away. "That's not me."

"That's what Digital Dust saw," says Schwartz.

"You put me in so much danger! I was literally in a sniper's crosshairs in that hotel room!"

Schwartz folds his napkin. "The hotel was crawling with agents ready to make an arrest. The snipers on the roof across the street were ours. We were closing in."

I point at him with my fork. "*You* killed Benoît."

"We took out the target once we had a clear shot," he says.

I guess two people having sex wouldn't present a clear shot.

"We didn't think Benoît posed a specific threat to you. But he is affiliated with a terror group, so we didn't want to take any chances."

I sit back. I've been nothing but a pawn to everyone. People were playing around with my identity and my life like it was a chess game.

"So for your protection, we took him out, and lost both the evidence and the suspect in the process," Hernandez finishes.

Because I handed the flash drive right back to the terrorists.

I picture that black glove slowly closing around the flash drive, and stab my fork into my half-eaten pancakes. "You knew everything that was happening every step of the way. Once I walked into a sting, why not just burst through the door the moment I entered that room if I was in any danger?"

But then I get it.

"Oh." I almost laugh again; this is so *vicious.* "You didn't want them to know there wasn't really a Mr. Preston, did you? You'd rather have them—*and the police*—think I killed Benoît so you could keep your mission intact." I glower at Schwartz. "Now I know what you mean by *trade-offs.*"

"We're handling the police," says Schwartz.

"Slowly but surely," says Hernandez. "As well as the media."

"You know where the Swans are headquartered. Why not just arrest them?"

"They hide too well," says Schwartz. "It's like they've been able to encrypt their entire existence. We don't even have enough to get a search warrant. Which is why we had to use the virtual decoy to—"

"Stop saying *virtual;* all you did was change my name. OWN THAT."

"Aidan, we're s—" says Hernandez.

"Oh, God, please stop." I cover my face with my hands.

These are the adults? The authorities? Their hideous desperation is making me physically ill. I wonder how many times I'm going to be betrayed by the people who are supposed to know better. I can't let this become a theme in my life.

Schwartz sighs and tries to touch my arm, some sort of a consoling gesture, but I pull away. "I'm a person!" I exclaim loud enough to make both of them recoil. "I can't be reduced to *digital dust*. You fed my image to terrorists, and told them I was their guy without my consent. I'm not even a legal adult!"

They're both just nodding, looking meek and sheepish. I hate them.

I want them to lose.

"The Swans are smart, though," I say. "They'd see through this whole Digital Dust bullshit. *This* guy? He'd see through something that seemed a bit too pat and perfect—like some adorable hacker genius. Are you sure you're not the ones getting played here?"

"We were very careful when we selected you," says Schwartz. "The level of authenticity was our safeguard."

"What *authenticity*? Tom? My brother? I was at Witloff, moving on."

Hernandez takes my hands again. "No. The suicide was recent."

That hits hard. I sit back in my seat, my mouth agape.

She clears her throat. "We knew how fresh that was. The Swans would respond to that."

I, too, loved someone who took their own life.

The way Hernandez is looking at me right now, I can tell

they've been combing through my life like it was a novel. And I'm the fictional tormented hero, now eating soggy pancakes in the flesh.

It was this past winter, after swim practice. The conversation went like this:

ME (answering the phone in the middle of jerking off, which is pretty much the only time my mom ever calls. It's like a sixth sense with her): Hello? *Mom?*

MOM: Honey, what's wrong? You sound out of breath.

ME (sitting back in my ergonomic desk chair, slamming my laptop closed, and hiking my underwear back up): I just got back from a yoga class.

MOM: Okay, well, don't strain anything.

ME: I'm okay.

MOM: I just read an article about how yoga can actually damage—

ME: Mom, why are you ca—

MOM: I'm so shocked by what I just heard! I had to call you. You remember our neighbors down the street?

ME: What neighbors?

MOM: Your friend, Shane. His father—

ME (almost falling out of my chair): What happened?

MOM: There must be marital strife, a divorce in the works. She's never around. That's what I'm hearing, anyway. I ran into Julia at the supermarket—

ME: *What happened, what happened*—

MOM: He—Tom—*Mr. Reid*—hanged himself! Oh, it's awful, Aidan.

Silence.

MOM: Honey?

ME (in a flat, faraway voice): Is he okay? Just tell me.

MOM: You seem upset. I didn't know you knew Shane's parents all that—

ME: Is he okay? TELL ME. JUST TELL ME.

Silence.

MOM: No, honey...he's not okay. He's dead.

I don't remember the rest of our conversation. But I can pretty much pinpoint the exact moment my stomach problems started—seven minutes later. Seven minutes after I learned my relationship with Tom ultimately led to that...which devolved into supermarket gossip that would perk up my mom's ears while sampling mini triangles of toothpicked Havarti cheese.

He hanged himself with his own belt, apparently.

The pain started in the pit of my stomach, and over the days, and then weeks, it did not let up, and it went from a dull ache to these sharp stabs. I'd go to bed with it. I'd wake up with it. Drinking soda exacerbated it. I couldn't go near alcohol (never was much of a drinker, anyway, as you know). And forget about spicy foods: I'd be sick for days if I had so much as a burrito. I started to miss sriracha the way junkies miss heroin. Eventually I saw the school nurse, who sent me to the doctor where I got the misleading EKG that started me on this whole road with my stupid heart.

What bothers me so much about Benoît and DirtyPaws is that after the whole thing with Tom and our breakup and his suicide, I realized certain actions of mine have dark consequences. I was heading down a self-destructive path. And I was aware of it. That's what really sucks.

I promised myself I wouldn't do anything like that ever again. But then, in a moment of silly stupid weakness, after the depressing anti-hookup with Darren Cohen, and feeling alone in a fancy hotel, there I was again hooking up with another rando older guy, thinking about Tom, pretending it was Tom.

It's like I just couldn't get past him. Makes me wonder if I ever will.

Even a computer program saw how damaged I was. Now that's just sad.

And man, have I lived up to what Digital Dust thought I was, this partially factual digital avatar of myself. I've killed two people. I've cavorted with terrorists, lied to my family and my friends, wiped a crime scene clean, stolen a wad of cash. I've been on the run for days. I've become Mr. Preston and everything anyone hoped he would be—except, ironically, the brilliant hacker part.

"So what's next?" I ask, shoving the plate away. The silverware rattles.

"We have a favor to ask," says Schwartz.

"We'd love your cooperation," Hernandez chimes in.

I shake my head at them, trying to feel something about their failure, unwinding their dubious motives in my head so I can understand them. They've devoted their whole lives to this, made untold sacrifices, and will get no public recognition, probably just a decent pension in the end, all in the name of national security.

But I don't feel anything. I have no sympathy for them at all.

"Why would I ever do anything to help you?"

They know I don't care. And they have their responses ready.

"We're the only ones who can end this," says Schwartz.

"We're your only option," says Hernandez, even though we all know she's not entirely correct about that. Digital Dust knows that, too.

But of course these bastards have a point.

I don't want to get mixed up even deeper with the Swans. I want to stay alive. I want my family safe. These agents are immoral, but at least they're sane, and on the right side of the law. They're my best shot.

And they know it.

"Can we count on your cooperation?" says Schwartz.

My mouth morphs into a leer. "After these amazing pancakes, are you kidding? *Anything.*"

CHAPTER 12

The Debrief

Schwartz and Hernandez drive me to an FBI field office about twenty-five miles away. There's some weirdness at first because it feels like I'm being arrested and booked, but they tell me that's not what this is. They just want to "verify me," which takes longer than everyone expected because I have no ID. I give them my Social Security number and my parents' address.

I'm photographed—against a white wall with a height chart—and fingerprinted.

I agree to be polygraphed. The questions mainly concern drug usage, if I have a criminal history, my identity, that sort of thing.

Then I'm debriefed by a bunch of agents with crude buzz cuts, wearing white dress shirts with the sleeves rolled up. I sit in an uncomfortable swivel chair in an office with low maze-like cubicles. They sit on the edges of desks, surrounding me, raining questions down.

I tell them everything I can about my interaction with Benoît and what happened after, with a heavy concentration on my time in the Merrick Gables. They show me a few photos. I identify Hardy Boy Joe, Hardy Boy Frank, and the bellhop I killed in that pool with a paper clip. They actually get a kick out of that. One of the agents jokes he never learned anything like that at Quantico.

When I ask him if he's ever been strangled to within an inch of his life as a child because a secret and probably illegal but definitely unethical government program picked him unknowingly to take part in a dangerous operation that would bring him face-to-face with psychotic terrorists, he shuts up real quick.

Someone goes over to a whiteboard with those same photos pasted on it. With a red marker, he writes DECEASED over Blond Bellhop's face. I guess his name was Vincent Davvio. They're all drifters, petty criminals, with a long string of convictions.

Troubled people, man.

I never saw the entire face of my dear friend who loves Martha and the Vandellas as much as me, and appreciates my tornado dreams, but they have a pretty good idea who he is.

"He goes by Scotty," says Schwartz. I'm waiting for some kind of punch line. But he's not joking. "Did you hear anyone call him that?"

I shift in my seat. "No. Are you, uh, sure that's his name?"

"Why?"

"It just...sounds like someone I would have a play date with in third grade. It doesn't sound like the head of a terrorist organization."

"Maybe that's on purpose," says Schwartz, consulting some notes.

"Okay."

"Take us forward," says Schwartz.

"You should all quit the FBI, start on macrobiotic diets, and become Pilates instructors."

"I meant in time. After you escaped the house."

"I got on a train."

"And then?"

"And then I met Shiloh."

"Shiloh," Schwartz repeats, nodding.

After another round of questions, where we go through every word that was said during every conversation with Scotty (that name! srsly?), we just begin to repeat ourselves, and my exhaustion mounts.

Sensing my patience wearing thin, Schwartz hustles me into a bare-bones conference room: foldout chairs, empty Starbucks coffee cups; it's just the two of us now.

"We let your parents know you're safe."

"I want to talk to them."

"We'll arrange that."

"Do I need a lawyer?"

"You're not in any kind of trouble."

"I meant to sue your ass. You know the Swans threatened my family? You got them involved in this shit, too."

Schwartz holds up his hands. "I promise they'll be safe. We're watching your whole family, keeping very close tabs. "We had good intentions, but the Digital Dust project went too far."

I look him in the eye. "Were you cool with your son... when he told you he was gay?"

He hesitates. "Yes, family counseling and everything so my wife and I would know how to best support him. And he's doing well."

"What's his name?"

"Eli."

Of course, this could all be bullshit. I almost ask to see a photo, but I don't, even though I'm curious.

"Well," I say, "I'm standing alone with you in this room, at this field office, I still don't have my phone, and you're going to tell me I need to keep pretending to be Mr. Preston. That's the favor you want, right?"

"Yes. And we'll get you your phone. It's being located. We'll announce you're not our man. In time."

"How much time?"

"Very soon. No one's released your name. Yet."

"That sounds like a threat."

"If the Swans figure out you're not real—if they know we're onto them—they'll do a whole purge of their ranks, and our agent risks exposure."

"Well, I'm supposed to be on spring break. So really... screw you all.

"You might feel differently when I tell you about our agent inside."

"Doubt it."

"It's Shiloh."

I sit at the table, push a paper cup away, and put my head in my hands.

Nothing was ever quite normal with Shiloh, and the way we met, but for some reason I never made that connection. Of course he's their stupid agent. Otherwise he would have just killed me in that cottage instead of calling 911, since the Swans obviously want me dead.

Of course he's not a handsome, well-dressed tennis player from Duke who materialized out of thin air to save me on a train. Life isn't like that; it's not a fairy tale. I think it would have been easier for me if Shiloh had turned out to be a backstabbing terrorist. Now it's more confusing. I don't know how much of him is real (or how real our chemistry was), and I can't even hate him—because he's risking his life to *fight evil*.

But I'm going to let myself be pissed that he lied to me. He steered me away from my justified doubts, my own instincts regarding his sudden entrance into my life. There was a little bit of gaslighting going on.

Agent Schwartz is watching me. "Shiloh broke his cover, risked the whole operation to go up to the Adirondacks to try to pull you out."

"He was the one who sent me there!"

"Those were his orders, and he was undercover. I don't think he knew they were going to try to kill you."

"Why *did* they? Scotty offered me a choice. He wanted me to get them the source code or join their cause. It was pretty clear."

"Because they're psychotic terrorists, Aidan."

"Or they already know I'm a decoy. And if they know I'm a decoy, they might already know Shiloh is an FBI mole. Have you considered all that?"

"We've considered everything. We're the FBI."

I wiggle my hands around in the air. *"Ooooooh."*

Schwartz sighs.

"Why was Shiloh taking photos of me at the Mandarin Oriental?" I ask.

"For our purposes, to keep tabs on you."

"But also to feed my image to the Swans, right?"

Schwartz looks solemn. "After Shiloh returned from the Adirondacks, we lost tabs on him."

"What does that mean?"

"He's supposed to check in with us at specified times, and he's gone dark. It's a very recent development, but...it hasn't happened before."

I sit up a little. "Is he okay?"

Schwartz notes my reaction. "You care about him?"

I don't know what I feel. I'm just dizzy.

No one ever risked so much to save me before.

But no one I know ever led me into a death trap, either.

That kiss, though. It was so soft...

"I think he cares about you," says Schwartz.

"Sweet." I'm trying to feel nothing. That would be easier.

"We're close to ending this. The best way to ensure your

family remains safe—the best way to help us move in and save lives—is to cooperate. I'm glad you're on our side."

I wonder which specific lives we're saving here: homophobic senators who don't see my human worth and will try everything to stop me from getting married or adopting children? People who are so low they'd picket the funeral of a gay teen?

"What does it mean that I'm on your side?" I ask. "What is it that you're asking me to do exactly?"

"We're working that out now." Schwartz looks at his watch, then flips on a TV mounted on the wall. On the news, the FBI director is giving a press conference about all the recent attacks. He's being peppered with questions, his face alight from camera flashes.

"All we know at this time...yes...just a person of interest. There is no name to be released. He's not an official suspect, more a witness on the periphery of events, who we'd like to talk to in regard to our ongoing investigation..."

The reporters shout more questions at him, drowning each other out.

"Turn it off, please."

Schwartz flips off the TV. "I wanted you to see where we're at with the media."

"Eventually you're going to announce publicly that this was all a mistake, right? So my future isn't totally fucked?"

"Yes."

But I don't trust this chaos to unwind itself.

"Why even give my picture out to the media in the first place?"

"The Swans would have expected that. We have to keep this operation looking legit."

Sure, at the continued expense of me, my life, my future.

Another agent comes to the door. Schwartz has a conversation with this person, sticking his head out of the doorway, so I can't hear what they're saying. Then he says "Okay," leans back in, and tosses me my phone, which I catch.

"Can I trust you not to make any calls or anything just yet?"

The phone is dead anyway. And no one's giving me a charger.

The feds place me in protective custody for my return to New York City.

At least I get to fly on a private jet.

That's kind of cool, and it sure beats the bus ride up here. I get a police escort onto the tarmac of a small airport, and then a bunch of government agents—they're not all FBI; I see NSA jackets, Homeland Security, Secret Service—escort me onto the small plane, with Schwartz taking the lead.

The plane is pretty sweet. My leather seat, resembling a comfy recliner, rises from a cushioned panel. The seats are in groups of four, two of them facing the other two across a high-finish wooden table. Laptops litter a conference table with leather chairs in the back of the plane. Across the aisle, Hernandez sits with three of her colleagues, chatting, consulting files. Schwartz sits across from me. The other FBI dudes who were questioning me earlier occupy the remaining seats around me.

We take off right away. There are no seat-belt or phone restrictions, although my phone is still dead, so who cares? They serve me Coke over ice in an actual glass, a really good chicken-salad sandwich with fancy potato chips, and I get a fleece blanket, which I snuggle under. TV screens display the route map. It'll be a short flight.

"Do you want to take a nap?" Schwartz asks me.

"I can't sleep on planes."

He leans forward, an iPad displayed on his lap. "This is our guy." There's an image of a good-looking sandy-haired man around his mid-thirties, wearing a black leather jacket, standing at a podium, pointing, with a wry grin on his face. I can't see his eyes, and I remember his eyes.

"That's him?"

"Scott Hewcott McAndriss III. Or Scotty. Has a master's degree in English from Columbia University. He's an academic, a professor. Untenured. Sarah Lawrence. UCLA. UConn. Brandeis. He bounced around, lots of affairs with students, apparently. Erratic behavior. Comes from money...*a lot of money,* actually. Family owned a supermarket chain. Grew up in New York City, but his family owned a summer home in Kattskill Bay, New York. That's near Mohawk State Park and Lake George, Aidan. Where he lured you."

"Oh," I mutter, hating the idea of being *lured* anywhere. I'm not some credulous kid. And Schwartz could be making this shit up for all I know. All of it.

"We think the Swans have a secret training facility nearby."

I sigh. "You *think*?"

"Aerial surveillance hasn't confirmed anything. Property records show nothing. And..."

I steel myself. "What?"

"The Warren County Clerk's office was hacked a few months ago."

Of course it was. "By them?"

Schwartz shrugs.

Everything is unsubstantiated. "Why did they pick that visitor center to hit?"

"We don't know."

I nod, unimpressed.

He goes on. "Parents are dead. No siblings. Had a partner for many years. The partner, Kenneth Swann, an accountant from Denver, apparently committed suicide."

I sit up, shook. "He did?"

"Swann had no immediate family that we could find, so we're a little hazy on those details. Our profilers are determining that's probably the turnaround point, though, where Scotty became radicalized."

"What did Scotty teach?"

"Queer theory. Gender studies."

Schwartz fiddles with the iPad, then plays me a TED Talk from 2009.

Scotty wears a conservative-looking black V-neck sweater with a light-blue shirt underneath and gray wool pants. I recognize his voice right away, though it sounds a little younger, warmer, less acerbic. He's striking to look at, but he tends to drone, in a heady way, about sexuality being a social construct and gender being fluid. At times he's hard to follow; he makes odd segues and is prone to dizzying tangents.

I guess that's a habit of mine as well, although I like to think I'm somewhat charming when I need to be.

Scotty is not a great public speaker—stiff, awkward, insular. He calls himself a disciple of Judith Butler, Simone de Beauvoir, Michel Foucault, Larry Kramer, Harvey Milk, and Queer Nation.

Schwartz tells me they're all philosophers, theorists, gay activists.

At some point, Scotty transformed from a boring, buttoned-up academic into a motorcycle-riding terrorist able to recruit followers with a virulently pro-LGBTQ agenda, all of them fearlessly willing to take on the government and kill anyone who gets in their way. It's almost too crazy to believe.

Maybe Scotty changed, like a comic-book villain, when he lost his partner. Maybe that's when the Swans were born. I know grief. I know how it can rip you apart. There's a fragile threshold. You can waltz into the darkness pretty easily. Or you can try to negotiate a way back into the light. Sometimes you get lost trying. And sometimes you even think you're in the light, but you're still stuck on the other side.

CHAPTER 13

Capture the Flag

We land at Teterboro Airport less than an hour later during a storm.

There's another police escort back to Manhattan. I'm taken to a penthouse suite in a midtown hotel. The suite is huge, bustling with agents murmuring into phones and staring into laptops, typing. I have no idea what's coming next. I sit in a comfy chair and watch the city, lit up in the wet hot night, get battered by rain. I see tiny twinkling lights for miles.

"We need you to sit tight for a bit," says Schwartz, coming over to me, his FBI jacket on, chugging a bottle of Poland Spring.

"How long am I going to be here?"

"Hopefully, not too long. Is there anything we can get you in the meantime?"

"An iPhone charger."

"Sure. Coming right up. But I'm going to ask you not to text anyone or make any calls. No social media posts, either."

Then what's the point of having the phone? "Why?"

"For your own safety. We need you to be mum right now."

A bulky agent with a shaved head, cell phone pressed to his ear, dangles a charger in front of me. I snatch it from him and plug it into the nearest wall outlet. When the phone turns on, there's a smattering of texts, but I don't read them because then I'll be tempted to respond. I want to play along, so this ends sooner.

My unlocked phone was in Shiloh's possession for a while. I wonder if...

Then I find it.

It's in the Notes app, dated yesterday evening, while I was in the hospital:

ATTACK ON VISITOR CENTER WAS US.

That's all it says.

Before I even have a chance to process this, my phone starts ringing.

I remember Scotty's fake area code quite well. Thankfully, the ringer is off. I hold the phone under my shirt and ask an agent where the nearest bathroom is. He points, distracted. I run in and lock the door, turning the sink on.

"I thought we had a deal," I say, through my teeth.

"We did. We're not the ones who tried to kill you at Mohawk."

"So the US government staged a terror attack on innocent civilians and got a state trooper killed in order to take me out? I'm supposed to believe that? There were *kids* there..."

"We would have been way more surgical. That was a mess. Honestly, I'm a little insulted they'd play that off as us." He starts laughing. "Gosh, Aidan, are you *sure* you haven't had any Special Ops training? Gotta say, I'm impressed."

"Nope, no training, Scotty."

"Ah, you've been debriefed—how charming! I like that you know my name. Brings us closer together. Now listen, hun, they're going to tell you they need you to make a drop."

"A drop?"

"They're going to tell you they need you to hand over a flash drive containing broken computer code to us. But it'll actually be spyware so they can get inside our system."

I don't trust anyone, and it's terrifying. I don't know what's real anymore. There are no good guys—only shades of immoral, compromised liars, everyone trying to play me to their own ends.

But I can't help thinking about Shiloh's oblique little message, and my neck gets all prickly.

And I have a growing hunch about something else.

I bite my lip. "You know, don't you?"

After a brief pause: "That you're a decoy? We figured that out a while ago."

"So why have me try to give you code you know I don't have?"

"Because I want *you,* Aidan."

"But you keep trying to kill me!"

"No, hun. You need to see the big picture. You became a liability to the government as soon as you fleshed out their little fiction. Can you imagine the fallout? Their whole counter-terrorism division would have to be flushed, rebuilt from scratch, years of work down the drain."

I have to remind myself that even though he can make logical sense and expertly tie pieces of fact together, Scotty is deranged—and dangerously persuasive.

But what if he's right?

And what if he isn't?

"You're everything I want," he purrs, "source code or no. A smart kid who's sympathetic to our cause. A smart kid *in need of a family.*"

"I never said I was sympathetic. And I have a family."

"What was coming out to them like?"

I pause. "One level below conversion therapy."

Scotty snorts at that.

"You seem like you're doing just fine without me," I say. "That sniper attack in Kansas was pretty ballsy."

"Go big or go home."

"But you have the wrong idea about me."

"We have enough in common where I can trust you. Because I feel I know you. To me, that's gold. We both think we break people, Aidan."

"...I don't think that."

"Your brother—"

"Stop." I press the phone hard against my ear.

"That older gentleman...poor thing...what was his name again?"

"Seriously, stop."

"These people were already broken in their own ways. Even though you loved them. But you didn't break them, Aidan."

"You won't win my trust by bringing them up. It just feels manipulative and cruel. That's a fail."

"We can take away your pain. Give you purpose. The unthinkable isn't unthinkable anymore. Before you know it they'll throw us in camps next to the refugee babies. We have to fight these craven hypocrite evangelicals. This is a war, hun."

"*Your* war, not mine."

His voice gets tight. "Don't be naïve. You and I are the same to the craven hypocrites. Time to pick a side. The feds used your brother—and that whole tragedy—as a lure. They have no respect for him, or what he was to you. But I know that pain. I've *felt* it."

"How far are you gonna take this, Scotty? Mass murder is still mass murder."

There's a knock at the door.

"I'M IN HERE!" I shout.

"Don't take too long," a voice says.

"Listen," says Scotty. "The most dangerous thing you can do right now is tell the feds we figured out there was never any Mr. Preston."

"Uh-huh," I say, somewhat dismissively, but he knows I'm listening.

"Sometimes you have to do ugly things to make change in this world. We did a lot of ugly things to win World War II. We firebombed Dresden. But we *won the war*."

"Those were the Nazis—"

"Are these evangelicals, wrapping themselves in their sad religious-freedom laws, any better?"

"Maybe a little?"

"They underestimated me, just like they underestimated you. Shiloh is still alive. Come find him. He's a beautiful swan now. And you will be, too."

Oh shit, *Shiloh*. I lean my head against the wall. "Is he okay?"

He snaps his fingers. "We're running out of time. See if things play out the way I told you. That's how you'll know you can trust me. In that moment, when you know for sure I'm right... cross the line."

"What does that mean, *Cross the line*?"

"Capture the Flag." He laughs a little.

"What—"

"They're about to knock one last time. We've been talking too long."

"I'm done being played, man. I'm taking myself off this chessboard."

"Oh, look at you, hun, all grown up."

He hangs up.

Someone immediately knocks on the door. "Hey kid, you okay in there?"

Are you fucking kidding me?

I stare at the closed door. "Yeah, sorry, upset stomach!" I flush the toilet.

"You're not making any calls, are you?"

"Haven't even charged the phone yet."

"Someone thought they heard you talking to someone."

"Someone was wrong."

They sit me down on the big plush couch in the middle of the suite. Schwartz comes over, surrounded by a bunch of other agents (it's like they're multiplying), hands on his hips. The pouring rain outside, reflected by the watery lights of the city at night, trickles dark shapes down his face.

Schwartz explains that the feds, posing as Preston, have been in further communication with the Swans. Since the Swans obviously know what I look like, it has to be me personally who makes the drop.

"Sorry, but what convinced them not to murder me *this* time?" I ask.

"We worked them over," says Schwartz.

"What the hell does that mean?"

"We think they tried to kill you at Mohawk because they didn't trust you anymore, didn't believe you were really one of them."

I draw in a sharp breath. Is he listening to himself? "They're right."

The most dangerous thing you can do right now is tell the feds we figured out there was never any Mr. Preston.

"So," says Schwartz, "continuing to pose as you, *as* Preston, we fed them fragments of actual malware to prove our legitimacy, our allegiance, and regain their trust. The FAA and the DoD were able to assist in this regard."

"Wait. What do you mean *fragments*?"

"Enough code for them to believe you're a legit black hat sympathetic to their cause and would have the know-how, for the right price, to finish the script. The rest of the malware will need to be delivered by you on a flash drive."

My hands fly to the sides of my head. "Sorry—you gave them *actual code* they need to hack military drones?"

"Some of the executable code needed to successfully sabotage military-grade encryption, yes. Problem is, now there's a ticking clock. Their hackers, who are simply more sophisticated than our team, could piece together the rest of the code fast and mount an attack within weeks."

"I see." This sounds utterly insane to me.

"You're going to make the drop in an hour with what they think is the rest of that code. But the flash drive you hand them will actually contain a different type of malware."

"Spyware?"

"Right."

Exactly what Scotty said. Jesus.

"Once we're inside their system, we can shut them down real fast. We've had our intelligence analysts go over this scenario again and again, and their recommendation is that this is our best course of action."

I'm so scared right now. *Scotty can't be right.*

When all the agents scatter, holding notepads, talking on phones and into earpieces, I pull Schwartz aside.

"Dude. I'm not feeling good about this plan."

"It'll all be over soon," he replies, pressing two fingers to his ear. "And then you can go back to your life."

He's not hearing me. "They already tried to kill me multiple times. You're seriously going to put me in their sights again? THEY JUST WANT ME DEAD."

"They won't get a chance to hurt you. We'll be shadowing you every step of the way. We'll have snipers on all the surrounding rooftops. And you'll be wearing a vest."

Right on cue, an agent with a ponytail steps forward and fits what she says is a Level II ballistics vest on me. The Kevlar is hot, but it's not as heavy as you would think. They give me new clothes: a loose white T-shirt with a red anarchist symbol (an A trapped in a circle) that fits over the vest, a pair of dark jeans that fit pretty well, work boots, a black hoodie.

I roll my eyes. It's like they Google-image-searched "hacker."

Another agent with surgical gloves comes over and tells me to open my mouth.

"It's a microchip," says Schwartz, circling me, "a GPS tracker with a wireless audio link. We'll be able to hear what's going on. Every word."

"Why do I need this?"

"For your own safety."

"What if I say no?"

Schwartz sighs, pats down his pockets. "Are you saying no?"

"I have that right, don't I?"

Schwartz nods, looks around. "Look, this is our shot. If we don't take it now, they'll just find you again. You may not be so lucky next time. What's wrong? Talk to me."

"What's *wrong?* You don't give a shit about me. I know the attack on the visitor center wasn't the Swans. It was you guys."

He looks genuinely startled. "What are you talking about?"

"Shiloh left a message on my Notes app."

"How do you know it was Shiloh? Lots of people had access to your phone."

Okay, I didn't think about that. I guess anyone could have written that note.

"If it was Shiloh," says Schwartz, "he could have just recorded a voice memo. So you'd know for sure it was him."

Okay, that's true, too, but who checks their *voice memos*?

"What did the note say?"

" 'Attack on visitor center was us.' "

Schwartz frowns and mulls that. "*Us*... that's rather vague."

I give him an exasperated look.

"You really believe the FBI tried to kill you at Mohawk, Aidan?"

"I don't know what to believe anymore."

"Think logically. You think we would have attacked children with tear gas? Killed a state trooper—"

I made that argument already—to Scotty. Maybe things got messy. "That part was an accident—"

"Chased after you in a national park with crossbows—"

"I don't know."

"He called you, didn't he?"

I fold my arms.

"They're all strung out on drugs," says Schwartz. "They're slowly unraveling. They're desperate. They'll say anything."

But I wonder who's more desperate.

"You knew he'd call me," I say accusingly. "And you knew

what he'd say. You've done plenty of profiling on him. If he persuaded me to join the Swans, you'd get another man on the inside with an audio link. Is that what you want now that you've lost contact with Shiloh?"

He looks tired. "I'm going to be straight with you, Aidan. At some point, this could get taken out of my hands." He shows me his palms to physicalize the bureaucratic metaphor *so I really get it*. "Digital Dust gets dissolved without a trace, we scatter, and the feds make their own determination. The Swans are ghosts. And then you're looking at Murder One. Evidence tampering. Grand larceny. Espionage. Whatever they decide to throw at you."

"That sounds like another threat."

"We may have lost Shiloh," he says. "He may have been killed, may have been turned, we don't know."

Everything he says is another escalating tactic to get me to cooperate, risk my life for them.

"*Turned?* I thought he went all the way to the Adirondacks to save me!"

"We don't know his true motivations. Our operation was nearly shredded. No matter his reasoning, he broke protocol."

"Look, I barely know him. It wasn't my fault he—"

"It's not entirely about the military drones," he says.

"What do you mean?"

"The Swans have something else planned that they're going to execute much sooner. That's what Shiloh's been trying to find out. The Swans put parallel plans into motion and compartmentalize info, and they do it well, so not everyone in this rather loose organization knows what's coming next."

That's when I remember, from the flash drive, that the drones were *Phase 3*.

We might still be in the middle of Phase 2.

"What are they planning?"

"Soft target. We think they're targeting children."

I think of the families in the visitor center. Annabelle, Sam…

Uncle Aidan!

Go big or go home.

"Do you know *any* specifics?" I press.

"Hold on," he says, glancing at his phone. "I have to take this call. Give me *one* second." As soon as he steps away, the agent with the ponytail comes over, adjusts the Kevlar under my clothes, and dangles the transmitter they want to put in my mouth.

"What is that really for?" I ask her.

"Just so we can hear everything going on, in case something gets said, in case we lose eyes on you."

I look around the hotel suite, at all the agents milling around. "Why was Schwartz chosen to lead this operation out of everyone in the FBI?"

"Schwartz is a good agent," she says, not answering the question at all. "You can trust him."

I clear my throat. "But it seems like, I don't know, he was *specially* chosen to work with me or something. Is that a thing you guys do?"

She's not really listening, crouching down and adjusting every inch of my clothing so the Kevlar is as invisible as possible. "He was assigned…"

"Is it because he has a gay son?" I offer, unsure.

"Son?" she says, still focusing on my clothes.

I tap my tongue against my front teeth. "Eli?"

"No. He has a daughter. I was at her bat mitzvah last year." She stands up, nodding. "You're looking good." She's checking her text messages as she speaks. "Schwartz is a good man, a family man. He's one of our best. You're in good hands." She pats me on the shoulder, walks away.

Schwartz returns. The Family Man. He looks up, sees my face, and hesitates.

He flashes me this phony reassuring smile and walks toward me with a quick shake of his head, like I'm a child objecting to soccer practice and he's about to school me about *letting the whole team down*.

That's when I step forward and slug him in the stomach with every ounce of my strength.

Fuck. That felt *good*.

Schwartz stumbles back with a huffing wheeze. The whole suite goes quiet. Everyone's eyes are on me, phones flat at their sides.

I stand there in the middle of the room, unmoving, staring at him.

Schwartz curses under his breath and waves away a couple of agents who were taking tentative steps toward me.

"My family, my friends—you're isolating me," I say, no emotion in my voice anymore, everything drained away. "I don't like it. I don't trust you. You're nothing but threats and lies, lies and threats. And I've just been a pawn. Guess what, I'm done. It's time for me to become a knight."

CHAPTER 14

The Handoff

We used to write each other cards."

Schwartz turns around with a muted smile.

"My brother and me."

I'm in the back of a Lincoln Town Car, and we're swooshing through the city in the rain in the night, an FBI agent at the wheel. I'm in back, next to another agent. Schwartz is in the passenger seat. Everyone has Bluetooth devices in their ears.

I got them to change the T-shirt. It's just an extra-large plain white tee now, under the hoodie, billowy enough to cover the Kevlar. No anarchist symbol. That was just fucking stupid.

Schwartz nods, vaguely. "Oh. I see."

He doesn't see.

"I know you think I'm just a means to an end. But there's more to me than all the pain and the shit in my past. My brother... Neil and I would write each other cards."

My parents used to send out Christmas cards to all our family and friends. But they'd always buy too many. So there would always be this huge stack of generic cheesy drugstore Christmas cards bursting out of the bottom drawer of my mom's desk. Neil and I would write cards to each other. It would be like Memorial Day, and Neil would write "Merry Christmas, I hope you're well!" and stick the card under my door, and then I'd write one back to him. We found this hilarious.

I explain this to Schwartz. He's nodding along, but mechanically.

"If he knew I'd had a bad day, if my mom told him something, he would try to make me feel better. So sometimes he'd get home late from practice or whatever. I would already be in bed, and then a Christmas card would get slipped under my door: 'Everything will be okay, I promise! I'll see you tomorrow and we'll play *GTA* and run from the cops and blow shit up.' He never wanted me to be unhappy. Never. And if he knew I was, he would say something about it to lift my spirits. My mood, what I felt, actually affected him."

"I'm sorry you lost your brother, Aidan. He sounds like a great kid."

"I'm afraid I'm going to forget what he looked like. Not just in photos, but what he looked like in person, how he smiled, how he'd blink his eyes. The sound of his voice is already starting... to fade away. I've saved all the old voice mails I have from him. I don't have many. I listen to them over and over. And I keep asking him, in my head, what I should do now... because I do that,

I ask him shit, sometimes I just talk to him...and there's nothing coming back now."

There's silence in the car as we go over a bridge.

It's like they took him away from me, like I lost Neil all over again.

Agent Schwartz puts his arm over the seat and flashes me one of his signature sympathetic smiles—but it's made of Styrofoam. He looks totally drained; guilt and loss painted all vivid on his face like he's finally realizing what he was complicit in, the actual consequences—in the flesh—of one of his *trade-offs*.

Who the hell knows what his story is? I've heard these guys spend years tracking terrorist cells and it all leads up to one moment.

"I asked Neil in my head what I should do about Tom—if I should e-mail him—and he told me not to. But I did anyway. I didn't listen."

"That's not on you," says Schwartz. "You didn't cause Tom to..." He trails off.

"Don't tell me I didn't cause something. Because you don't know."

Two years. Two years I was e-mailing him.

Tom and I started e-mailing each other when we were still together, for scheduling purposes mainly—no gurgly swaths of romantic poetry, just logistical shit—when he would have the house to himself, when my parents would be gone, that kind of thing. Basically when we could have sex.

I bet Digital Dust saw those e-mails.

What a find. What a score.

After Tom told me we were done, I stopped. I didn't try to contact him again. Like I said.

Not for a while, anyway.

When I got to Witloff, things seemed to stabilize for me.

At least at first.

I was in a new environment. I joined the swim team. I made friends: Jackson, Leo—there were some great kids there, and I could talk to them. I really could. But I was a little lonely, too—far from home, and on my own for the first time. Sometimes being surrounded by lots of people made me feel even lonelier.

But I felt like I had grown up a bit, too, that I was kind of a new person—no parents hovering, or Neil's empty room, his empty chair at the dinner table staring me right in the face every night.

There was a period of adjustment where I started sliding into these sticky funks. Being away provided a certain distance, a distance I didn't previously have. And Neil crept into my thoughts a lot during those times. So did Tom. And Tom was someone I could still talk to—sort of, anyway.

I just missed him. I was still in love with him. Which sucked.

So I started e-mailing him.

Ugh. I know.

Just to tell him how I was, what my life at Witloff was like, not that he really cared. I didn't have any illusions like that, but I'd e-mail him anyway. And yeah, he'd never respond, but I knew he was reading my e-mails. I felt it. It was like he was reading a diary I was writing just for him. He became my silent audience in a dim theater at night, all creaky and ghost-lit. But of course Digital Dust was watching, too.

I met this kid at Witloff named Sebastian. He had been through some real shit, too. No one knew what exactly, but this kid was on so many SSRIs and other meds that one of his eyelids would involuntarily droop down whenever he'd talk to you. He changed his Instagram handle to ZombieMud and for a while would post only photos of dead birds.

I didn't want to become like Sebastian.

As I began to reflect more and more on Tom, and what we had together, and how it ended, I began to feel a raw, fresh bitterness rising up. And I wanted to address that with him because it wasn't going away.

I should have talked to a professional, maybe even gone on meds myself—at least for a while—but my experience with therapists back home, after Neil died, hadn't yielded much; probably because it was family therapy, which wasn't what I needed at the time. I didn't want to examine my grief when I was just numb, so I felt the whole thing was bullshit.

That's when these thoughts started creeping into my mind that Tom had *stolen something from me*. At first it was vague; my *innocence*, something flowery and amorphous like that. But the more I thought about it, and him, the more I realized I was never going to have another first: he had been my first. And sure, he could move on and forget about me, but I was having a hard time doing the same.

Tom took something from me. And I wanted him to take

some responsibility for that because all he did was turn his back on me at the end—to protect a family that he still had, when mine was shattered into a million pieces.

He never once wrote back. I accepted that at first, but then it would just make me angry because, at a certain point, I didn't even know if he was reading my e-mails anymore. I stopped feeling him on the other side. I started picturing him just deleting them the moment my name flashed across his screen. Like he had deleted me.

Eventually, I got sick of him never responding. So I did something kind of dark.

I told him he had left scars on me, and I couldn't take it anymore and was thinking about killing myself. It wasn't true. If it were true I would have turned to Jackson or Leo, because they knew about my past and cared about me, and I could always talk to them.

I just wanted to see if he would respond, if he would *say something*. I wanted to get a rise out of him. I didn't know about his personal travails, whatever was happening with his marriage, and it was definitely a messed-up thing to do. Anyway, soon after I wrote him that e-mail (probably Digital Dust's personal favorite), he must have...done what he did...because I heard about it from my mom only a few weeks later.

And then I knew he had probably read that e-mail, had probably been reading *all* the e-mails I sent to him. He probably loved me, had maybe never stopped loving me. Or at least that's what I'd like to believe. It's what I tell myself. He just had to let me go and was hoping I would do the same. But I didn't. I couldn't.

And I had to grieve him in private, which was very different than grieving Neil in public; so everything began to filter into my subconscious, and the dreams began, the tornado ones, but also the ones of my house on fire, lots of that kind of thing.

What I realized back at the hotel, with all the feds buzzing around me like worker bees, is that I have to finally escape the tornado. I have to get out of the burning house. And maybe I can take Shiloh with me.

I can't get that fool out of my head.

What if he really did risk everything to try to save me? That means something.

Whether or not I'm more of a liability to the government or to the Swans—well, I don't know if that even matters anymore. I'm not a totally innocent bystander. The feds did some pretty unscrupulous shit getting me involved in all this, but I made mistakes, too. We all walk into things, fate blowing us cruel little kisses.

Aunt Meredith and her Death Rays. Drew and the avalanche...

Whether or not Schwartz has been telling me the whole truth, or trying to manipulate me this whole time—which, let's face it, *he has*—I do know Scotty can get creative. And I believe the Swans may have set another, deadlier plan in motion already—especially if Shiloh was feeding the feds that specific intel.

What if something horrible happens that I could have prevented? To little kids? How many goddamn tragedies do I have to leave my imprint on?

I guess I want to prove to everyone, and myself, that Digital Dust was wrong.

So I let them implant that microchip in my back molar. And seal it with pasty goo, and do what they could to make it look like it's a cavity filling.

And I'm going to let them think I'm just going to make a handoff.

The city flattens out and the sky opens up as we head through an industrial section of Brooklyn near the East River, neon reflections drowned in its depths, the windows of warehouses aglow with secrets, rooftop parties hopping in their own strobing hubs, water towers like stoic shadow puppets against the sheet of swirling chemical-blue sky. Tons of hollow, skeletal buildings in the midst of construction sprout from everywhere, dotted with work lights, like something gutted and awaiting consumption.

I've lost track of the time. My phone, never fully charged, is dead again.

The car pulls to a stop on a quiet street. The scrolling LED sign by the entrance to a school announces mundane stuff like class schedules and special events. Its lights dance across the wet windshield, reminding me I'm no longer an ordinary kid—and may never be again. The rain has slowed to a pesky misting. The windshield wipers squeak. The noise gets under my skin. "Where are we?"

"Near McCarren Park," says Schwartz.

"What time is it?"

"It's nearly one a.m.," he replies, then turns away. "Go

ahead," he says into his headset. "They want to test your transmitter, Aidan. Say something, please."

"Blah blah suck my dick and go to hell."

After a beat: "All right, we're good," says Schwartz, giving me a thumbs-up. "Remember, Aidan, all you have to do is hand over the flash drive. Don't talk to us directly. Just talk to them. We'll hear whatever you both say. We're gonna be unseen, but surrounding you at all times. We want them to think you're alone, so you may not see us. Act natural."

I don't even know what acting natural means anymore. "Where's the drop?"

"Walk in that direction—" he points to my right in this blasé sort of way like I asked him where I could buy a candy bar—"and when you hit the park, find the tennis courts. Only one of them should be occupied."

"Okay."

"Yes?" says Schwartz into his earpiece. "Okay, Aidan, just give us a minute...we want to sync our operation here."

Five minutes go by. I feel like I'm melting into the leather seat, liquefying with anxiety and impatience. And then they tell me to open the door and *go*.

I step off the street and slosh through a patch of grass. The rain has pretty much petered out by now.

I cross a quiet, leafy street with lines of parked cars. There are benches and picnic tables off the sidewalk. I enter an expansive court through an open gate, but it's the wrong one—this has basketball hoops, a batting cage. It's untended. The asphalt is cracked; grass pokes through the cracks in a messy swirl, like cinnamon on a breakfast bun. Brand new high-rise buildings loom in the near distance, proud and incandescent.

I hear the sound of a tennis ball being hit, sneakered feet on a wet court. The noise is at once entirely ordinary and spooky in its ordinariness. I go back out and circle around. The tennis courts are right next to where I was.

Behind another fence are seven blue refurbished hard courts, in the shadow of an automotive school with caged windows on its lower floors. The courts are empty except for the one in the middle. Everything is lit by the sherbet-colored exterior sodium lights of the school.

Two dudes in tennis whites are playing a match—in the middle of the night.

Through the holes in the fence, I see who they are.

The Hardy Boys.

I stop in my tracks and exhale a thin whistle of air through my teeth. I pull up my hood. "They're here, two of them," I say, under my breath.

I open the gate, which clanks, and walk onto the courts. I splash through a fresh puddle. The Hardy Boys stop when they see me and sling their rackets over their shoulders. The abandoned tennis ball bounces once, twice, and rolls away.

There's something intensely ghostly about this whole scene. The two HBs stand stock-still, illuminated in the mist. I move forward. As I do, they move to the opposite end of the court from where I'm approaching, like we're here to play a game of Canadian doubles. Anything could happen right now. Anything.

Slowly I approach the net, my heart pounding, telling myself: *There are snipers everywhere, I'm wearing Kevlar.*

HB Frank approaches from his side, like we're about to have a coin toss. We meet at the net. He sticks his hand out. I put the flash drive into his upturned palm.

"There you go," I say. "The source code."

HB Joe approaches the net as well. They're both grinning at me, prepster jack-o'-lanterns, their teeth shining, probably not from moonlight, but I want to believe it's moonlight.

"Are you one of us?" says HB Joe.

"I am."

They stare at me, as if assessing. Both of them seem vaguely amused, like two sadistic kids watching a small animal being tortured.

"Is Shiloh okay?" I ask.

More grinning. "He wants to see you," says HB Frank.

"He" could mean Shiloh, Scotty, Kanye, anybody.

"So you've figured out who you really are," says HB Frank.

"I have."

"Well?"

This existential chitchat with two terrorists on a tennis court.

"I'm Aidan Jamison. I am sympathetic to your cause. Take me with you."

The feds are listening. This is the point where they could swoop in—if they wanted to. This is the turning point.

But I know they won't. I knew they wouldn't.

Slowly I walk past the net to the other side of the court.

Cross the line, Scotty said.

The HBs acknowledge my compliance by turning their backs and walking off the court. I follow them through another gate, off the tennis courts and to their Tahoe, parked on the street outside. HB Joe holds the rear door open for me.

This is what I had hoped—that they wouldn't frisk me this time.

I'm one of them now, after all.

I pause for one final second, biting my lip. The feds can see I'm getting taken. But there's no sniper fire. No Schwartz coming to the rescue. No Hernandez, or the woman with the ponytail, or any of the other feds hurtling out of the darkness.

No gay son, either, probably.

I get in the car. The Hardy Boys take the two front seats. They change out of their tennis whites into sleek black athletic gear. Both of them are well muscled, and both of them have those swan tattoos on their forearms—the one Benoît had, with those same numbers. It is a cult. A murderous one.

Hardy Boy Joe turns on the ignition. He lowers his window and throws the flash drive I just gave them out onto the street. I hear it land on the sidewalk with a weak little clatter.

But it's the loudest sound I've ever heard.

Any question whether they know about the feds' little operation—about me, Shiloh, the fake malware—is instantly answered.

It's me they really want. Just like Scotty said.

Scotty got taken in by Digital Dust, whether he realizes it or not. It snared both of us. He sees me, somehow, as the compatriot he's always longed for.

So I'll give him that.

We screech away, zip through the night, over yet another bridge, the city rising in the distance, on my left, and then we're on a very familiar highway.

No one says another word.

CHAPTER 15

An Army of Lovers

Welcome to Merrick Gables.

I gulp a little when I see the sign again. *Yeah, great, thanks.*

The house is dark as we pull into the driveway. My car door is opened and I climb out.

I follow the Hardy Boys through the house, which is much bigger than it looks from the outside. I see flickering and hear voices and music. The house is more alive the deeper in we go. The backyard pool appears to be where the action is centered. I'm walking down that same hallway where Blond Bellhop confronted me.

I didn't look closely at the photos on the walls last time.

A small blond boy—it has to be Scotty at maybe ten, eleven years old, standing stiffly, with his severe-looking parents by a lake. No one is smiling. The mountains, rising up in the background, look familiar.

Out those tall windows, I see the pool lit up. The glowing water refracts blue kryptonite light over everything. There's a firepit on a lawn beside it. Boys in white tees and bathing suits hold marshmallows over it, speared on long metal sticks. There's a full bar lit up with Christmas lights and a young dude pouring drinks. A DJ behind a booth spins vintage disco.

It's a pool party. Except no one is swimming.

And everyone is wearing rabbit masks.

I walk outside, toward the pool. People are cavorting, dancing, drinking. Someone blithely hands me a rabbit mask, too. I put it on, trying to blend into the crowd, as I look around for Shiloh. The mask is heavy and hot. There's a stark unreality to what's happening here. I think about *BioShock* splicers coming undone as they leave their deranged masquerade ball. I think about Frank, the demonic bunny from *Donnie Darko*. This is an acid-tinged bacchanal.

A boy wearing a black bunny mask, pink bathing suit, and nothing else is passing around a silver tray with tablets that resemble SweeTarts in pastel hues. Everyone is taking one, placing them on their tongues. When he gets to me, I take one, too. But I only pretend to put it in my mouth; I actually shove it in my pocket instead. A few people turn their bunny faces to look at me—I'm wearing more clothes than everyone else, and no bathing suit, so I stand out.

Only two people are unmasked. They're cuddling on a chaise longue by the pool. I recognize Scotty right away. His wavy sweep of thick sandy hair, longer than from the TED Talk I saw, is hard to miss, and he's aged well. He's a good-looking dude.

Though not buff, he's trim and toned out of that leather motorcycle jacket, with long, muscular soccer legs. He's wearing a white polo shirt, brick-colored shorts that taper above the knees, and blue boat shoes, half kicked off. He resembles a Silicon Valley playboy on a weekend retreat to Martha's Vineyard.

The dark-haired dude nuzzling his neck is tall and shirtless, with a lithe swimmer's build, barefoot, wearing tomato-red swimming trunks. He turns his head and a sharp jawline comes at me, glinting in the light from the pool.

Of course, I'm a young gay man, so I instantly have a visceral reaction to this boy, to the image itself—until I see who it is.

Shiloh.

The back of my throat is itchy and raw. It feels like I have all the symptoms of the flu at once. From the way they're lying there—touching each other, gazing into each other's eyes—it's pretty clear they're an item. And have been for some time. That shit is hard to fake.

Shiloh isn't just undercover—this is definitely something else.

"I, uh, have eyes on Shiloh," I say, under my breath. "He's alive... but..."

The caresses are soft and meaningful. Shiloh's little nibbles on Scotty's ear fill me with a primal envy, an uncomfortable recall to the emotionally humid days after my breakup with Tom, when everything felt like moving through thick mud and I could barely get myself out of bed, or keep myself upright in the shower without collapsing into noiseless sobs that hurt the muscles in my lower gut.

I had to choke back all that crying so my family wouldn't hear me.

But why do I even care . . . I don't care about Shiloh . . . I barely know him. And he lied to me. Over and over.

I hate this thing inside myself, this need to become attached to people, this brutal loneliness that drives me, drives all my mistakes. I hate that Digital Dust saw all that. Everything that's wrong with me appealed equally to the feds and to the Swans, everyone doing amoral things—to me—for their own gains.

I hate that this is happening, that I'm here, that I'm seeing this.

Maybe it was on purpose. Maybe they wanted me to see them together to hurt me, some sort of revenge.

But it doesn't matter anymore—I've just been spotted. Scotty and Shiloh sit up, untangling their legs, and stare at me, an overdressed anomaly in a sea of dry, shirtless bathers who are all skittering around the edge of the pool like no one ever learned how to swim.

Then Scotty and Shiloh get distracted, because Hardy Boy Joe, also unmasked, walks outside, holding a white rabbit in a cage, and everyone *oohs* and *ahhs,* forming a loose circle around the edge of the pool—a throng of bunny faces peering at a real bunny, all tense and twitchy in his cage, nervously staring back at everyone.

This would seem like a death cult—like some sort of deeply creepy ceremonial offering or witchy animal sacrifice—if there was any kind of hushed reverence to the proceedings. But instead there's Donna Summer blasting, drinks being swilled, and a lot of stifled giggling. Still, Scotty takes the cage with the rabbit, steps forward in front of the pool like a Grand Wizard, and displays the rabbit for everyone.

"Noooo," a kid whines, burying his head in the shoulder of another boy, who comforts him by running a hand through his hair.

The music is turned down as Scotty opens the cage. He holds the rabbit out by the scruff of its neck, like he's a magician at a kid's birthday party. There's an air of malevolent anticipation. And then, without a word, Scotty drops the little white bunny into the pool.

My first thought is: *Can rabbits swim?*

I think they can, actually. But we never get a chance to find out. As soon as the rabbit hits the water, it makes a horrible screeching sound, contorts, goes instantly still.

There are a few soft gasps from some of the boys in bunny masks, and some of them look away.

The rabbit floats there, twisted in on itself in a really disturbing way; its eyes black marbles, reflecting the dying firepit and the embers unleashed into the night sky. One would know what happened only from the tiny plume of smoke and the faint hiss.

Suddenly I understand why no one's swimming in the pool.

It's electrified.

Well, that's one way to have a pool party, I guess. Get people drunk, give them pills, gather them around an electrified pool, and hope no one slips.

"Our hacker brothers can do amazing things with their code," Scotty announces. "Our brave soldiers stormed the battlefield in Kansas."

I think of those photos of a young Scotty at a lake with his parents.

...His family owned a summer home in Kattskill Bay, New York. That's near Mohawk State Park and Lake George, Aidan. Where he lured you...

Schwartz wasn't lying about that after all.

Scotty spent summers in the Adirondacks. He knew the lay of the land there better than anyone.

I think back to the Mandarin Oriental with Shiloh and Tats.

We're so sorry, Mr. Jamison, there must have been a mix-up on our part...

We have a message for you...from the other guest.

From who?

A...Mr. Preston.

The Swans are the expert hackers, able to scramble anything—not the feds, who have been playing catch-up this whole time. They said so themselves. The Swans latched onto Digital Dust's bullshit and took things into their own hands.

Everyone used the empty shell of Mr. Preston to their own advantage and simply filled in the blanks.

The Swans are the ones who led me to the Adirondacks.

They're the ones who tried to kill me.

And Shiloh helped.

He was curt. He gave me directions to a location. As well as info on a bus you're supposed to take to get there. And he said no matter what: come alone.

Shiloh argued with me, told me I shouldn't go. But that was an act.

He knew I'd go. He knew I had no other choice.

"While we wait for Phase 3 to be finalized," says Scotty to

the rapt crowd, "turns out all I needed was a blueprint, a well-placed sympathizer, and a really good electrician."

Shit. Phase 3. They already figured out how to hack military drones.

Hopefully the feds heard that. It'll look suspicious if I keep talking to myself.

Scotty walks away and Shiloh follows, leaving everyone to silently stare at the dead rabbit floating in the pool. After a moment there's a needle scratch and Donna Summer comes back on. People start murmuring again. Two boys even start to dance again, reluctantly. A few people mosey over to the bar.

The dead rabbit floats away, toward a corner of the pool where I hadn't noticed a giant white inflatable swan. A heavy hand lands on my shoulder. I turn around and see my old crime-solving pals, the Hardy Boys, standing behind me.

"Scotty wants to see you," says Hardy Boy Frank.

I really don't want to be alone with Scotty, but this whole place is a terrorist cell, so it's not like I'd be safer anywhere else on the premises.

And this is what I came here to do, so…

"Are we having chlorinated rabbit stew for supper?" I mutter as they lead me inside the house. I'm amped up on fear. The possibility of my impending death ripples through every cell of my body. I'd rather go out a hero, but if this is what it takes, I'm not sure I fit the definition. My knees are shaking so bad I can hardly walk.

CHAPTER 16

Heaven-Ender

I'm led into a different, larger room this time. It's more of a library—tall bookshelves line the walls. There is an antique chess table. But the room's biggest quirk is the vintage-looking sky-blue globes on every surface. Maps and atlases are draped everywhere, too—on a large oak desk, over chairs.

Wraparound windows face a giant yard on a different part of the property, the moonlit night partially curtained by scarlet velvet drapes. There's soft gray carpeting and the walls are painted a plum color, with more yellowed maps framed on them.

One of those pricey HD home projectors, perched on a shelf, splashes an old movie across a large screen in the front of the room. The sound is off; I don't recognize the film. There's a woman with intense lipstick, screaming at everyone.

Scotty is sitting in a leather chair in front of the screen, but facing me. Shiloh, still in his bathing suit but now also wearing a white shirt, unbuttoned, stands behind him, portrait-like.

"You can take off the mask," says Scotty. I do, and place it on an upholstered armchair in the corner of the room. "We should chat, face-to-face, both of us unmasked. Don't you think?"

"Sure," I reply. I've grown used to Scotty's voice lately. It's almost comforting.

He regards the mask on the chair for a moment, then turns back to me. "I cleared the room of any stray paper clips." He laughs, brushing a sweep of hair behind his ear.

"So, the feds..." he says, comically looking all around the room.

I wait.

"...know where I live, who we are," he goes on. "They know close to everything there is to know about me. Yet they don't... want...to...move...in." He makes a face, shoots his hands out: a flamboyant show of bewilderment.

I keep trying to hold eye contact with Shiloh, but his eyes are iced over like he's in some kind of trance. Every time our eyes meet, his gaze flits away.

"Why do you think that is?" says Scotty.

I shrug. "Do you have a mole in the FBI or something?"

Which side *is* Shiloh on?

He glances at Shiloh. "I knew a lot because of what *this one* was feeding me. For a long time they had no hard evidence of anything. Their hands were tied. And we know how to stay invisible. But now they're afraid to move in because they know we're about to pull the trigger on something. It's like we've wrapped the world in a bomb and they don't want to snip the wrong wire. We've just tied their hands in a different way."

I wonder if Shiloh appreciates the bondage symbolism as much as I do.

"So here we are...drinking mai tais by the pool," he says, smugly.

I never got my cocktail, but sure.

"What is it you have planned, Scotty?"

"I am a twenty-first-century Queer Nation soldier," he announces, plainly. "There was a manifesto already written and waiting for us, long before the Swans took flight."

I'm feeling more and more uneasy by everything happening in this room right now, which honestly I have no right to be surprised by. "Yeah, 'An Army of Lovers Cannot Lose.' I read it online."

"Oh, good for you," he says, and points at me. "*That's* the Aidan I know."

"Well, you texted it to me—right before sending me threatening photos of my parents."

The door swings open and a dark-haired boy in a rabbit mask comes into the room. He's holding a silver tray with lines of crystalline yellow-brown powder on it. Scotty leans forward and snorts a line with a thin metal straw he takes from a pocket. Shiloh does the same. I didn't expect this at all. Drugs, seeing people using, freaks me out.

Bunny Boy heads over to me with the tray but I quickly wave him away; he plops the tray down on a coffee table and leaves the room. Scotty stands and does a shake-out, whipping his hair around, making little gasping sounds.

The movie flickers across his body.

He grins at me and points at the projector playing behind us. "*Mommie Dearest.* Faye Dunaway playing Joan Crawford? It's a camp classic."

He looks disappointed by my non-reaction.

"We used to have a real culture," he says. "It had some bite to it. We created these icons so their glow would shine on us, and we'd be lifted by their light, and out of the shadows. Judy. Liza. Bette. Cher. Madonna..."

I nod along.

"We're partially responsible for allowing ourselves to be victimized. There's no real unity, no community, no *depth* anymore—it's all falling to pieces." He mimes someone looking vapid and texting.

How dare he bemoan gay culture with Lady Gaga walking the earth?

Scotty sits at the chess table and starts moving the pieces around in a frenzied way. "Some of us have to do all the work. And not one of them"—he holds up a finger—"not one of them will even say thanks."

Shiloh sits on the edge of the desk, violently running his fingers through his scalp.

Scotty studies me. "Sometimes I think we can't win, and

that's why I work *so hard*. But Aidan," he flashes me a mischievous smile, "look where we invaded." He raises his arms triumphantly. "The very place that symbolizes the Family and All Its Precious Little Values. American suburbia!"

In my head I hear a thunderclap.

Soft target, Schwartz had said.

I narrow my eyes at him. "What's your plan here, Scotty?"

C'mon, c'mon, c'mon…

He rises, walks over to me. "Tom became your emotional link to the rest of the world, didn't he?"

I didn't expect to hear Tom's name, and it feels like suddenly being throttled.

"Your umbilical cord," says Scotty. "There to feed you all the love you were starved for once your heteronormative nuclear family dissolved after your brother's tragic death. And then he, too, was gone." He snaps his fingers. "I'll bet it felt, at times, like you wouldn't survive the pain."

I feel like a judge at a trial: *I'll allow it*. "I thought it might break me," I admit.

"Especially when you keep blaming yourself."

I glance over at Shiloh. He just watches Scotty talk, his eyes wide, empty, bloodshot.

"I understand," says Scotty, nodding, rubbing his chest in wide circles.

"This isn't some gift you have," I tell him in a clipped, salty way. "You only know all this shit about me because the feds put my whole life on the fucking internet."

"They reduced your pain to ones and zeroes! Well. I'm just saying I relate."

"What are you planning next?" I counter.

Scotty sticks his tongue through his teeth, lasciviously, and makes a wet sucking sound. "I feel like *The Lavender Scare* isn't being taught in schools these days," he says, his eyes wild.

Jesus, *what*?

"In the fifties they purged homosexuals from the federal government, linking them to communism, claiming they posed security risks. Everyone's forgotten, it's so terribly sad—we're losing our grip on our own history, which then mercilessly repeats itself. Seventy years later, our rights are still being carved up, siphoned away."

"But are you going about this the right way? Killing innocent people?"

Scotty either didn't hear me or is ignoring me. "Do they protest the death penalty? Are the right-to-lifers rioting in the streets over gun control? Why is it *us* they hate so much?" He glides around the room. "I think their hatred becomes a kind of addiction. It turns into a thirst that gives their empty lives a bit more *meaning*. If I were wrong, they'd be passing legislation to ban psychics and gossip sites. The Bible isn't so keen on those, either."

"You're not wrong." And he isn't. Their hypocrisy is pitiful—these knuckle-dragging politicians who speak reverently about the sanctity of religion, hiding behind their phony devout veil to curtail the rights of others—rights they so freely enjoy themselves. Whenever one of these voices rises over the rest, you can pretty much bet this closet-case homophobe will be found in a bathroom stall at a rest stop doing the nasty with some trick. They think they can repress that part of themselves by hurting those like them, those who trigger their unwanted desires.

Scotty's brilliant at making his rage infectious. He knows how to weaponize his intellectualism, his privilege, and his snobbery, distilling it into its own unique poison.

And it works because he's basically right.

Scotty is fulfilling so many fantasies of destroying these bullies and everything they stand for. He's onto something for sure, and I sympathize with their cause, I really do. But I'm not willing to kill innocent people and have their blood on my hands. I'm not one of those weak, damaged runaways so easily seduced by Scotty.

Digital Dust saw only metadata, but that doesn't make up a person. It didn't—*couldn't*—see what's inside my heart. I feel too much for people, even *awful* people, because they're just... people. Human beings are frightened, ignorant, complex creatures. I'm only seventeen, but I know that much.

I got hella educated on that shit early on.

My shattered parents; poor, tormented Tom; confused Darren Cohen; the feds lost in their ethically questionable maze. They all hurt me, in different ways, to different degrees. But we can't hold on to so much fury that we succumb to pure evil and become worse than those we hate. Then *we're* the hypocrites.

If this is going to be an epic religious war, it didn't end with the Crusades, and Scotty's not about to end it now with his cabal of puppyish hackers and creepy midnight parties.

Scotty's gotten up real close to me now. He hasn't raised his voice once; he's kept his white-hot anger contained to a low boil. "They want us to lie down while they choke us with their legislation," he says. "Time to rise up. Let's make them feel vulnerable in the way they've made *us* feel vulnerable for decades."

I take a breath. "How?"

"Our cyber-warriors can get inside their computers, their bodies, and every place they go to practice their *religious freedom.*" He puts those last two words in mocking air quotes. "Those places won't be safe anymore. And, just like a throng of Pied Pipers, we'll finish off the rats, then take their children."

I lick my lips, anxiously. "What does that mean?"

"We are an army of lovers because it is we who know what love is."

The room gets brighter as the night outside improbably gets even darker, the moon moving behind some night clouds. Shiloh looks up at me, his face a watery blank, and I give him a sad, weary look. Something in his eyes softens. Scotty—who even hopped up on drugs is hyperaware of everyone and everything—notes this.

He looks at Shiloh, and back at me.

"You want to ask Shiloh something?" he says.

"I want to know where he stands...on all this. You make some valid points, but we could just protest in the streets. Stand in front of government buildings. ACT UP did it. They got in people's faces. They made change."

"Aidan, I appreciate your historical and cultural knowledge—I *do*. But you can be a bit lacking in the broader-view department.

That's a flaw I'll chalk up to your feckless youth. These are different times we're living in."

I smile in spite of myself. "If you can use your hackers to get inside their computers...and expose their hypocrisy, you can out every closeted senator who supports anti-gay legislation. The world can know about every homophobic baker who actually has that secret boyfriend. Right? You can use what you do, your gifts, to destroy these people's lives and their shams without *murdering them*."

"Oh, Aidan." He's shaking his head at me.

Now, this I don't like: being patronized by a terrorist who's a little bit in love with his own (admittedly quite hypnotic) voice.

"That leaflet talks about love, Scotty. It doesn't talk about *killing*. You've misinterpreted decades-old activism. You can fight for what you believe in without carnage."

He's still shaking his head at me.

"But it would bring you less glory than killing and blowing things up and making a big fucking show. Less *infamy*, right? And that's what this is really about, isn't it?"

Scotty gives me a charged, slightly dangerous look. "They're moving quicker, more insidiously than ever. They've taken over all three branches of government. We need to fight on a bigger scale. Tactics must change. It's time for the Swans to take flight. And you, hun, you need to spread your wings."

"What is it you're about to do?"

He peers at me like I'm not living up to some grand expectation. "When I said we were connected by loss—*you and I*—I meant it. We can both understand—and empathize—with the very personal, human costs of this war. And I will be the soldier who fights it in the name of those who no longer can."

"Is that what any of those people would want you to do?"

He looks affronted. "You think I *want* to be a martyr?"

I didn't use that word, but as soon as he says it I realize that's exactly his plan. He wants to go down in a blaze of glory. Eventually, like all extremists, he wants a firestorm.

"I want to ask Shiloh if he's really a Swan." I look at Shiloh. "Do you think people should be murdered? They're bigoted assholes, sure, but *murdered*. And innocent people too, if they get in the way? You, who told me in my hotel room, when we were *alone,* to listen to my friends and family and let them help me and call the police and that I need to grow up blah blah blah."

Scotty is blinking rapidly, his jaw sliding back and forth as if on a broken hinge; he didn't expect this. I got under his skin. Shiloh is his weak spot. Just like I thought.

15–love, bitches.

"I want to hear you say it." I pout like a heartbroken schoolboy, overplaying my part maybe just a tad.

Scotty looks back and forth from Shiloh to me. Shiloh doesn't respond.

"And yet here you are," I continue, "snorting drugs with terrorists and killing bunny rabbits. Who *are* you, dude?"

"Hotel room?" says Scotty. He turns to Shiloh. He points the silver straw, coated with powder, at him. "I didn't know you two were alone together in his hotel room."

"We weren't alone," says Shiloh, finding his voice at last. "And it was only for a few minutes."

"No, it was longer, and we *were* alone." My voice rises. "*Why are you lying about us and what happened?*"

Scotty hops over to a wall. He opens the hidden door to a walk-in bar and steps inside. Round vanity lights automatically click on; they surround a mirrored wall that reflects bottles. Scotty frowns, considering his reflection. Then Shiloh and I both jump as Scotty drives his fist into the mirrored wall, smashing it into glittering dust.

Scotty punches what's left of the pulverized mirrored wall again and again in this terrifyingly focused way. And then I have to look away because his hand is nothing but a bloody pulp. Yet he keeps on punching.

The sound of that. Jesus.

Shiloh lunges, grabs my arm. "I know what he's going to do," he whispers into my ear, "so just play dead."

His swift movement startles the hell out of me. "What?"

"*Play dead!*"

"They know you're an agent," I whisper to him. "They know who you are."

"I know," he says. "But they think they turned me."

"*Did they?*" Kind of a dumb question, I guess. Could someone answer if they've been brainwashed?

"No," he replies.

He does seem, all of a sudden, focused, agile, and articulate; but also groggy and spent, like he's fighting his way through a thick cloud.

"You wrote that note on my phone. *Attack on visitor center was us.*"

"What?" His face is ashen. Sweat coats his forehead and glosses his upper lip.

"Was that you? Who did you mean? The feds or the Swans? Whose side are you on?"

He shakes his head, his eyes rheumy, cloudy. "It's the drugs..."

"Who was 'us' supposed to be?"

Shiloh just shakes his head.

I hear bottles clanging, a glass banging down. Scotty emerges from the walk-in bar holding a tumbler with brown liquid. In his other hand is a stainless-steel .44 magnum.

Oh, shit, what now?

Scotty grins at me. "I'm sorry, my dear, you're up for elimination. The time has come for you to lip-synch for your life."

"Scotty," Shiloh rasps.

"Wait," I say.

For the first time, Scotty raises his voice. "MILO!" he bellows.

Milo?

That's when Bunny Boy enters the room again. This time he's holding a different silver tray. There's a lone gold object on the tray.

"So let's find out if you're a Swan," Scotty tells me.

Bunny Boy picks up the object.

Bunnies and swans—what is it with Scotty and backyard wildlife?

"Open your mouth," Bunny Boy tells me.

I step back. "Uh, what is that?"

"We liquefy our serum, hun," says Scotty. "It's what we call the Heaven-Ender."

"N-n-n-no thanks."

"*Yes,* Aidan. A single spray on your tongue. So I know for sure you've been dosed. It's the first step. It's how we begin our flight."

I think of flocks of ducks honking across a winter sky. My house. My backyard. We had a stream. I would feed the ducks. Neil and I would.

I look closer. The gold thing is an atomizer.

"Open your mouth," Bunny Boy says again, coming at me with that atomizer like I'm a flowering plant he's about to water. I step back. "One spray on your tongue."

"You have to shrink down to fit into Wonderland," says Scotty, dancing around the room, his mangled hand dripping blood everywhere.

"Stick out your tongue," Bunny Boy commands, still coming toward me at a steady pace.

"Only then can you fly," says Scotty.

Is this where I'm supposed to play dead? That... doesn't make sense.

"ENOUGH!" says Shiloh, pushing Bunny Boy away from me.

The room goes very still very fast, like evil fairies were pulling this whole terrifying performance together with cruel little strings—and they all just got snipped. Bunny Boy freezes in place. Scotty stops flailing.

"I guess you're not a Swan," says Scotty, petulantly, like a child playing with a dangerous toy that an adult just took away. He turns to Bunny Boy. "Get the fuck out of here, you're *boring.*"

Dat's wight, Wabbit! I almost say out loud.

I exhale.

Bunny boy quickly exits the room, taking his stupid tray and atomizer with him.

"I *knew* you weren't a Swan," Scotty tells me in a low voice. Although he legit seems disappointed by the realization.

I'm trying to catch my breath. "If you knew...why did you have me...why did you want me..."

"To come here?" He gives me a small smile. "Because if I brought you here, Aidan, I could settle all my doubts once and for all about *this one*." He tilts his head toward Shiloh and hands him the gun.

I love how he keeps referring to Shiloh as *this one*. Adorbs.

"He's who I really care about," says Scotty. "Sorry, hun."

It's the way he says those final two words: full of malice, devoid of emotion, and I know, with a flooding dread, what he's about to do.

"Now I'll know for sure which side Shiloh is really on," he says.

I can't find the words to make this stop. I just spew nonsense noises.

Scotty turns to Shiloh. "Shoot him," he says, gesturing lazily at me.

"No, *no*," I plead, holding up my hands. "Wait—"

There is no pause or hesitation.

Shiloh takes a few steps back, aims, and fires.

CHAPTER 17

Quest Gardens

He shoots me twice.

There is a bright flash and an incredibly loud bang. My ears are instantly ringing so bad I can't even hear myself scream; what feels like a battering ram is thrust with incredible force into my chest, under my right shoulder. And then, when I'm down on my back, there's a second bang, and another battering ram comes down on my stomach, right above my navel.

There's incredible pain everywhere, and an insistent fear that the bullets penetrated the Kevlar and I'm going to die in seconds. But I still somehow manage to remember what Shiloh told me, and now it makes sense:

Play dead.

So I roll onto my stomach, capture my terrified breathing into the crook of my arm, and do not move.

I hear animal sounds: Scotty rasping, lurching, moaning, cursing in high-pitched whelps, kicking over a chair, then swiping a bunch of papers off the desk. I hear Shiloh grabbing him, flesh on flesh, whispering to him, calming him down, like someone reassuring a runaway stallion. "I need to know now," says Shiloh quietly. "You have to start letting me in more."

Scotty mumbles something else, and Shiloh says, "Okay, okay..."

Shiloh finally gets Scotty to leave the room, saying, "No, it's over, it's over, it's over..." and Shiloh closes the door behind them.

Okay, then I pretty much fuck things up.

I sit up, peel off my hoodie and shirt, undo the side strap, and rip off the vest, because I'm freaking the hell out. I want to know if the bullets penetrated the Kevlar. They didn't. Despite being high as a kite, Shiloh knew where to aim, and what distance to shoot me from. I have two horrible-looking bruises forming on my body, but the bullets didn't go in. That's when I hear footsteps right outside the closed door.

I leave my hoodie, shirt, and the Kevlar on the floor like a snake that's shed its skin, and hurtle myself into the walk-in bar. Broken mirrored glass crunches under my feet. I peek through a small crack in the door. The Hardy Boys rush into the room, huffing and puffing like big bad wolves. They stare down at my discarded clothes.

HARDY BOY JOE: Oh, shit.

HARDY BOY FRANK: Where did he go?

HARDY BOY JOE: I don't know.

HARDY BOY FRANK: He was wearing a vest. We didn't frisk him.

HARDY BOY JOE: Oh, shit.

HARDY BOY FRANK: We gotta tell Scotty.

HARDY BOY JOE: Oh, shit.

HARDY BOY FRANK: He escaped.

HARDY BOY JOE: Find Scotty.

HARDY BOY FRANK: Shiloh knew.

HARDY BOY JOE: They're both moles. They're feds. That's a vest.

HARDY BOY FRANK: We gotta find Scotty.

They leave the room and I begin to understand two things right away. One: holy crap, those two are really stupid. Two: there's a very good chance I might not make it out of this thing alive.

That's when I start to realize some stuff.

I could have run away. I could have gone into hiding. But I penetrated a terror cell in the hopes I could help Shiloh, who I believed to be a good person, and prevent something truly awful from happening.

Okay, yes, I didn't have *too* much of a choice, with everyone pulling at me and coming after me, but I think I made the right decision for once. And I did have a decision to make. This was brave. I'm officially one of the good guys.

I didn't have a great start to my smudged-up adolescence. I didn't do the right thing with Tom. I didn't behave well for a good portion of my life, and that includes with my brother. It's hard even to think about that stuff.

After what seems like close to an hour, I step out of the walk-in bar and throw my shirt back on. I take a bottle of whiskey and pour it on the floor. I wrap a bar towel around it and smash it in two so the neck is a jagged weapon.

I search the room. Papers are scattered all over the floor; one of them catches my eye because it seems out of place. It's the schematics of the wooden Mind Melter roller coaster, the iconic ride at Quest Gardens.

Everyone knows Quest Gardens. It's a famous amusement park in Lollaby, New York. It's been in a lot of movies, mainly during montages halfway through rom-coms. I've even been there a few times, when I was much younger, on summer getaways with my family. It's probably pretty close to here.

Why am I looking at a diagram of the Mind Melter roller coaster? Next to it are printouts of computer code I can't understand, and next to those the schematics of the Quest Pool. There are also schematics for the Derby Racer Carousel, one of only two like it in the nation.

An article reprinted from a local paper states that due to consistent warm weather—or, as the park euphemistically puts it, "climate re-alignment"—Quest Gardens will have its Grand Opening three weeks early this year, at a time when lots of kids are on their spring breaks. Although I bet there are some economic factors involved as well—I heard Quest Gardens almost went bankrupt during the last recession. The opening is tomorrow. Or, as I gaze out the window, I guess it's *today.*

The sky is lightening. It's already dawn. I see a discarded

rabbit mask lying on the grass outside, and I think about the electrified pool.

Look where we invaded. The very place that symbolizes the Family and All Its Precious Little Values. American suburbia!

Jesus, I know what they're going to do next—something aimed directly at the notion of apple-pie Americana.

We'll finish off the rats, then take their children.

Schwartz was right: they're targeting children.

Quest Gardens isn't some big, national chain; it's a small, local amusement park. No one's eyes are on it. No one's eyes were on the funeral in Kansas, either, or that random visitor center in the Adirondacks. The Swans are clever that way. They're never going to attack a big city or some important monument.

They're going to directly smear the very idea of "The Family" and "Family Fun"—paragons of the religious right—while operating behind the well-tended trees and shrubs of the Merrick Gables.

Leave it to a gay terror organization to have a matching theme.

Turns out all I really needed was a blueprint, a well-placed sympathizer, and a really good electrician.

Holy shit. Scotty has someone on the inside at the amusement park.

Suddenly remembering my FBI-sanctioned dental work, I say out loud, "Hello, FBI? I think the Swans are going to hack the rides at Quest Gardens Amusement Park. They're going to electrify the public pool."

I have no idea if the feds can hear me, since I can't hear them.

I have no idea if this implant is operational, or ever was.

I need to get out of this house. But I hear voices and running footsteps outside the library, so I wait, aiming the broken bottle at the door, ready to thrust. And then I wait some more. And then I wait even longer, my whole body aching and throbbing where I was shot.

I cautiously move to the closed door. Suddenly the door is thrust open. I pounce with the broken glass in my hand. But it's Shiloh standing there, breathing hard, Scotty's gun at his side. "Whoa, whoa!" he says, jumping back.

"Shit, sorry. Sorry!" I back off, throwing down the piece of glass.

"Jesus, Aidan. It's okay," he says, one of his hands raised defensively. "We need to get you out of here." I notice he's fully dressed now, with a perfectly tailored light-blue shirt, navy-blue jacket, and slender beige slacks.

I stare at him. "What did you...hit a Barneys outlet?"

"I just got dressed."

"Your eyes are clear."

"Scotty likes to keep everyone docile, in a state of perpetual intoxication."

He's probably sleeping with every dude here.

"I was already sobering up," says Shiloh, "but Scotty keeps an IV drip in the house. I used it to flush out my system."

"Why did you take the drugs?" I anxiously rub the sides of my face. I cannot get a handle on this boy.

"You have to do some seriously messed-up shit when you're

undercover. You have to play their game to an extent to give yourself credibility."

Yeah, to an *extent.* "So they didn't turn you?"

"No one turned me."

"The feds lost track of you."

"Things with me and Scotty took a . . . bad turn."

"Where is he?"

"He escaped. With his henchmen."

"Why didn't you stop them?"

Things are moving too fast for me to fully appreciate that the word *henchmen* can now be dropped in casual conversation with nobody batting an eyelash.

"They were too fast. There were . . . obstacles."

"He's going to attack Quest Gardens," I say.

"Yeah. I know. Mass electrocution. I found out the plan, he finally just told me, which was why I was undercover for so long. I needed to build up that trust. It took time."

"I think he also sabotaged the rides."

Shiloh's eyes widen (in this totally cute way). "Oh."

"I saw diagrams on the floor."

"I didn't know about that part. We have to get you out of here."

"I'm not going anywhere with you. I want some answers. When we met on the train, what was your objective? Try to kill me as soon as you got me alone?"

"No, Aidan, *then you'd be dead*. I was supposed to get you to Lake George. The Swans have a base there, where they train new recruits."

"Recruits? Scotty had already tried to kill me by then."

"What, Vinny drowning you?"

"*Who?* Is that the bellhop—?"

"Yes. That wasn't on Scotty's orders."

"But the next one was, right? Why that random visitor center, with all the kids?"

"After he told me to send you to Mohawk, Scotty changed his mind and decided to take you out—send a message to the feds that he knew you were a decoy. Also, hitting a random spot populated by tourists and families was sort of a dress rehearsal for Quest Gardens. Scotty was super impressed you survived."

"I'm *so* flattered—"

"Aidan, please, let's discuss this later—"

"They *for sure* know you're a mole now... both of us."

He nods. "I figured."

"They saw the Kevlar on the floor."

He glances at the floor. "You took it off?"

"Yeah, sorry, I'm *new at this*. We have to call the police."

"I'm cut off," says Shiloh. "No cell. There's no working landline here, either. Do you have your phone on you?"

"It's dead. But the FBI put an implant in my molar." It's only now I notice blood on his hands and arms. "What the hell happened to you?"

"Obstacles," he repeats. "I'm sorry I had to shoot you."

"Twice."

"Twice, yes. I had to make it look real. I'm sorry."

"*Sorry* doesn't cut it. That was an uncomfortable moment in our relationship. Among several so far."

"If the FBI allowed you to get taken by them, I knew they'd put a vest on you."

"WHY THE FUCK DIDN'T YOU JUST SHOOT SCOTTY?"

"The rest of them would have killed me immediately! And you, too. I had to protect my cover as long as I could. The feds want him alive; they know so little about any of the Swans' future attacks." Blood is dripping down the side of his face. Now that I look closer, it looks like the upper tip of his left ear is missing.

"Dude," I say, pointing at his ear.

Shiloh touches the blood with the tips of his fingers. "I know."

"Are you okay?"

"Yes. What about you?"

"It hurts when I breathe," I say, with an accompanying wince to drive the point home.

"You may have a cracked rib. That's common."

"COMMON FOR WHAT?"

"Getting shot." Shiloh gives me this very sorry, pleading look, which is adorable.

But, n-o-o-o, I'm still not won over. "You led me into a trap."

He sighs. "Well, really you led *yourself* into a trap. More than one. First at the Mandarin Oriental, which wasn't quite your fault, but then at Mohawk, which was."

"Are you serious, dude? You *sent* me to Mohawk."

"Aidan, I had to keep my cover. I needed to find out their plans. I didn't know they were going to try to kill you. Please believe that."

"What did you *think* they'd do?"

"Recruit you. That was the original plan before Scotty changed his mind, which he does constantly. And then I could have taken it from there."

"But Scotty knew I was a decoy."

"I didn't know he'd figured that out. And Scotty was already a little bit in love with the idea of you."

I snort. The idea of me. Tom probably fell in love with the *idea of me* as well. The reality of me is a little bit more of a handful.

"Scotty goes ballistic sometimes. He plans, he organizes, and then he goes off the rails, with no rational thought behind his actions. He's always vacillating. It's impossible to keep up with him. He's a psychopath, Aidan."

By steering me toward the Adirondacks, Shiloh had to know there was at least a risk I would be killed. And his mission came first.

I'm always the collateral damage.

"When I found out, I went up there to try to save you," says Shiloh. "But it was too late. Scotty likes making theater. I couldn't get to you in time."

"You had my phone on you. I had the iPad! You could have just texted me to tell me what was going on."

"Everything was being monitored. I'm sorry, Aidan, they hacked into your devices a while back. We need to get out of here."

"What did they want to spray in my mouth? Heaven-Ender?"

"Probably liquid molly. The Swans traffic in these designer drugs. Not just MDMA. Stuff that's so experimental it hasn't even hit the black market yet. That's partially how they fund this organization." He takes a breath. "Which is why...I'm going to lead you out of the house now and I'm going to ask you not to look, okay?"

"What?"

"Keep your eyes closed."

"I'm not a little kid. Seriously. You keep treating me like—"

"Trust me! Stand behind me. *Okay*?"

"Okay, okay."

I stand behind Shiloh as he leads me out of the room. We tiptoe around a corner, then out into that long hallway with those tall windows facing the pool. I try not to look. I really do. But I hear these loud slurping sounds coming from the open glass doors, over the sound of a forgotten record-player needle scratching the inner rim of vinyl, through speakers that were never turned off. That's when I can't help myself. I peek outside.

There's blood everywhere.

The pool is hissing, sparking, and I see at least five rabbit-masked bodies floating facedown in the sludgy water, electricity coursing through them, causing these horrific twitching tremors I'll never forget as long as I live.

Other bodies are splayed around the pool, covered in blood. The slurping sound is coming from a corner of the pool. A rabbit-masked boy, his blood-smeared back to us, is crouched over one of the bodies. He's making sharp, unnatural pulling motions with his head.

"Shiloh. *What the fuck is happening?*"

"I told you not to look!"

"I looked."

"Told you, they're all on these crazy drugs. Stay behind me."

Just as we near the wooden gate that leads out of the backyard pool area, a blood-splattered boy in a rabbit mask, totally naked otherwise, confronts us, foaming at the mouth like a rabid animal. He has a bloodstained kitchen knife, and he slices the air with it so violently you can hear the *whoosh*.

Shiloh pushes me back and holds out his hand in a calming manner. "It's okay, it's okay," he says soothingly, keeping the gun low, by his hip. "Hey, hey, it's okay..."

The boy, teeth bared, knife raised, lunges.

BANG BANG BANG.

Shiloh shoots the kid. He goes flying back, while I clap my hands over my ears. "Jesus! Oh, my God!"

I guess these are the *obstacles* Shiloh was referring to. Got it. Okay.

"Keep moving!" says Shiloh, pushing me past the kid's body and out the wooden gate leading to the front of the house.

We reach the driveway. I notice Shiloh is limping. He fumbles with a set of car keys. "What happened to your leg?" I ask him.

"I got attacked by one of them while chasing Scotty. And the drugs...my head isn't one hundred percent clear yet, but I'm getting there. Can you drive?"

"Yes."

He tosses me the keys and we get into one of the black Chevy Tahoes parked in the driveway. Another Rabbit-Swan-Splicer-Boy comes at us, pressing his frothing horrible face against the car window as I screech out of the driveway and down the street, whispering: *Oh my God, oh my God, oh my God.* I make a quick hairpin turn in case we're being followed.

The sun is up. And, according to the weather report displayed digitally on the dash, it's going to be a warm, sunny day, in the eighties. It might even get up to ninety.

So basically a perfect day for an amusement-park trip.

As I barrel through suburbia, I realize Scotty did an incredible job of infiltrating this lovely little bedroom community. That was a pretty badass and subversive move. People just waking up to their cappuccinos and the morning news, casually deleting morning spam e-mails on their smartphones while breaking apart multigrain muffins, have no freakin' clue what's going on down the street from them—that the Creepiest Terror Cell of All Time is right next door.

"I'm taking you to the train station," says Shiloh, wincing as he holds his leg.

"What? Why?"

"I want to get you to safety. Call the police from the station. They'll direct you to the feds. Keep using your audio link in case it's working. Narrate your actions."

"Do we have time?"

Shiloh checks his watch. "The park opens in about two hours."

"How far away is it from here?"

He sighs. "About two hours."

"Then no, no way. We need to get there."

"Aidan. I don't want to put you in any more danger."

"Says the man who just shot me! Twice!"

"I had to! You know that."

"Plus, you can't drive."

Shiloh sighs.

"I'm not stopping this car until we're at Quest Gardens," I inform him.

Shiloh curses to himself, puts his head in his hands. "Then take the next left here, onto the highway. Stay at sixty, sixty-five, but don't go over; don't speed."

I turn onto the highway. "And what happens once we get there?"

"Either the authorities will already be there, which is what I'm hoping, or I'll have to flag down the park staff, make sure they don't let anyone inside. We should stop at a gas station and call 911 from a pay phone, or borrow someone's—"

"Uh. I don't think we can stop."

Loud engines have pierced the usual morning highway din. Shiloh whirls around to look out the rear window. There are two motorcycles coming up behind us; two green visors sparkling in the morning sun.

"Shit," he says under his breath, "they followed us."

The two bikes fan out, surrounding our car.

"Their movements are synchronized," I say, frowning.

"Sena Bluetooth," says Shiloh. "They can talk to each other."

A third bike comes up from behind, then speeds ahead of us with a deep throttling roar, going at least ninety, clearly on its way to fun and magical memories at Quest Gardens.

I take a breath. "What if they start shooting at us?"

"They won't start shooting at us."

"What if they do?"

"They won't."

They start shooting at us.

The first shot takes out my side-view mirror. It just *plinks* away like it was never there.

"Fuuuuuck." I instinctively slam on the brakes, but thankfully the highway isn't jam-packed so I don't get rear-ended. Then I floor it and swerve into the motorcycle on my left, where the helmeted asshole is aiming a gun right at my face. I bump up right against him and he nearly tips over, then veers ahead, speeding up to avoid being sideswiped again.

Shiloh grabs the wheel. "Aidan! You're drifting! Stay in your lane!"

I fight him off. "Do not grab the wheel when I'm driving!"

"I'm trying to help you."

"You're not helping, you're throwing me off, I'm doing fine!"

"I'm just trying—"

"LET ME DO IT."

The second shot pops out the rear window with a tremendous explosion and makes a neat round hole in my windshield. They shot clean through the car.

"Jesus!" I scream. "This is so scary. *Holy shit…*"

"Okay, speed up!" says Shiloh.

"You don't have to keep telling me what to—"

Gunshots cut me off.

But they're Shiloh's—firing out the broken rear window at the motorcycle quickly gaining on us. I can see it swerving, but then the Swan biker speeds up again, sidling up on the passenger side, his mirrored insectoid helmet staring us down.

He aims his gun.

"DUCK!" we both shout.

I duck my head down but manage to keep my grip on the wheel.

The third shot takes out the passenger window and the driver window simultaneously, crystallizing my field of vision with a mist of broken glass.

I spring back up and step on the gas.

The motorcycles keep pace, flanking us.

Shiloh fires out both windows, making my ears ring. Both motorcycles swerve, slow down, hang back.

"Speed up," says Shiloh.

I do, and the motorcycles slowly disappear behind us.

"Did we lose them?" I ask, going about ninety now. I hear distant sirens.

Shiloh looks out both broken side windows, looks behind him, then at me. "For now, yeah. They did not expect me to have that gun. I think I got that guy in the shoulder. Keep your eyes on the road."

"I'm going ninety."

"Go eighty."

I slow down to eighty. "I'm bleeding." I raise my arm up.

"Okay, keep your hands on the wheel." Shiloh produces a towel—*why does this boy always have a towel?*—and wipes my arm down, then picks lightly at my skin. "They're not serious cuts, just little shards of glass embedded in your skin. I got most of them out. You'll be okay."

"They can come back, right? Shoot out our tires?"

"We'll get there soon," he says, uneasily. "Just keep your eyes on the road and stay focused. I think we scared them off. Good work."

I can't help fighting off a grin, and slap the wheel. "I'm a freakin' superhero! Okay, maybe both of us, but I'm driving, so I win."

Shiloh gives me a half-smile. "Look, after our meeting at the motel, I finally had a chance to read over your Digital Dust file. I hadn't previously."

I stop grinning. I suddenly feel extremely naked and exposed.

I can only say, "Huh."

"Well, you mentioned your brother's death and I wanted to get the whole story."

"I wish you hadn't done that. That's not really fair."

"Maybe. But I'm glad I did. Because there was some stuff I wanted to tell you."

"What stuff?"

"Look, I was part of Digital Dust myself. They found me in a similar way, except they trained me to become a field agent. I had some serious issues in my own life. I had substance-abuse problems. I was heading down the wrong path."

"Looks like the government Philip K. Dicked us both over."

"They actually saved me in a way," he says. "I never had purpose before. My parents died when I was very young. There was an... accident."

Avalanches... death rays...

"I was bouncing around the foster care system for years. I started drinking myself to blackouts at twelve."

"I'm really sorry."

"I buckled down, got myself into college, but I still struggled with depression and anxiety, feelings of worthlessness. I got into some trouble. But the feds, with this program, gave me a chance to make something of myself—to make my life matter in a way that it never would've otherwise. I could save lives."

"What kind of trouble? Was it some sort of plea deal?"

"Not exactly," he replies.

"Well, I never asked for any of this. I'm just a normal kid."

"Normal? You've had serious stuff happen. We both know that."

I shake my head, stare ahead at the road, clutching the wheel.

"The thing I wanted to tell you," he says, "is that I understand you were involved...romantically with this older man...the father of a school friend, right? I think I get why and how it happened."

"You wouldn't, because you don't know me, and I didn't tell you about it. Reading about my data in a manila folder doesn't count. It doesn't tell you who I am as a real person."

"You're right, but it tells me something."

"This is bullshit," I mutter.

"Your brother dying, an older sister out of the house already, your parents basically rejecting you—"

"Shut the fuck up, man—"

"I get it, I'm just saying *I get it*. But the thing I wanted to tell you...is that none of it was your fault."

Scotty's been saying something similar to me this whole time, but it feels different coming from Shiloh. It hits hard. Tears blur my vision. This is bad, since I'm driving very fast on a busy highway where armed terrorists on motorcycles could reappear at any time. "You don't know."

"You were a minor. I *do* know."

"I don't want to go into this right now—"

"What was his name?"

"Tom," I say under my breath.

"Tom was in the wrong. Not you. You were the child. He was the adult."

"I made mistakes."

"Yes, you did. And you know better. You can't keep going down this path—the meaningless hookups, getting attached to much older men when you're not a legal adult yet. Just like I couldn't keep going down the path I was headed down. You don't feel like you're a child, but in some ways you still are. You can't emotionally process certain things that you could with a little bit more maturity."

Now he's Confucius all of a sudden.

"I just want someone to love me," I say, reciting a future Adele song title as the crying finally begins. Snot and tears start leaking out of my face at the worst possible time. "I didn't mean to hurt anyone..."

"I know," he says, placing his hand lightly on my wrist. "It's okay."

God, I've been crushing on him so hard ever since our first train ride, and now he's seeing me like this. I hate it. "I like you, Shiloh, *a lot,* which doesn't even make total sense. It's been scary for me 'cause I don't know you at all. And it's even scarier now because I guess I *really* don't know you."

How much has been a game, a manipulation?

"You do know me, Aidan. My name really is Shiloh. I am—or was—attending Duke. That stuff is real. And I am a snappy dresser—can't help that. I'm just an undercover agent for the FBI on an interim basis, so they can capture the Swans. I'm one of the good guys. And so are you."

"Part of why I agreed to infiltrate the Swans was because of you," I tell him. "Just thought you should know that. I know I get attached too easily—dude, I know. But I just...think there's something good about you. Complicated and kind. Killer combination."

Several emotions crisscross his face, too fast for me to read. But then he seems to push them all away. "Thank you."

"Yeah."

"I've battled my own kind of loneliness too, Aidan. And guilt. Everyone does, to an extent. Doing something I cared about helped." He smiles at me. "And I like you, too."

I flick my eyes over to him, smile through my tears, then turn my attention back to the road. "What's next for you after all this?" I ask him. "Assuming we survive."

"I'm going to have to go through detox. But...you know...one step at a time. Let's get through the rest of today."

I point at a green road sign that says QUEST GARDENS, directing us off the highway at the next exit. We seem to have lost the bikers—at least for now. "Should we pull over, find a phone?"

"No, it's too late for that," says Shiloh. "Let's just get there."

I turn off at the next exit, drive down a long tree-lined road, and suddenly a giant sign looms: QUEST GARDENS AMUSEMENT

PARK. There is an image of one of the Derby Racer horses with an almost angry expression on its face, showing bits of teeth, catapulting into the sunlit sky as if it died and is now entering Derby Horse Heaven. Or maybe the horse is just on some kind of magical quest. Let's go with that.

I pull into one of those endless, sectioned parking lots. My heart sinks when I see the parking lot is almost half full this early in the morning when the park isn't even open yet. I guess a lot of families are on vacation.

Now I remember that Quest Gardens sits on the glimmering Long Island Sound. The sky is crystal, with only a few fluffy milky-white clouds.

This place is going to be packed.

The park opens in twenty minutes. In the distance I see the columned entrance with QUEST GARDENS written in puffy banana-yellow lettering with candy-blue trim overhead, sword-and-shield insignia beside the words—symbolizing quests, I guess.

The wooden framework of the Mind Melter roller coaster rises in the distance. I remember, as a kid, you could hear the *whoosh* of the ride and people's distant synchronized screams from anywhere in the lot.

We park and hop out of the car. We both scan the lot for the motorcycles, but I don't see or hear them. As we get closer to the entrance I yell, "Look!" and point at the line of people and families snaking around the entrance waiting to gain admission. The glass-walled ticket booths, on both sides of the entrance, are still unmanned. "This is a shitshow," I say.

"We might have gotten here just in time," says Shiloh.

"That's optimistic."

"There's gotta be security keeping that line in check," says Shiloh. "We'll just tell them to call 911."

"Do you have any FBI credentials on you?"

"I'm undercover!"

"So they're just going to believe what we tell them? To close the park?"

"They'll have to. There's going to be a terrorist attack."

We both walk quickly toward the entranceway. "Have the pool and the rides already been tampered with, do you think? Or does Scotty hope to—"

"Whatever he engineered, it happened last night. I didn't even know about it. During the pool party, Scotty sent a small team to Quest to rendezvous with whoever he has working with him here on the inside. I guess the party was supposed to be a celebration of that, the completion of Phase 2."

"What the hell is the point of you infiltrating them, and going undercover, if you can't let the authorities know what he's about to do? They said you went dark."

"Yeah, Scotty confiscated my cell phone and locked me in the basement."

"He did what?"

"He gets paranoid. He's super jealous and possessive, in case you may have missed that. And violent."

"Yeah. I noticed."

"He figured out I was an agent a while ago. But that only thrilled him more. He relished the challenge, thought he could twist the situation to his advantage. He was confident he had turned me, that I was brainwashed by him. But all of a sudden he wasn't so sure anymore. When you escaped the Adirondacks, he got a clever, nasty idea: he could test my allegiance once and for all by bringing you here."

That's a twist to this dark little fairy tale. I guess that's why they didn't try to kill me on the tennis courts. I wonder if the feds knew about this.

"He didn't think I'd be wearing a vest? The tooth implant?" I ask.

"He hasn't been thinking clearly in a while."

"I saw you guys cuddling together by the pool. That looked pretty real."

"Scotty felt bad about freaking out on me. That happens. He'll do crazy shit, then feel bad after. The makeup sex is amazing, though."

I stop walking. "You guys were...having sex?"

"I was undercover, but yeah." Shiloh points at the entrance line. "We really need to keep moving—"

"Whoa." I wave my hands around. "Hold on, hold on. How could you have sex with him? He's a psychotic terrorist."

"It was part of my cover."

"Did you feel something for him?"

"It's hard to feel nothing."

"Were you attracted to him? I mean...*are you*?"

"Scotty? He's not a bad-looking guy."

My hands go flat at my sides. "I don't know what to do with this."

"What did you think was going on?" says Shiloh.

"Part of you is in love with him."

"Here's the thing," says Shiloh, turning to me, "maybe yes, maybe no. But the Swans have no precedent. In the history of foreign and domestic terror, there's never been anything like them. Not in the way they're able to organize, recruit, attack, and remain secretive in the way they do. They're a total anomaly."

"I know all that already! I've been debriefed!"

"Well, I had to get as close to Scotty as I could. And I had to make him believe, at every moment, that I was his lover, his partner, his soul mate...so don't be naïve enough to think when you give yourself over to someone like that, despite the false circumstances, that you don't start feeling something back. That would be impossible. I know what side I'm on. Did that get blurry at times? Maybe a little."

I'm getting a little tired of people calling me *naïve*. "So at no point did you maybe start to sympathize with him and his radicalism?"

Shiloh puts his hands on his hips. "Did *you*?"

I look away and sigh.

"It was hard not to, Aidan. And I'm just the type, as Digital Dust knew, who would be a perfect fit for the Swans. But he never turned me. I'm not a terrorist. I never will be. The FBI knew that, too. Or *should have*. I know right from wrong. My reason is still intact."

I nod. "Yeah."

There's a silence. My ears are still ringing from the gunshots. Sounds—including Shiloh's voice—remain kind of muffled. I think I hear the rides going, people screaming, and the gentle lap of Long Island Sound against narrow rocky beaches—all of it at once. But I may just be imagining all that from a distant memory—an aural mirage.

There is a crazy, illogical, serpentine madness to everything Shiloh is telling me. It simultaneously makes me trust him less and like him more, if that's even possible, and I don't know if it is. He sacrificed a hell of a lot to go undercover.

"You said you were an addict," I say.

Shiloh nods. "Some of my biggest weaknesses became my biggest assets. It is tricky and messed up...I acknowledge that. But I achieved a lot. I was able to feed the feds a lot of intel they wouldn't have had otherwise. You helped, Aidan! You did good. You helped expose them, smoke them out. The FBI needs evidence—proper justification to move in—in order to protect civil liberties and all that. We're finally giving them what they need."

I look away. "You have this habit of talking down to me, Shi. Like I'm a slugger on a Little League team in a slump. I always feel like you're either scolding me or cheering me on in a slightly patronizing way, and there's no middle ground."

"Aidan, I—"

"No, dude, you're talking very heroically and majestically, and I'm glad you found your path, that you lifted yourself out of shitty circumstances for the greater good, but let's look at the whole game, okay? You lied to me. On the train, in the motel, you lied to my face."

"I had to—"

"All that bullshit about me not having faith in *human kindness*—"

"Not all of it was a lie. We do have a connection."

"Was it manufactured?"

"Not that part."

"But you're still a liar. Say it. I want you to admit it to me."

He looks me in the eye. "I lied to you, yes."

I shake my head. "This whole Digital Dust thing...that they did this to me without my even knowing...it isn't right. You have to realize that. And you took part in it."

"A lot of things went wrong."

"Well, they shouldn't have," I say.

"You're right. There were mistakes made. The rules keep changing, the game keeps changing, and when the bad guys are faster, more insidious—when they get even more cunning—we have to do what we can to keep up, in order to save as many lives as possible. There are trade-offs. That's all I can say."

He's parroting Schwartz a little, but clearly this is what he was told, and this is what he has to believe.

"You know I have a crush on you, Shi."

He smiles. "I like when you call me that—"

"You're cute, smart, sweet. But every time you open your mouth, I feel like I know you less."

"I understand," he says. He looks a little sad.

It's like he just realized the thing he sacrificed for all his heroism was a chance at me. Or maybe that's just wishful thinking on my part.

I have no idea what Shiloh's really like outside his guise, what he's like outside these extraordinary, terrifying, adrenaline-pumping circumstances. He's been playing a character the whole time I've known him.

I don't know how much of the real Shiloh I've experienced. I see goodness in him, but I also see a lot of other crap, and anyway I have to stop getting attached too quickly. Being alone is not always a bad thing; it's not always a sign of some sort of inner failure. Maybe I need to start knowing myself a little more before opening myself up so willingly to people—hurling myself at them and hoping they'll drop everything to carry me away into the sunset.

I look at Shiloh, and okay, *yes*... I want to make out with him really badly right now. I want to fall asleep with him next to me, his arms wrapped tightly around my chest. But I'd rather do those things with a future version of him—a version of him that's come through the fog of all this. Someone I know is the real Shiloh.

He might be on the right side of things, but he is a trained liar. And that's something I have to consider. It's time I started taking care of myself instead of waiting for other people to do it for me.

Anyway, what the hell am I doing standing here, thinking about all this crap?

The amusement park is about to get attacked.

CHAPTER 18

The Last Tornado Dream

As soon we run to the front of the line, about three families—already exhausted, with crying, screaming kids—start making a big show about how we're cutting. Shiloh reassures them we're the authorities (ha ha), which all the angry, tired parents refuse to believe. Then park security ambles over: two big guys with earpieces and scowls on their faces.

"Is there a problem?" says one of them.

"Line's back around there," says the other.

"This is an emergency," says Shiloh. "You have to close the park down and get all these people out of here. This place is about to be attacked."

"Shiloh!" I point beyond the security guards.

The ticketing booths have opened, and people are already

streaming into the park. Shiloh checks his watch. "You opened early?" he asks one of the security guys.

"Big crowds today," the guy replies.

"What time does the pool open?" I ask him.

"In about fifteen minutes," he responds.

Shiloh tries to explain the situation, but it sounds too crazy and unbelievable, even to my ears. We sound like pranksters. They ask for IDs, of course. We have none, and then things escalate in a really inconvenient way.

"No way am I calling the cops on this joke," says one of the security guys, laughing. "I'll bounce you out myself."

"Just call the cops on us, then!" says Shiloh. *"People are going to die!"*

But they're hustling us away from the line of people, because they don't want to cause a panic (which kind of needs to happen).

"Shoot your gun in the air," I murmur to Shiloh.

"What?"

"Shoot. Your. Gun," I say under my breath.

"I've had enough," barks the security guy, who obviously heard me. He gets Shiloh in a headlock, then the other guy grabs me; they spin us both around, and they do it with unfortunate choreography and tragic timing.

Because as soon as we switch places, in a really balletic, super-fast way, they both get shot with arrows.

I yelp and cover my head, diving to the ground. The arrows just, like, appeared. They didn't even make a sound. They're the same kind from Mohawk—with the green fletching—arrows clearly meant for us.

The first guy was shot through the shoulder, the second guy through the upper thigh. Looks like we all got lucky.

That last archer—the one I killed, Katniss Fuckerdeen—was obviously a better shot.

Guns and arrows. The Swans came to Quest Gardens well armed.

The two security guys stumble back, each of them instinctively grabbing the carbon arrows sticking out of them, all bug-eyed with pain and shock. Shiloh and I look behind us, through the entrance to the park. "They're already inside," says Shiloh.

We grab the two wounded security guys and move away from the entrance fast, ducking behind a nearby car. "Is there another way to get inside the park?" I ask one of the profusely bleeding security guys, crouched low on the ground.

"Along the beach," one of them croaks. "The park is on the sound. You could get in that way."

"On motorcycles?" I ask.

"Sure," says the other guy, "if you can deal with wheelspin and don't care about getting sand in the engine. The sand is thin."

Then, right on cue, comes the *vrrrrm vrrrrm* of motorcycles from inside the park. And then, finally, I hear the sound of sirens—distant, but growing closer. Helicopters, at least six or seven of them, suddenly appear, surrounding the park from the sky.

I breathe a sigh of relief. "They heard me. They're here. Thank God."

"What's going on?" says one of the security guys, his face crinkled with pain.

Shiloh puts a hand on the guy's knee. "Let the EMT guys take the arrows out. Don't try to do it yourselves."

"Shit," says the guy, spitting on the pavement.

"You'll be okay," says Shiloh, "but we have to go inside the park now, and we have to cordon it off so no one else can get inside."

"I'm going in there," I tell Shiloh.

"No way," says Shiloh.

No one saw the crossbow attack. People are at the ticket booths, wallets out, streaming into the park in droves. When they open that pool, about a hundred impatient kids are going to jump in all at once. "There are only two of us right now," I tell Shiloh, "and we may not have much time. You stop more people from getting into the park. I'm going to warn the people already inside."

"They're going to try to kill you," says Shiloh. "You took off the Kevlar."

"The rides are death machines! The pool is electrified. We have to stop them!" I run toward the entrance.

"Aidan!" Shiloh screams after me.

I sprint through the gates.

Most of the park is set on a wooden boardwalk, which wraps around the whole park, facing the water. Booths line the boardwalk: shooting games, throwing games, ring tosses, Whac-A-Mole, Skee-Ball, hot-dog stands, innumerable cotton-candy vendors, stuff like that.

There are already lines outside the entrance of all the major rides, including the Mind Melter and the Derby Racer. This isn't good.

Then something chilling happens. The music coming out of the omnipresent sound system is blaring Top 40 like Taylor Swift and Ariana Grande, but then in a staticky hiccup it goes away. There's a brief moment of silence, replaced by faint classical music—a weird choice.

The classical music slowly rises in volume.

I stop in my tracks, because I know the music. I know what they're playing. But I can't place it. I press my fists against my temples. It's Tchaikovsky. And a moment later, I know what it is.

Swan Lake.

I run up to the historic Derby Racer. The carousel is under a round wooden honeycomb roof. There are no poles; the horses simulate galloping, faster and faster, as the ride goes on.

One "race" is just ending, and kids are already filing on for the next.

I start yelling at the ride operators, but no one can hear me over the bugle call that begins each ride, *Swan Lake* blaring, and the instructions the ride operators are shouting to the kids—to lean their bodies to one side, brace their feet. Once the race begins, the spinning track of the ride itself is pretty deafening, too.

Finally, I'm able to grab the ticket attendant. "You have to stop the ride!"

"Is someone sick?" she asks.

Let's just go with that. "Yes. YES! But don't let anyone else on the ride! Get everyone out of here RIGHT NOW!"

She looks confused, but she's smart and can tell I'm not messing around. "Why? What's going on?"

In answer to her question, an arrow embeds itself in the side of a passing horse. Another arrow meant for me, but it could have hit the little girl who was riding it. I turn around. Across the boardwalk I see the motorcycle, skidded on its side, facing me, and the green-visored biker reloading a crossbow from a black quiver on his back. No one saw the arrow except the ride attendant and me. She turns to me, eyes wide. "*What the hell is that?*"

"Is there an emergency stop on this ride?"

"Yes."

"HIT IT. And get all these kids off the ride, get them out of here, tell them to run and keep their heads down! Alert security, whoever you can, tell them the park is under attack, *but get people away from this ride*!"

She jumps into action. I hear the sound of an alarm, the ride creaking to a stop, and emergency instructions over a loudspeaker. I run back onto the boardwalk. Another motorcycle zooms down it from the other direction. I'm trapped in the middle of both bikes. I look at one, then the other. Both the Swans are loading crossbows. And I'm wide open, totally vulnerable. I'm not sure where to run.

But then gunshots ring out and one of the Swans flies off his bike. Shiloh appears from behind him, gun aimed with both hands. The gunshots create an almost instant panic, which is probably good, as people scream and grab their children, running for the exits.

I can see people pouring off the Derby. Within seconds, it's totally evacuated. The other motorcycle revs, turns, and speeds away down the boardwalk. But I get the feeling he's not going far.

I run over to Shiloh. "Thanks!"

"I got them to shut the pool down," he says.

"I got the Derby Racer evacuated."

The sirens are getting louder. In the distance, on Long Island Sound, I see the lights of police boats approaching the beach.

We both glance up at the Mind Melter. No one on the coaster heard the gunshots. It's whizzing by, and it's loud (*whooshing, rushing, clacking*), full of screaming kids, their arms in the air. We run over to it, and on the way we reach the downed biker.

It's Hardy Boy Frank. He's taken off his helmet and is coughing up blood. He's also bleeding from his shoulder. Shiloh was right; he nailed the guy from the car.

"How many of you are here?" says Shiloh, aiming the gun down at him.

"Traitor," growls Hardy Boy Frank, spitting blood at Shiloh.

Shiloh grabs the crossbow from him and leans down. "You would have killed all those kids in that pool?"

"You nearly shot a little kid on a carousel," I add.

He never answers. Hardy Boy Frank coughs up more blood, then his face goes still and he dies right there in front of us.

This guy has been chasing and terrorizing me across the entire State of New York for days, and now he's gone just like that, so fast and quiet. It's weird I don't feel more about seeing him die. I didn't even get a chance to say some clever final zinger like "Enjoy hell!" that would have been the last thing this asshole heard.

Shiloh straightens, puts a hand on my shoulder, "We have to get you—"

I know he was going to say *out of here,* because that's what he's been going on about all morning, but he doesn't finish the sentence. Instead he stumbles backward with an arrow sticking out of his shoulder.

"AH, CHRIST!" he says, his voice choked by pain as he grips the arrow. I reach for him.

"No, don't touch it!" he screams. "Get out of here! Run!"

The other motorcycle is speeding toward us across the emptying boardwalk. People are jumping out of its path.

There are too many people, still running, scattered about, for Shiloh to shoot back at this distance. But the bike is getting closer. "Run!" Shiloh yells at me again.

The park is suddenly flooded with police officers and feds. They must have just arrived and rushed through the gates. They all have their guns out.

And then they all get knocked to their feet by an enormous explosion, followed by a terrifying, apocalyptic fireball, angry orange and hellish black. The Derby Horse Racer just exploded, shooting projectiles of wood and metal and splintered glass and whole derby horses into the air.

Weirdly, this now justifies the completely nonsensical Quest Gardens welcome sign we saw on the way here, with the horses flying into the sky.

Shiloh and I duck behind a juice bar to take cover from the falling debris. After a moment, I peek out. It seems everyone had gotten far enough away from the Derby ride in time, and the police hadn't moved in yet. I don't see any injuries. That's a goddamn miracle. People are shouting and screaming. The cops are trying to contain the chaos.

Then all I hear is one collective whine of police sirens, coming from everywhere. "I can't believe they bombed the Derby!" I shout at Shiloh, whose mouth is wide open, his face bloodless.

"They probably tried to hack it," he says. "But these rides are too old. Those idiots. It's all manual. There are no computers. So they just blew it up."

"What about the coaster?"

We run out from behind the juice bar. The Mind Melter has come to a halt now, and cops are quickly leading people off the ride.

Two more dudes in green-visored motorcycle helmets, masked by the havoc, hop off their bikes and dash over to us.

One of them wraps a leather-clad arm around my throat. The second one flanks me on the other side, sticking a pistol against the side of my head. They drag me backward, toward the entrance to the Mild Melter.

Shiloh lunges at them, even with the arrow sticking out of his shoulder and blood running down his arm, but they pull me away. "Keep back, Shiloh," says the one with the gun—Scotty. He presses it harder against the side of my head. "Or *bang bang*, your boyfriend's dead."

"We're not really sure what our relationship is yet," I say quietly, but panicking. *"It's burgeoning."*

"Quiet," says Scotty.

"WHOA WHOA WHOA!" the police yell, seeing Scotty, training their weapons on us. It's a standoff. And I'm on the wrong side.

"I'm not a Swan!" I scream.

First of all, this is probably already obvious—no one could

possibly look more like a hostage than I do right now. Secondly, *and this needs to be said,* that is probably the dumbest thing anyone has ever uttered during a police standoff.

"Put your weapons down or I shoot the kid," says Scotty, addressing about, oh, three hundred armed police officers. I wonder how this is going to go down.

"They won't do that!" says Shiloh, standing between the cops and us, like a referee, both arms out even with the arrow in his shoulder, forming a one-man barricade, which is totally useless but *so adorable.*

Scotty ignores both him and the cops, keeps the gun aimed at my head, and says, "Let's go for a ride."

"I'm not really a fan of roller coasters."

Especially not now, knowing Scotty's been using them as terror toys. There are so many horrible ways to die on a roller coaster. My mind starts ticking them off as we slowly shuffle toward it.

"Had any more of your tornado dreams, by the way?" Scotty asks.

I actually think about that for a second. "Since this whole thing began, nothing more about tornadoes. Maybe the tornado's already caught up with me."

"Maybe you're about to get spun up into the sky," offers Scotty.

Now I'm sick to my stomach.

Scotty waves his gun around and shouts demands.

A ride operator nervously runs over, hands over his head, hostage-style, to start up the Mind Melter again.

I don't like this. I don't like that we're going on the ride, and

I don't like the way Scotty keeps checking his watch. Like something, somewhere, is timed. Shiloh doesn't like this, either. "Do not let them get on that ride!" he yells over to the cops.

"I'll kill him," says Scotty. "I'll shoot him right now. I just want one ride."

"He's booby-trapped it!" Shiloh screams. "Take him out. *Take him out now!*"

I can see the police officers shift, eyes roving, analyzing the situation, but Scotty is careful to stay out of anyone's sights, thrusting me in front of him as a human shield, his gun jammed into my lower back. "If you stop this ride while we're on it I will kill the kid. Do not stop the ride!" he yells.

I stare up at the huge cartoonish pink brain perched over the coaster that twinkles red and gold from a million tiny lights inside. 'Cause this is the Mind Melter. *Get it?* The brain is actually a winding, spiraling tunnel. The coaster spins you around within it, turning the riders themselves into a bizarre personification of insanity, scrambling the brain from the inside. From what I recall, it feels like being trapped inside a gigantic piece of glowing bubble gum. Then the coaster spits you back out, at the highest point, right before the main drop.

Hardy Boy Joe opens the gate, and the three of us enter through it. Scotty keeps me in front of him the whole time, his pistol pressed hard into the back of my neck, as we board the coaster, facing sideways, so he remains out of anyone's crosshairs.

Then we're inside, undercover.

There are three yellow trains with six cars each, faded red lightning bolts on the sides. The lightning bolts make me think of Jackson's tattoo. Thinking of Jackson, my gorgeous best friend who knows me better than anyone and takes no shit, calms me down a little. I think: *There are good things in this world among the bad.*

Scotty pushes me into the last row of the last train. He sits beside me. Hardy Boy Joe takes the gun from Scotty and sits in front of us, turned around, keeping the gun aimed at my face.

"Can I Instagram us?" I say. "All right if I tag you?"

Scotty and Hardy Boy Joe remove their helmets and place them on the empty seats. Scotty removes his gloves. His right hand is bandaged up. He unzips his jacket.

The ride operator, who can't be much older than me, gives me a tremulous look. He's sorry because he knows he's most likely leading me to my death. Against his will, of course, but still. It's not a facial expression you see often. It gives me a chill, though. I'll tell you that.

I nod at the kid. The kid nods back at me. Nothing anyone can do now.

I hear even more sirens now. And helicopters. I turn to Scotty. "What'd you do to the ride, huh?"

He smiles, all crooked and mean. "Oh, how'd you guess?"

"Blaze of glory, right?"

He makes this *tsk tsk* sound. "And you have a family, friends, a fresh romance on your hands. Still in the flush of youth."

"So why do this, man? Why take me with you?"

"If it was just me, no one would care." He pats me on the back. "Now they'll remember. Plus, you ruined everything else I set in motion."

"You took this too far."

And something about that disappoints me.

Scotty glares at me. "So, just to be clear, you were okay with us hacking drones and bombing government buildings in flyover states, mowing down homophobic picketers. It's just Quest Gardens that put you off?"

I shake my head. "No, I was never okay with any of this. You stirred something up inside me, I'll admit that, but I'm not this. That's the problem with extremism."

His eyes widen, amused, mocking. "Oh, do enlighten me, hun."

"It goes off the rails. You succumbed to the same ugly hatred the religious right has for us, Scotty. And you were going to kill little kids."

"I'm the only chance any of us has left. I told you—sometimes you have to do ugly things to win a war. Fighting. Slaughtering. It's human nature."

"It doesn't have to be."

"*When they go low, we go high.* That didn't really work out, did it? Look where the pendulum has swung." It's the clarity in his eyes that frightens me the most right now; he's sober, not clouded by drugs.

"Homophobes, okay... but why innocent people?" I hear the desperation coating my voice, fraying it.

"*Innocent people*—that's an oxymoron."

"Children, Scotty—*little children.*"

He looks at me with disgust. "*Their* children."

Jesus. To him, everyone has become the enemy.

The train starts to move. There's something eerie about only three people on this rumbling old coaster that should be filled with excited kids and parents. It feels wrong. *It is wrong.* And so is that gun being pointed at me. "Take the gun off me, please," I say. "This is a roller coaster. That thing could go off."

Hardy Boy Joe only sneers back at me.

"Do it," says Scotty, and Hardy Boy Joe lowers the gun.

I grip the seat with both hands, trying to suppress my pulsating fear. I look straight ahead. "What happened to you, Scotty?"

"We never truly appreciate what we have until it's gone. But you understand that, of course." He looks me in the eye. "Don't you?"

"What happened to your boyfriend?" I ask, trying to tighten our connection, hoping that might stabilize him, if that's even possible at this point.

Scotty sighs and leans back in his seat. "He wanted children."

"He...did?" I'm baffled. His answer is so honest and simple and weird.

"He was basically straight." Scotty gives me a wistful smile. "He worked with numbers. He listened to Wilco. He wanted a house in the suburbs, a family. His own family rejected him. They all turned their backs." He leans in to me close, brushing his shoulder against mine. "They were *religious.*" He hisses that word as his eyes settle on mine.

"You didn't...want those things?"

"Children? A family? Are you out of your mind?"

He's asking *me* that—hilarious.

"I wasn't interested in conformity," he says. "I wasn't interested in breeding. But Ken loved the world. He loved it too much, and that was his problem."

"How could you love it *too much*?"

"It's why I fell in love with him. But it was also why I fell out of love with him."

I place a hand against the back of my neck.

"Ken loved his little nephews. After he came out to his family—at my insistence—all he had left were Instagram posts of smiling people on lawns who he loved deeply...who would never speak to him again. He refused to delete the app, would just sob over these fucking photos every day."

"That's awful."

"And that's why I left him."

There's a heavy silence for a second as we roll along.

I bite my lip. "But...*why*?"

"I can put up with a lot, but I can't put up with *pathos*. I can't put up with people needing things they will *never get*. It's Charlie Brown and Lucy with the football. I'm not attracted to weakness. I love throwing parties, but not pity parties."

Despite the random *Peanuts* reference, an unexpected heaping of sadness gets poured over my escalating terror.

"Then poor Ken, he had no one left," says Scotty. "So he checked himself into a sad little motel off a highway in Connecticut and slashed his wrists in a bathtub. Did I know he would do that?" He moves his head, slightly, from side to side. "Nah..."

"I'm sorry." Man, this story is a real downer.

"But...I realized, over time, no one would ever love me like he had." Tears brim his eyes. "I fucked up. I want him back. And I feel like I get him back—parts of him, in flashes—by fighting everything in the world that hurt him."

"I don't think he was weak," I say, "I think he just wanted to be loved. I think he just wanted to have a family..."

"That's not what we're on this earth to do," Scotty intones. "We're engineered not to be burdened by children, and our ambitions should be greater than upholding the Traditional American Narrative. We are the superior race."

My eyes flutter. "Says who? What does that even *mean*? Who says what we're on this earth for? No one has those answers. You're fighting for equal rights, aren't you? To get married, adopt children, live normal lives—"

"Right!" Scotty claps a hand to his chest. "Because we deserve those things! We are human beings and we deserve the same rights, dignity, and respect as everyone else! It doesn't mean I want what everyone else does, *but we deserve to be treated equally.*"

I guess I expected more from an evil mastermind so adept at the Art of the Mindfuck than general misanthropy, confusing self-contradictions, and a whole lot of generalized bullshit.

Scotty can be downright boring and disappointing in the harsh bright sunlight. In the end, there's not much depth to his sparkling wordplay.

He smiles at me, sadly. "If I had tornado dreams, I'm pretty sure I wouldn't be running away from them. I'd be standing still, waiting to get blown into the sky and shredded up for taking everything for granted, for being cruel and coldhearted to someone who never deserved it. But the storms never come for me. Not when I'm awake and not when I'm asleep. Don't you know, Aidan, what that tornado really means?"

"No," I tell him, even though we both know it's *death.* It's always been that.

And then that awful memory punches me in the face like it so often does:

You're not my goddamn brother.

I sit upright in my seat as we continue to climb, higher and higher, with this *clickity clackity* sound, remembering the last time I spoke to Neil. Remembering that whole thing yet again.

I know I said that I was "muddy" on the last time I spoke to Neil.

That's not quite true. The last time I spoke to Neil, the night before he died, we had a pretty vicious fight. And it was about the weather.

How lame is that?

He had to be at his game the next morning. And my mom had to be at her stupid Saturday morning Pilates class. So there was only one car. And we had only one dad, obviously. And I really needed to be at GameStop, so I could get some dumb video game on the day it came out. Before it sold out.

I could have downloaded it from the PlayStation store. I could have just done that. But I wanted a physical copy—the physical copy came with a limited-edition booklet of fan art, *and I wanted the booklet.* And also...I was trying to prove something.

There was supposed to be a storm. Lightning, hail, everything. And our dad hates driving when it's storming. So, really, before the storm, there could be only one car ride, and it was going to be either Neil or me.

And I just got pissed that Neil's basketball game was going to take preference (yet again) over me doing something, over me getting this video game. For once I just wanted to count, I guess. I felt Neil always counted more—'cause he was older and a jock superstar—and I just wanted to count for once in my goddamn life. I wanted to get that one ride before the stupid storm. For once I wanted it to be about me.

So I got into it with my dad and with Neil, about how every weekend he takes Neil to his game and this one stupid time *why couldn't he just take me somewhere.* One of those irrational things you get into when you're a kid and you're helpless. Neil said fine, he'd just get a ride to the game with a friend, but my dad was all like: *No, no, no, Aidan needs to learn patience, he needs to learn to wait, he needs to learn he can't always get his way.*

FYI, I never got my way. *Never.* So fuck that shit.

In my head, I had this whole stormy weekend planned out—me happily sitting in front of the TV playing this video game, flipping through the fan-art booklet, and eating Cheetos. The fact that my perfectly imagined plans were going to get ruined—that I wouldn't have the video game, and that I'd be stuck at home during a thunderstorm without it—made me furious. I was a turd about it. I was overdramatic. *I was a little kid.*

It was my dad who made it into a whole thing when it didn't need to be. But the fact that Neil was so *nice* about it made me even more pissed, because I felt like he was trying to one-up me, make me look petty.

Why did Neil always have to be so goddamn perfect?

He wasn't perfect, though. He was just kind and generous. I knew that. I knew it even then. But I didn't always appreciate it as much as I should have.

So I took out all my anger on Neil. I got red in the face with rage about how everything is always all about him. And at the end of my little tirade, I said to Neil before I stormed off:

You're not my goddamn brother.

It's such a stupid thing to say, too, like *what does that even mean*? Of course Neil was my brother. But it was the last thing I ever said to Neil, and that sucks—a big kick in the nuts from the universe. And of course he was all like, "Oh, c'mon, Aidy, of course I'm your brother," and "Dad, just let me get a ride with Jason, don't make this into such a big deal, let him get his video game, it's fine, maybe it won't even rain."

But I wasn't hearing it. I ran up the stairs to my room, slammed the door shut, threw myself facedown on the bed and pounded the pillow, drowning in my own stupid selfish sorrowful eleven-year-old tears.

It's just typical family shit that happens. But, yeah, that was the last thing I ever said to Neil. And obviously that will haunt me forever.

"You're thinking about him," says Scotty, pointing his finger at me. "I remember that look on your face."

Maybe it's that, Shiloh had told me, looking at me, in the cab.

What?

The way you suddenly get sad like that.

That thing Scotty said about how I think I break people. He was right.

I never got over the idea that maybe I broke Neil's heart.

Digital Dust wouldn't have known that. That was all Scotty. Props to him.

I look at him. "There are things I want to do. Things I want to see. He'd want that for me, too. I'm only seventeen years old."

"There's Paris and Rome," says Scotty, "the Egyptian pyramids, the Great Wall of China. Castles in Scotland. London. Berlin. Hong Kong. There is so much…so much beauty and so much pain. There is a whole world out there. Ken knew that. Ken knew that better than anyone. The things we wish we could undo."

He laughs a little to himself, thinking about the world, I guess.

And then we nose-dive.

Scotty and Hardy Boy Joe cheer like little kids as the wind pummels us and my stomach drops, and the coaster, feeding off the momentum of the first plunge, speeds around a bend, and up another climb, down another, steeper drop, and straight into the twinkling gummy-looking brain.

Everything's all muffled and dizzy and pink and Scotty and Hardy Boy Joe's cheers echo crazily inside as we zoom around in there. And then we're spat out, rising again, the sky on all sides of me.

I can see the whole world now: the Ferris wheel spinning to my right, helicopters like huge black insects suspended in the sky, police lights flashing beneath us, the sun sparkling on Long Island Sound. There are sailboats, too, triangular and noble. In an abstract way, they resemble swans.

Scotty grabs me, puts his arm around me, and gives me a big wet kiss on the cheek as the coaster continues to climb to its biggest drop. "I wanted people to think about fate and choice. What if I sit in this car, or another car instead? What if I go on the ride today, or tomorrow? I wanted people to think about the choices we make without knowing what they'll mean...That's why I put the explosive charges at random, scattered points along the coaster."

"Sorry, you did what?"

"Because it's not about *choice*. It's about *fate*."

And then it happens.

A string of flashes nearly blind me, followed by several thundering booms, like an explosive necklace was wrapped around the whole coaster. The empty train ahead of Hardy Boy Joe gets torn apart by a blast and blown skyward. I watch, incredulous, as comic book–colored cars shoot like bullets into the gleaming azure sky.

With incredible force, right before we reach the top of the biggest drop, the coaster comes to a screeching stop, and we teeter there at the very top.

"Oh, they stopped us!" Scotty screams, slapping his thigh.

I don't hesitate.

I stand up and kick forward, driving my foot straight into Hardy Boy Joe's throat. He falls back with an *oof,* gripping the sides of the car to steady himself; his gun flies out of his hands. He tumbles, stands up halfway, and apparently that's exactly what the police were hoping would happen. There's a sudden crack of a sniper rifle from the distance, and then Hardy Boy Joe is just gone, over the side of the coaster.

I fall back into my seat, breathing heavily as Scotty stares downward at his falling comrade, fascinated by what just happened. Cautiously, he leans forward and peers over the brink of the Mind Melter, where we were just about to drop. He turns around and looks the other way over his shoulder, where we just climbed. And then there's another crack of a rifle, and Scotty quickly ducks down, wrapping his arm around my shoulders. "Well, that's just rude!"

"JESUS CHRIST!" I shout, trying to wriggle away.

"I can't believe they stopped the ride. After all that! What the hell do they think is going to happen now?"

In answer to his question, there is a terrible cracking of wood from the damaged, blown-out tracks, and the rail beneath our car comes apart, tipping the train over at a sharp angle.

Scotty slides right out of the car.

Like someone just ripped me out of my body and I'm observing everything from above, I hear myself gasping for breath and making a petrified, voiceless "UGGGHHHHHHHH" sound. A scream from someone too scared to scream.

Scotty's hanging on to the edge of the car with both hands, his legs dangling in midair.

I clap my hands over my eyes and then slide them down my face like this is all a nightmare that I can wake up from. Then I find my voice, and all I'm saying is, "Holy shit, holy shit, holy shit...."

I see the public pool, empty and serene, directly below him.

There's so much terror I can't even feel it anymore. It just becomes a shudder through my body, a rapid, forceful tingling. Then it's like a switch gets turned off and I feel almost sedate, my vision narrowed in a primal way, every breath measured out.

"Help me," says Scotty, trying to hold on, grasping, his face strained.

He reaches out a hand and I grab it. But it's his injured hand, and the bandage starts to come undone in a way that we both know means the undoing of him.

"I'm scared," he tells me plainly—the last thing I'd ever expect him to say.

"I am, too."

"How are we different?" He looks genuinely inquisitive.

Of course the answer to that question is obvious: despite everything, I stuck out my hand for him. But I think he meant *why* are we different? And that, I guess, I just don't know.

He wallowed in the darkness, but I saw something else on the horizon.

I mean, Neil died, and I was destroyed. Tom broke up with me, and I was destroyed. Tom killed himself, and I was destroyed yet again. I was this boy who kept getting blown to smithereens and put back together again, like I was made of magnetic fibers and everything just had to recombine because the rules of time and space demanded it. Except there'd be more cracks in me each time. More nicks in the facade.

I guess I knew I'd always be damaged in some ways, but I knew I could try to become better anyway, maybe because of all the pain. I didn't want to give in. Or give up. Neil wouldn't have wanted me to. Neither would Tom. That's what Digital Dust got so wrong; that's why I could never be a Swan.

The irony is, Scotty is the weak one here.

He chose hatred, and I chose love. They both hurt in different ways. But one is a kind of pain we need to feel, I think. The other is a kind of pain we choose to feel. Hatred and anger lead you nowhere.

I feel sorry for Scotty.

"You're nothing like him at all," he says to me.

He's slipping out of my grasp. "Hold on, Scotty. Who?"

"Preston," he says. "We all got it wrong, didn't we?"

"Yeah," I say quietly. "Yeah…you all did. There is no Preston."

His eyes sparkle, but it might be just the empty sky reflecting in them. I'm not sure. "Now I know what it was I really saw in you all this time," he says.

"What?"

"You remind me of him a little."

My arms feel like they're going to be ripped off. "Who?"

"You love the world, Aidan."

"Jesus. *Hold on.*"

I realize tears are streaming off my face, dripping down into the void, and Scotty does the funniest thing: he catches one of my tears on his tongue.

"See it all," he tells me. "The whole wide world."

"I will, I will."

"Forgive yourself."

More tears fall onto his face, into his eyes now.

"Stop punishing yourself, Aidan."

"I will."

He looks like he just had some kind of revelation. "There won't be any more tornadoes for you," he says. "They've all blown away, tucked back into the sky."

And for some reason I believe him. I believe I've had my last tornado dream. I don't remember the last one I had. I can't remember the last time I even slept. Of course, the tornadoes turned into burning houses, but I don't feel the need to point that out to him. And I have a feeling I won't have any more of those, either.

I try with all my might, using both arms, to lift Scotty up, the blood rushing to my head with the effort, thinking: *Let me save this one fucking person in my life.*

But he's too heavy and I'm not strong enough and his bandage is rapidly unraveling.

Scotty continues to slip from me as my grip weakens.

Something changes in his eyes, this rabid dissonant light flickers out, and he gives me a wan little smile full of sadness and relief.

"You're going to fall out if you keep trying," he says.

"Please hold on!"

Suddenly, he's Neil.

And then he's Tom.

And then he's Scotty again.

"Only one of us can make it out of here alive," he says, gazing up at the sky. "Oscar Wilde said we're all in the gutter. But some of us are looking at the stars."

"I'm trying to—"

"Time to let go," he says.

But it's Scotty who lets go.

I watch him fall through the sky, his bandage chasing after him, a mad kite tail in the wind.

And he does get part of his wish, I guess. He does go down in a blaze. Not exactly glory, though, more like *infamy*—but it is pretty spectacular. When his body hits the electrified pool about a hundred feet below, it's like the inversion of fireworks, sparks and streamers of smoke spiraling from below instead of above. The redistribution of weight rights the car a little, and the train stabilizes on the broken track, but just barely.

"I'm going to survive this," I say out loud. And I know I will.

I curl up in the train car, teetering on the edge of the tallest point of the Mind Melter. I laugh a little. I place my hand over my heart and I say *thank you* to whoever is listening, if anyone is, for my healthy heart and for letting me survive all this. Not that I believe in anything like that—I don't—but I do it anyway.

I let a couple of Taylor songs play in my head. I even sing some of the lyrics out loud over the sound of the helicopters.

I think I can feel their blades whipping the air.

CHAPTER 19

So How Was Your Spring Break?

In a delicate rescue operation, firefighters from half a dozen departments throughout neighboring towns on Long Island use ladders and the ole' bucket-brigade technique to get me down from the destroyed Mind Melter.

How very analog, I think, crying and laughing at the same time.

It takes almost an hour, but then I'm down and it's over.

A foil Mylar rescue blanket thrown across my shoulders, firefighters, police officers, and EMTs lead me out of the Quest Gardens amusement park. The front parking lot is just a gigantic sea of blinking, blaring emergency vehicles now, as far as the eye can see.

I look around for Shiloh. They try to load me into an ambulance right away, but I tell them I'm not injured and need to find my friend.

But I don't see Shiloh anywhere.

Running through the throng of emergency workers and now the media (reporters with cameras and microphones and vans pulling up, the cops trying to hold them back) come my parents and my sister. "Aidy, honey!" my mom says, running into my arms, nearly knocking me down. She grabs my face. "Are you okay? *Baby, are you okay?*"

"Yeah." I hug her back, hard, and accept her many violent kisses. "What are you doing here?"

"You're all over the news," says my dad, putting his hand on the back of my head. "They're calling you a hero."

"My little brother," says Nicks, hugging me, "a hero."

"I thought they said I was a terrorist?"

"Is that what you'd prefer?" says my dad, gruffly.

"No," I tell him, "I just did what anyone would."

"That's what heroes always say," says Nicks.

I'm confused. "How did you get here?"

"The FBI collected us," says Nicks. "They gave us the low-down, kept us at a field office overnight while this whole thing played out. We were terrified." She wipes at her eyes. "I have never been so scared, Aidy. *Never.* The whole thing on the roller coaster played out on live news."

I cover my eyes with my hands. "Oh shit, am I famous?"

"You might be a little bit famous," says my mom. "I mean I'm sure you'll get a book deal, at least." She looks at my dad. "Oh, maybe I can bring it to my book group!"

"Okay, calm down," says my dad, patting her on the back.

"We never even got to visit Aunt Meredith!" says my mom, shaking her head. "She had already moved on to another casino, in Arizona this time, can you believe it, and your father *refused* to change our plane tickets again."

"No more plane tickets," he confirms, grumbling something else I can't hear.

Someone hands me a bottle of water. Of course something very particular is gnawing at me, and it isn't my aunt's gambling addiction. "So, listen," I say to my family, clearing my throat, "when you say the FBI explained everything... um... how much did they tell you about... me?"

"They just said you had been randomly selected online or something to trick a terror group," says my mom. "Something about a photo you once posted. I don't know. Can you believe this shit?" she tells my dad.

"We'll let the lawyers work all that out," he says. "Have a feeling his college will be paid for. Important thing is that he's okay. I told you the internet is evil. Nothing good comes from the internet. We won two world wars without twatting to anyone."

I roll my eyes. "Jesus, it's *tweeting*. Twatting? *Seriously?* I mean you know it's not *twatting*, Dad—you have to know that."

A few cops come over with EMTs and ask if I'm doing okay, and if I need to go to the hospital. I tell them I'm okay. A paramedic gives me a cursory examination anyway. I ask the cops if anyone got hurt. They said there were a few injuries, only one that's serious (shrapnel, from the Derby blast), but no one was killed. And no children were hurt. Some feds approach, wanting a bit of my time.

I ask for a few more moments with my family and they say that's fine—the police are keeping the media at bay—but soon they'll need to clear everyone out so they can begin their work, since this is an active crime scene. Also, they want me to come with them to a field office for a debriefing. I ask them where Shiloh is. They say they'll try to find him, but he may have been taken to a nearby hospital already.

When my dad and my sister get pulled into a conversation with one of the cops, my mom grabs me again, saying "I love you" and kissing my forehead.

Something's churning inside me. "I wish you had told me that sooner."

"What?"

"That you love me. You haven't said it since Neil died, and you're just saying it now because of all the drama."

My mom looks like I slapped her. "Aidan!"

"When Neil died, you and Dad went nuts. I get it. But I was alone—*I was grieving him, too, Mom*—and realizing I was gay, which isn't easy, and then you just shipped me away so you wouldn't have to deal with me—"

"You wanted to go to Witloff! You told us you wanted to leave. We all discussed this with Dr. Boardman, and he thought it would be a good idea—"

"Mom, seriously, I came out to you, and you and Dad had

no reaction, except that awful letter he gave me, which was so *cruel*—"

"What letter? I don't know about a letter!" she shrieks.

I shake my head. "You need to start seeing me as a real person. I've become just a blur to you and Dad. Just some blur of a boy you once knew."

My mom starts to cry. "Aidy. We just wanted you to be happy."

"Well, I haven't been. And nothing you did helped. You shut me out."

"No one is perfect! We all tried!"

I feel like I'm being a little harsh, and this isn't really the time or place for this. I squeeze my mom's arm. "It'll be okay, we'll... talk things through."

My sister, who's pretty much always the most emotional person in any situation but seems to be holding it together right now, untangles me from my mother and pulls me aside. "Listen, people are going to suggest that you need to talk to someone. A professional. *Do it.* Okay? Talk to someone."

"I'm not keen to go back into therapy, Nicks. We tried that."

"Try it again. You've seen some terrible things"—she puts her hands in a throbbing circle around her stomach—"and we can internalize that, we can repress that. I did this chakra-cleansing workshop in Westport with a Hindu healer who had been reincarnated from a Natterjack toad. He was on his, like, forty-fifth life—"

I snap my head up to the sky like a Pez dispenser. "Nicks, you're killing me. Not now with this shit, *please not now*—"

She grips my arm. "No, just listen. I don't believe that crap, either—although it was an *amazing* workshop—but just talk to someone. Okay? Trust me."

"Okay, I will. Good point."

"The FBI spoke to me first. Before they talked to Mom and Dad."

I close my eyes and take a breath. "Oh?"

"I know a bit more than they do about how this whole thing came about. I asked them not to tell Mom and Dad, you know... *everything*."

I nod. "Thank you. I see now why you think I should get help."

She digs through her purse, finds a lozenge or something, throws it in her mouth and clicks it around her teeth. "I'm gonna tell you something..." She holds up her hands, and I'm not sure if she's holding off a sob, a cough, if she's going to sneeze or what, but then she gulps in some air, and just says, "I knew."

"About?"

She moves her hands and head around like, *you know.*

"Uh-huh."

"I should have said something. I should have done something. I'm a terrible sister. I'm sorry. I just didn't know what to do or if I should."

"How did you know?"

"I just sensed it...I don't know, something you said, something I caught. I'm incredibly intuitive, you know."

"Right. I'm glad you didn't intervene. That would have made things a hell of a lot worse. I handled it. And I'm okay now."

She takes a big dramatic breath. "I knew about it, that it was going to hurt you in the end, that it was not good, and I did nothing."

I put my hand on her arm and grip it tight. "I am okay. I love you. You are making this about you in a weird way, like you always do. But all you need to know is, what happened with Tom was kind of a complicated thing and hard to quantify; I am a strong person, and I am okay now...about that, about him, about everything. And I forgive you. *Okay?*"

She nods, lips pursed. "You are strong, stronger than me. We should talk more about this."

"All right. If you want to, we will."

"I know basically nothing. Nothing about you, nothing about what happened. *I want you to know my babies.*"

I notice my parents looking over. "We'll talk. Not here, though. Not now. Okay?"

She nods, digging through her purse for something else, probably a Xanax. "To think we could have lost you today..."

"But you didn't."

I see a hand rising up, over the crowd, waving, beckoning. "Hold on a sec," I tell Nicks, squeezing her shoulder. I walk through the mass of emergency workers rushing around, gently pushing people aside, until I find Shiloh. He's leaning against an FBI van, right next to an ambulance, with two paramedics bandaging up his shoulder. He doesn't look great.

"They got the arrow out?"

"Yeah," he says. "I'm going to be okay. But they gotta get me to the hospital soon. They don't want it to get infected or anything."

"Of course."

"We did good," says Shiloh.

"Yeah, we did."

"Can you give us a quick minute?" says Shiloh to the paramedics. They nod, take their kits, and disappear into the swarm. "Are you all right?"

"Yeah. I think."

"I'm sorry you had to go through all that."

I laugh. "I've had better trips to amusement parks. And I've never admitted this to anyone, but I'm not a huge fan of heights."

Shiloh grins. "You're a great kid, Aidan. I really liked getting to know you."

I fold my arms. "*Kid?* You're like four years older than me..."

I want to tell him how much I liked getting to know him, too. But I don't know if I really did get to know him. Although I like everything I *think* I know about him.

So instead I say, "Will I see you again or what?"

"I'll see you around," he says, but it's not a cold, rejecting kind of thing; he's grinning. And he takes my hand in his, and rubs his thumb over my thumb.

We stay like that for a moment.

"I want to wait," I tell him, surprising even me.

But Shiloh only nods.

"I want to go to college, maybe see where I am after a little while before we move forward with anything."

Who is saying these things? Is it me? We've had a really interesting start to something, and I'm feeling a lot of emotions, but

I hear myself saying these things, and although I want to stop myself from saying them, I know they are the right things to say. I feel it in my bones.

Shiloh gestures around. "Whatever happens, it shouldn't be about this... this nightmare we've been through."

"I think there are certain things worth waiting for," I say, taking my hand back, and breathing in deeply.

Shiloh moves in, kisses me on the top of my ear, and whispers, "If it's meant to be, it's meant to be."

"I hope it is," I say, keeping a little spark lit. "I'd like to get to know the real you."

"You've already done that," he says. "More than you realize. And more than anyone else has."

We both need to let the insanity of this experience dissipate and see where we are when the dust settles.

"Cool," I say, rocking back and forth on my heels.

He gestures behind me with his head. "Is that your family over there?"

I look behind me and see my parents wildly gesticulating at each other. "Yup."

"They look completely crazy," he says, laughing.

I smile at him. "You have no idea."

He points at my chest. "Get your rib checked. Let them do an X-ray."

"Okay."

The paramedics return, along with some guys in FBI jackets. "I have to go now," he says.

"I'll see you around," I say, a lump rising in my throat.

He gives me a little wave.

I watch him get into the ambulance, and I watch the paramedics close the doors behind him. Several police vehicles, sirens letting out single piercing retorts, escort the ambulance out of the parking lot, then onto the road. I watch the ambulance disappear over a hill, flashing lights melting into the sun streaks in the sky.

I didn't realize that would be the last time I ever saw Shiloh.

No, he didn't die—nothing like that. In fact I heard he fully recovered, was doing well, going through detox. We just never spoke again. Or haven't yet.

But six months later, I'm not sure we ever will. Shiloh seems to have been absorbed back into whatever mysterious system created him. His phone doesn't work. I haven't been able to contact him, and no one's been much help in that regard. I'm guessing that's on purpose.

It makes me wonder, all over again, who he really was, and how much of him was real. The jigsaw puzzle of things about him that I liked so much may not be the parts of him, all put together the right way, that make up who he actually is. It's all so knotty and cryptic. He was undercover, after all. He was trained to play a specific role. He was, however briefly, this chimerical presence in my life.

I never forgot what he said to me, though, after I told him I'd like to get to know the real him.

You've already done that. More than you realize. And more than anyone else has.

That made me feel special, still does, and I think about those words often.

Sometimes I think I see him in crowds. But it's never him.

I worry Shiloh thought I was too damaged. Or maybe he thought he was too damaged, and wanted to spare me all the broken stuff about him I still don't know about.

I would have accepted all his darkness. I would have helped him get through it. I hope, wherever he is, he knows that. What an intense romance I could have had with someone who saved me on a train and then, only a few days later, shot me twice at close range.

Long sigh.

So I suppose you're wondering what happened after.

Well, right after, I went to the hospital. I had a cracked rib, but no internal injuries from getting shot. There's nothing they can do about a cracked rib, really. I got painkillers. I told the FBI everything that happened. We went over it a million times, and then I went home. A few days later, just like they said in the Lake George hospital, our family cardiologist confirmed my little ol' heart is perfectly fine. It's not enlarged.

Briefly I became a media sensation, because the opposite of what I thought was going to happen *happened*. Instead of the feds retracting their initial statement that I was a person of interest in the terror attacks and removing my photo from circulating in the media, the whole thing came out about me and Digital Dust and the Swans.

I never gave a single interview. I never spoke to a single reporter. My family shielded me from all that. I watched these fools on ratings-grabbing cable-news networks sitting in their comfortable chairs with their six-figure salaries debating the ethics and morality of Digital Dust and the concept of collateral damage. Because that's what everyone determined I was: collateral damage. Is it right, they all mused, to endanger and "inconvenience" an innocent kid if scores more lives could be saved as a result of infiltrating a terror group and stopping future attacks?

They called in experts, all the usual pundits. Many said *no,* some said *sure.* They gave the whole we're-living-in-a-new-world-so-the-game-has-changed argument. I'm so sick of hearing that.

Also, there was an undercurrent of homophobia to the debate as well, as Scotty would have happily pointed out:

Look where the pendulum's still swinging, hun.

Since the Swans were a gay homegrown terror organization and all that.

Ultimately there was a huge shitstorm about it, and blowback from the public, everyone worried about their own kids who spend half their waking consciousness on Snapchat and Kik and Instagram. If I could be fed to terrorists like mutton to a lion, so could their own kids.

Meanwhile, I was the one having nightmares about trying to hold on to Scotty on that roller coaster right before he fell to his death. There have been no more dreams about tornadoes or burning houses. But there were definitely messed-up dreams about that final roller coaster ride. And every time, Scotty said something different to me right before he fell.

Once he said, *I always wanted to be a poet, but I can't rhyme, and I don't understand meter. Will you write a poem for me about a garden at night?*

Another time: *I always wanted to visit Tangier.*

The worst thing he said was, *You'll never find love, Aidan. You're going to be known for this forever. You'll never be anonymous... until the day you die, all alone, in a crumbling lighthouse on a forgotten seashore.*

Typical Scotty: theatrical, over-the-top.

I never saved him in any of those dreams. He fell every time.

There were many investigations into the Digital Dust program: how it came about, and how it went so wrong. Congressional hearings. Litigation. And settlements. We lawyered up, and my dad was right—my college (and beyond) is paid for now.

I'll never know what the FBI's endgame really was on those tennis courts. I know they were hoping to get that spyware to the Swans, believing it really did have to be me who delivered it. But I think they secretly hoped the Swans would kidnap me again so they'd get ears on the inside, since they'd lost contact with Shiloh. I'll always be proud of the fact that I stopped caring what they did or didn't want from me, and made my own call. I did what I thought was right. And it worked. My finest hour.

Agents Schwartz and Hernandez and many other people involved in the formation of the Digital Dust program—most of whom I never heard of and never knew existed—resigned. I never saw or spoke to Schwartz or Hernandez again.

My dad said not to worry about them (I don't), that they'll all land high-paying consulting jobs in the private sector. Part of me wishes them luck.

Part of me wants them all to go to hell.

And yet...

What Shiloh and I did mattered in the end. With the higher-ups in the Swans now dead, the FBI was able to dismantle the rest of the terror network of hackers and lost boys the Swans comprised, effectively wiping them out for good. I guess that's why some counterterror experts had a good argument that Digital Dust saved lives.

On the other side of that coin, though, gay rights continue to be endangered. Scotty would have been real smug about that.

Told ya, hun.

I called my college and asked about LGBTQ groups on campus, and how I can be involved when I get there in the fall.

Like a sheltered, privileged tool, I'd never even thought to ask before.

There are plenty of political and support groups. There's even a queer resource center on campus with books and research materials. I'm turning eighteen soon, and I'll be able to vote. I plan to become way more politically active now, or at least *aware*. Gotta start somewhere.

I've also done some research on suicide prevention. I think that might be something I dedicate my life to, I don't know. It would be kind of a weird tribute to Tom, and to Scotty's partner Ken, who I never even knew. And Neil would have been proud of me. I can always volunteer for hotlines and stuff.

I listened to my sister. I went into therapy.

So did my parents, but they saw a different therapist, which worked out better for everyone.

With my sister at my side, and on the advice of my therapist, I told my parents about Tom, and what happened. It felt good to get all that out. My mom cried. My dad just listened and looked somber.

They've come to terms with the fact that their grief over Neil led them to start treating me in a way I felt was unfeeling and kind of removed. We're all still working through this, but things have gotten better. And our relationship has improved. They never fail to tell me they love me now, every day, sometimes several times a day.

Now I'm like, *Okay, fine—I get it.*

With prompting from my therapist, I wrote a series of letters.

The first letter I wrote was to Neil, telling him how much I love and miss him, and how sorry I am about our silly fight the night before he died. He deserved better from me.

The second letter I wrote was to Tom, apologizing for my behavior after our breakup, even though everyone unanimously agrees there were other factors in his life that drove him to do what he did and it was in no way my fault AND I NEED TO ACCEPT THAT.

I also scolded him a bit. I was just a kid, after all. He should have known better, that he had all the power. He should have known that he was my first, real, true love. He should have respected that. And protected me. I deserved better from him.

I wrote to Scotty. I told him I'm sorry I wasn't able to save him. I admitted we had a connection, although a complicated one, but in the end he disappointed me by fully crossing over to the dark side. I told him I will try to make change in the world my own way, partly as a tribute to what the Swans *could have been,* but mostly to further my forever quest to prove that Digital Dust was wrong about me.

I wrote a letter to my Aunt Meredith, the only person I wrote to who is still alive. I said I'd like to get to know her better, and maybe we could have lunch once she's feeling better and talk about those Ethan Hawke novels. I haven't heard from her yet. I hope she takes me up on my offer. I hope she knows I was serious.

Lastly I wrote to Drew, the kid who died in that avalanche, who I never knew. I told him I was sorry for making fun of his (admittedly extremely preppy) death. Wherever he was now, I told him, I hope he didn't hold my occasionally snarky sense of humor against me. I said we have a lot more in common than he probably realized. I said he sounded like a great kid, and I wished we could have been friends. I said I'm a lesser person for not having known him—but that might have been overdoing it just a tad.

I returned to school to finish the year. It was all about regaining normalcy. That's what I asked for, and that's what I got. So I enjoyed that last chunk of senior year. That prolonged twilight, dotted with fireflies of random memories and the last wisps of minor friendships, where you watch the waning days of your childhood burn out until you're ejected into the next phase.

"So how was *your* spring break?" I asked everyone when I got back, when I was still all over the news every moment of every day. That joke never got old.

I spent most of my free time with Jackson and Leo, as well as with my other dorm mates. Jacks and Leo both got the summer internships they were hoping for, and Jacks got back together with Tats (for now; we'll see).

Jacks and Leo were really good friends to me. They helped me through that whole nightmare, and they were protective and sensitive during the never-ending aftermath, with news vans parked outside the school grounds, reporters hoping to nab me, cajole me into a sound bite, any kind of comment. The media never got one. They never will.

"Man, the shit that happens to you," Jackson said when he first saw me again, laughing himself into a whirlwind, slapping at himself, like he does. Then he gave me a big bro hug. "I'm so glad you're okay," he said, squeezing me hard, which still hurt because of my rib. I realized how much I love Jacks and how sad I'm going to be when I no longer see him on a daily basis. But knowing Jacks, he won't let our friendship fade away.

Okay, so one weird thing, and you're not going to believe this.

Darren Cohen.

He sidled up to me as I was walking toward my dorm a week or so after we got back from break. His hair was all wet and he was carrying a soccer ball, wearing white Adidas shorts, a plain gray T-shirt, red high-tops, and black Nike socks pulled up right below his knees. "Jamison," he said, dropping the ball, kicking it around while I watched him, and certain parts of him.

When I didn't answer, he stopped kicking and turned around. "Hey."

"Hey."

"Want to take a walk?"

"Um. Okay."

We wound up at the empty football field at Lynch Stadium. I looked up at the bleachers. I saw, in the distance, all the old brick buildings on campus I soon wouldn't be seeing anymore. Darren juggled the soccer ball for a few minutes, letting it bounce off his feet. "Uh, so you had like a lot of shit go down after we met at the Mandarin, huh?"

"You heard?"

He laughed.

"Thanks for keeping things discreet," he said. "Between you and me, I mean."

I nodded, not sure where any of this was leading.

"How are you doing now?"

"I'm okay."

"Listen, I'm sorry."

"For?"

Darren stopped juggling the ball, resting it under his foot. He puffed out his cheeks, forming a thought that looked more and more painful as it coalesced. The way the light caught the ends of his hair made them look like spun gold. He looked down at the apple-green turf. "I didn't treat you right. It's been bothering me."

I looked at him, slowly nodding, unsure how to respond.

"I just wanted to say I'm sorry. I was an asshole."

"It's okay. I mean...are you just saying this now, though, because you feel bad about everything that happened to me?" I realized, all of a sudden, none of it would have happened if things had gone better that night with Darren. I never would have gone back on DirtyPaws, or found Benoît. I laughed at this fact, softly, to myself.

He took a step back. "What? What's funny?"

I waved him off. "Nothing. Nothing, man."

He got a jittery, vulnerable look in his eye. "Look. Can I make it up to you?"

"How?"

He juggled the soccer ball a little more, then kicked it away. "Want to go see a movie or something?"

"A movie?"

"Yeah."

I scrunched my mouth around. "Uh. Sure. We could do that. Sure."

"Cool."

We both nodded at each other for a full minute in the middle of this field.

"What about Ashley?" I asked.

"Uh, we're taking a break. Plus...I meant...let's hang *as buds*. You know?"

"Sure. Buds."

I thought about it some more, then decided to give Darren a second chance.

I signed out with my housemaster that Saturday night, and Darren and I went to see an indie movie at an art-house theater called the Post Office, fifteen minutes from campus. The movie was a quiet, syrupy drama about a family with an alcoholic father and a manic-depressive mother on vacation in Nantucket.

The mother is a famous photographer known for snapping her family, and her kids, at their worst moments. Their teenage son has just come out as gay. She wants to capture his confusion and despair rather than really be there for him as a mom. She's kind of a self-involved, horrible person. The movie was a little slow at first, but then it got kind of engrossing.

Halfway through the movie, Darren put his hand on my leg.

I sat back in my seat and exhaled quickly through my nose. Obviously, I didn't expect him to do that. Darren kept his hand there and I put my hand on top of his. Then he moved his hand off my leg but kept his hand intertwined with mine, so we watched the rest of the movie holding hands.

After the movie, people filed out of the theater and Darren and I were left standing alone on a quiet, darkening street lit from the golden glow of the box-office window, not saying anything. The late-spring evening felt like blue cotton.

I said we should probably head back, but Darren pulled me aside, past the movie theater, in front of a closed stationery store, and put a hand on each of my cheeks, smushing up my mouth. He went in for a kiss, but I pushed him away.

"I'm not sure," I said.

Darren looked at me, his eyes buzzing, and sort of nodded internally. "Okay."

"I thought you wanted to be buds."

"I thought that, too," he said. He looked down at his feet.

"You're not...you need..." I finally just said it. *"You're not a very good kisser."*

"Ashley said that, too," said Darren.

"She did?"

"Yeah, she did. So I guess I'm not. But...I can get better at it. Right?"

"I'm not sure...if it's one of those things people are just good at or not."

Darren looked a little sad. "Oh."

"But, uh, if you want..." I looked behind and around me, not sure why, not sure what I was looking for. "I mean, I..."

"It's okay," said Darren. "I don't care if people see us together anymore."

"Okay."

"I want to kiss you," he said, firmly.

Back in my dorm room, ignoring the "three feet on the floor" rule, we did kiss. It was rough going at first. I gave him a lot of direction, tilting his jaw, saying stuff like: *Too much teeth; relax your tongue; go slower;* but we got there. Eventually he got gentler, there was intention behind what he was doing, and it was kind of nice being with him and forming a connection I never thought could happen.

We binge-watched a show on Netflix, lying next to each other. By the end of the night his head was on my chest, his arms wrapped around me. This time he *wanted* to be near me. It wasn't simply because I was there. And he never changed his mind.

Oddly enough, Darren and I have stayed in touch. It's just one of those things in life that surprise the hell out of you, I guess.

I'm in my freshman year now. I love college. I've made friends. I love my classes. I love the freedom. College is about learning how to think in different ways, not just learning how to take tests or memorize stuff. It suits my brain better, even if there is a shit-ton of reading.

I even met a dude I like. His name is Christoph; he sits behind me in my Introduction to Medieval Literature class. We've been on a few dates, and so far so good. Darren teases me about him. I think Darren is jealous. Darren, weirdly, has been texting me more than Jackson or Leo lately. Sometimes I think about Darren, too. And what might have been if we both hadn't been heading off to college just at the time when we connected, in the right way, and I taught him how to kiss properly.

And I think, too, what might be. Because you never know. You really don't.

And hey, I get a little jealous, too, thinking about Darren using my top-notch kissing skills on someone else. I taught that boy well. I should reap all the rewards. He's doing well at Dartmouth, too.

Everyone at college knows who I am; there's no getting around that. I'm the kid who: Saved Quest Gardens, or Took Down the Swans, or Was Exploited by the NSA. I'm the Collateral Damage Kid, the Preppy Suburban Gay Reluctant Hero or...whatever you want to believe about me. There's been so much written and discussed about me by people who don't know me, that I've nearly regressed into Mr. Preston again—a fiction outside myself, dissembled and manipulated by forces beyond my control...but whatever. No one really cares here. I'm just another college kid trying to fit in. People are cool. And that's a relief.

I don't know who I am yet, either. I want to find out.

The nightmares, gradually, faded away.

And, since I've been so busy with schoolwork and acclimating to college and being in a new environment, everything that went on during that crazy-ass spring break is starting to seem like a distant memory, too. Sadly, that also includes Shiloh. But I'll meet so many people yet in my lifetime. I like meeting new people. Every new person is like a different world to me.

Sometimes, though, late at night, lying in bed, about to fall asleep, I'll think about storms. And I'll think about what Scotty said to me on that roller coaster:

The storms never come for me. Not when I'm awake and not when I'm asleep.

My storm never came, either. The one that was supposed to come when I was eleven, the one that caused my fight with Neil that awful night. It never stormed. The fight we had was unnecessary. Pointless. We could have easily had two car rides the next morning—one to his basketball game, and one to GameStop. It would have been fine.

I sulked in my room for the rest of that night and I sulked

the next morning, after I woke up. By the time I finally got over it and saw the Christmas card shoved under my door, Neil was already gone—off to his game—and most likely, gone from this world, too.

I saw the sunlight glowing behind the corners of my window shades and I laughed, feeling like a total jackass. Then I sat on the edge of my bed, fought back a smile, and read Neil's card:

Aidy, don't be mad at me. I love you. You're my brother no matter what you say, you dumbass. It didn't rain! It didn't hail! The storm never came.

Be happy. Smile, for God's sake. Look out the window! There is so much sun! There is so much light!

ACKNOWLEDGMENTS

Thank you, with all my heart, to:

Jenny Bak, my deeply intuitive, funny, courageous, and brilliantly talented editor. It was a joy working with you on this book.

James Patterson, for all the kind support.

The whole Jimmy Patterson team for their incredibly hard work and passionate commitment to their authors: Julie Guacci, Sabrina Benun, Erinn McGrath, Diana McElfresh, Tracy Shaw, Stephanie Yang, Sammy Yuen, Elizabeth Blue Guess, Lisa Ferris, Aubrey Poole, Sasha Henriques, Linda Arends, Allan Fallow, and Josh Johns.

Everyone at Little, Brown and Hachette.

Victoria Marini & the folks at Irene Goodman Agency.

Lia Chan & ICM.

Brian Murray Williams.

Jordan & Lorin Milman.

Evelyn & Harvey Milman.

My deepest gratitude to:

April Henry, Lindsay Champion, Kara Thomas, Kit Frick, Maxine Kaplan, Cale Dietrich, Emily Wibberley, Austin Siegemund-Broka, Lissa Price, Karen M. McManus, David Levithan, Melissa Albert, Penelope Burns, Beth Kingry Northington, Henry Kessler, Fernando Hernandez, Sarah Henning, and Naomi Grossman.

ABOUT THE AUTHOR

DEREK MILMAN has worked as a playwright, screenwriter, film-school teacher, DJ, and underground humor-magazine publisher. A classically trained actor, he has performed on stages across the country and appeared in numerous TV shows, commercials, and films. Derek currently resides in Brooklyn, New York, where he writes full time. *Swipe Right for Murder* is his second novel for young adults.

JIMMY PATTERSON BOOKS FOR YOUNG ADULT READERS

James Patterson Presents

Stalking Jack the Ripper by Kerri Maniscalco

Hunting Prince Dracula by Kerri Maniscalco

Escaping from Houdini by Kerri Maniscalco

Capturing the Devil by Kerri Maniscalco

Becoming the Dark Prince by Kerri Maniscalco

Kingdom of the Wicked by Kerri Maniscalco

Gunslinger Girl by Lyndsay Ely

Twelve Steps to Normal by Farrah Penn

Campfire by Shawn Sarles

When We Were Lost by Kevin Wignall

Swipe Right for Murder by Derek Milman

Once & Future by Amy Rose Capetta and Cori McCarthy

Sword in the Stars by Amy Rose Capetta and Cori McCarthy

Girls of Paper and Fire by Natasha Ngan

Girls of Storm and Shadow by Natasha Ngan

You're Next by Kylie Schachte

Kingdom of the Wicked by Kerri Maniscalco

Daughter of Sparta by Claire M. Andrews

It Ends in Fire by Andrew Shvarts

The Maximum Ride Series by James Patterson

The Angel Experiment

School's Out — Forever

Saving the World and Other Extreme Sports

The Final Warning

MAX

FANG

ANGEL

Nevermore

Maximum Ride Forever

Hawk

The Confessions Series by James Patterson

Confessions of a Murder Suspect

Confessions: The Private School Murders

Confessions: The Paris Mysteries

Confessions: The Murder of an Angel

The Witch & Wizard Series by James Patterson

Witch & Wizard

The Gift

The Fire

The Kiss

The Lost

Nonfiction by James Patterson

Med Head

Stand-Alone Novels by James Patterson

The Injustice (previously published as Expelled)

Crazy House

The Fall of Crazy House

Cradle and All

First Love

Homeroom Diaries

For exclusives, trailers, and other information, visit jimmypatterson.org.